I'VE GOT A SECRET

A mysterious smile, which he was unable to suppress, passed over Old Harry's rosy face and he lowered his eyelids coyly. "I reckon you'll hear of another death today," he said idly.

The old man rose with agility and stood for a moment to stare into the white glare of the eastern sky before going off like a cracked alarm clock.

"Three in a row, three in a row," he chattered, turning 'round. "There's allus three in a row."

"Oh." The investigator settled back. If it was only a case of superstition, he was not interested. "I don't know so much about that."

"Aha! But I do," Old Harry exclaimed, laughing with ancient glee. "I do!"

Other Albert Campion Mysteries by
Margery Allingham

THE BLACK DUDLEY MURDER
THE CASE OF THE LATE PIG
THE FEAR SIGN
THE GYRTH CHALICE MYSTERY
MORE WORK FOR THE UNDERTAKER

Coming Soon from Avon Books

THE CHINA GOVERNESS
THE MIND READERS
CARGO OF EAGLES
MR. CAMPION AND OTHERS

AN ALBERT CAMPION MYSTERY

MARGERY ALLINGHAM

THE ESTATE OF THE BECKONING LADY

AVON BOOKS  NEW YORK

None of the characters in this book is a portrait of a living person nor did the incidents here recorded ever take place.

Originally published in Great Britain as *The Beckoning Lady*

AVON BOOKS
A division of
The Hearst Corporation
105 Madison Avenue
New York, New York 10016

First Avon Books Printing: January 1990

AVON TRADEMARK REG. U.S. PAT. OFF. AND IN OTHER COUNTRIES, MARCA REGISTRADA, HECHO EN U.S.A.

Printed in the U.S.A.

RA   10   9   8   7   6   5   4   3   2   1

This book is
Affectionately Inscribed
to my
Old Friends and their
Merry Wives

"But who," said Florizel at last, "who is this lady who is for ever beckoning?"

"That," replied he, "is beyond my knowledge. Some aver that she is Love, or Dame Fortune. Some, honour in the field. Some, the Muse herself. And the old have an unpleasant idea that she is Death. But all I can tell you about her for certain is that her eyes are laughing, and that she is without mercy."

CONTES DE FÉES

from the translation by Anthony Greene
1929

CONTENTS

DRAMATIS PERSONAE
(APPEARING)

ALBERT CAMPION, thought to be on holiday in Pontisbright

RUPERT, his son

DETECTIVE CHIEF INSPECTOR CHARLES LUKE, recuperating in Pontisbright

TONKER CASSANDS, friend to Campion, inventor of the Glübalübalum, married to Minnie

MAGERSFONTEIN LUGG, a London fellow, attracted by Miss Diane

OLD HARRY, a country person, protector of Miss Diane

SIDNEY SIMON SMITH, alias "the S.S.S. man," a palindromic V.I.P.

WESTY STRAW, step-great-grandnephew to Minnie, an American subject

GEORGE MEREDITH, friend to Westy

"FANNY" GENAPPE, a millionaire

SUPERINTENDENT FRED SOUTH of the rural C.I.D.

SOLLY L., a bookmaker

WALLY, friend to Tonker

THE POLICE CONSTABLE at Pontisbright

CHOC, a dog

THE IMPERIAL AUGUSTS, a celebrated troupe

THE LADY AMANDA, married to Albert Campion, mother of Rupert

MINNIE CASSANDS, née Miranda Straw, celebrated woman painter, A.R.A., owner of The Beckoning Lady, married to Tonker

Obituary

Mr. William Faraday

Mr. William Makepeace Faraday, author of many amusing librettos, died last Saturday in Pontisbright, Suffolk, at the age of eighty-two.

He was born in Cambridge in the late sixties, the son of Dr. James Faraday, one-time Master of Ignatius, and Mrs. Caroline Faraday, whom all who knew the University in the days preceding the First World War will remember for her dominant charm and, without ingratitude, for the overawing hospitality which she dispensed to the undergraduates of that remote and golden age.

William Faraday was educated at Charterhouse and St. John's College, Cambridge, and when he left the University he settled down to a curiously retired existence in the home of his parents, and it was only after the death of his mother in 1932, when he was fifty-nine, that his remarkable talent became evident.

His first publication, *The Memoirs of an Old Buffer*, which appeared in 1934, was one of the most successful humorous books of the decade, and in a matter of months he discovered himself a literary figure, but it was not until the late James Sutane perceived in the volume of pretended reminiscences the ideal libretto for his forthcoming musical show, *The Buffer*, that William Faraday's true gift was fully appreciated.

The Buffer, which ran at the Argosy Theatre for five

1

hundred and twenty-four nights, was followed by many other extravaganzas from his fertile imagination, amongst them *Uncle Goat, Sweet Adeline,* and the outstandingly successful *Harrogate Ho!*, a revival of which enlivened the late forties.

Mr. Faraday's influence on contemporary wit has been considerable. His was the charm of artless prevarication, never crude or overdone, but endearing to those who could appreciate the gentle absurdity of Dignity skating on the thinnest of ice with the placid sang-froid of the truly courageous.

As a man he was generally beloved, and a host of friends will miss his shy smile and air of bewildered pleasure at their delighted reception of his sly tall stories. His latter years were spent in happy retirement in the country. He was unmarried and died at the house of a friend.

CHAPTER I

Two Dead Men

I

It was no time for dying. The summer had arrived in glory, trailing fathomless skies and green and gold and particolour as fresh as sunrise, yet death was about, twice.

All through what was left of the first day, one body lay hidden between the steep sides of the dry ditch, secret on a bed of leaves. From the moment when it had toppled so suddenly from the plank bridge leading to the stile it had vanished from sight. The green waves of ribbon grass and periwinkle which fringed the verges had parted as it passed, to swing up again immediately, so that there was now only one way of catching a glimpse of it. That was to step down on the other side, where the chasm was wider and less overgrown, stoop under the bridge where lichen and black fungus made an evil ceiling, and peer into the translucent tunnel beyond.

On the second day only one person did that and no one else passed that way at all.

On the third day in the very early morning, when the sky was a dazzling white and the grass was grey and beaded with dew, there was much unusual foot traffic on the path which led over the stile from the house to the village. Among the first to pass were two rather alarming old women. Each carried a sinister bag, wore very tidy clothes, and spoke with hushed excitement. They rested at the stile, discussing death and the grisly office they had

3

come to perform for it, but neither glanced behind her at the hanging grasses or dreamed for one moment that beneath them lay a second waiting form whose stiffened limbs would have, by that time, taxed all their experience.

Later on that day, when the sun was up, there was much coming and going. Several people from the house made short cuts to the village, and one shook out a shopping bag over the ditch so that with the dust three small items fell idly through the leaves. These were a pin and a paper-clip and a small bronze bead.

The undertaker himself walked that way, since the journey was so much shorter from his wheelwright's shop than if he had got out his car and gone round by the road. He tripped through the meadows, looking incongruous in his black suit with his rule sticking out of his breast pocket and his face carefully composed for his first glimpse of the bereaved.

After him, in the afternoon, came the ladies, walking in twos and threes, wearing hats and gloves, and carrying kind little notes and nosegays to leave at the door. Nearly all paused on the stile for a first glimpse of the water-meadows, flower-spangled and lace-edged in the yellow light, but not one noticed if there was any new and unusual wear on the planks, or observed that there was something dark and different on the edge of a rusty ploughshare which lay on a bald patch under the oak overshadowing the bridge.

It was dark before the one person who now knew the way dared to clamber down under the planks and, with head bent to avoid the lichen, lit a single match and held it high. The body was still there.

It was still there on the next night and the next, but by now it was limp and shrunken into the earth which would not open to receive it.

On the evening of the sixth day there was a quarrel at the stile. Two country lovers met there and the boy was restless and importunate. But the girl, who was at that strange age when every sense is sharpened, took a sudden inexplicable loathing to the place and would not listen. He argued with her and his smooth face was hot and his hair-grease reeked of roses as he nuzzled into her neck. He whispered that the place was so deserted, so hidden with the spreading tree above them making for darkness, and the steep artificial slope of an embankment providing a screen on one side. But her disgust, which was not for him as she supposed, was overpowering and she thrust him off. He caught at her dress as she climbed away but she struck out at him, caught him more sharply than she had intended, and rushed off down the path sobbing, principally in apprehension. He remained where he was, frustrated and hurt, and he was almost in tears when he dragged the packet of cigarettes out of his pocket. He had only two left of the posh kind which, together with the hair-grease, he kept for courting nights, and when he lit the second one he threw the empty carton over his shoulder into the periwinkle fronds. It slid down out of sight and came to rest on a crumpled lapel.

The boy finished his angry smoking very quickly and kicked the stub into the planks at his feet. Finding he derived a sort of satisfaction from the exercise, he went on kicking, doing a certain amount of damage to the surface of the wood, and afterwards, when he stepped into the meadow, he kept clear of the uncut hay-crop from force of habit but trod the other way under the tree and kicked a lump of iron he found there, lifting it up at last with the toe of one of his best shoes and sending it neatly into the path. It was grey dusk by then and he did not look at the thing at all closely, but suddenly wearying both of the pursuit and of all women turned abruptly and walked back to the village and the telly, which would be showing in the back bar of The Gauntlett.

He had been gone a full twenty minutes before the watcher, who had been sitting up behind a bramble bush on the high embankment throughout the entire proceedings, came sliding down to the path. Once again the nightly performance with the match took place, but this time the glance in the flickering light was perfunctory and the investigator withdrew hastily and went along the path

for the ploughshare. A foot turned it over gently and the
match flame spurted once more, but by now the stains
which had been dark were brown as the rust on the iron.
The feet slipped away.

A police constable in uniform, taking a walk in the
scented night in an unenthusiastic search for something he
would have described as "certain activities only natural
but about what there have been *complaints*," found the
ploughshare by falling over it. He picked it up, saw what it
was by the light of the stars, and carried it almost into the
village. On the outskirts he passed a rubbish dump sunk in
the hollow of a dried-up pond and decently screened by
shrubs. The constable had size and strength and in his
youth could fling a quoit with any man in Suffolk. Spreading his chest, he swung his arm once, twice, and at the
third time sent the share with the stain and the single shred
of fur-felt still upon it, high and free into the arch of the
sky. Seconds later he heard the satisfying crash and tinkle
as it came to rest amid a nest of old iron and broken
bottles.

On the seventh day, the one person who had watched
over the body robbed it systematically. It was unpleasant
work but it was done thoroughly, in daylight at dinner-
time, the one sacred hour in rural England when all visiting is taboo and no one walks abroad. There were no
observers and it was entirely fortuitous that when the
pathetic shred of a thing was again at peace the cigarette
carton lay under the withered right hand.

On the eighth day the inevitable occurred and a large
and sagacious dog came into the field.

II

"Good morning. What a nice little funeral it was, wasn't
it? Just the right time of year for flowers. That always
makes it so much more gay."

The sensible-looking woman with the white collar on
her neat cotton frock went on cutting faded blossoms out
of the wreaths on Uncle William's grave, and the wind,

which always played round the hilltop church at Pontisbright, ruffled the few strands of grey in her glossy hair.

Mr. Campion, who was standing rather foolishly holding a belated wreath which the village postman had given him, because he "didn't think it quite the ticket for the old P.O. to deliver direct," wondered who on earth she was.

"That's another, is it?" she inquired, scarcely glancing up. "Give it here and I'll see what I can do with it. Dear me, it has got knocked about, hasn't it?"

She rose easily to her feet and, taking the tribute with firm capable hands, held it at arm's length, turning it round to find the card.

"From all in the Buffer Company, Swansea, to the best old Buffer of all," she read aloud. "How extraordinary. Oh I see, they're acting one of his musical comedies. How inefficient theatrical people are, aren't they? Two days late and not really a very suitable message."

"Better than 'best wishes,' " said Mr. Campion, his pale face flushing slightly.

She stared at him and laughed. "Oh yes, of course," she said, only too obviously turning up his card in some mental filing system, "you're so amusing, aren't you?"

Mr. Campion took off his spectacles and gave her what was for him a long hard look. She was coming back to him now. He had seen but not spoken to her. She had sat some pews ahead of himself and Amanda at the funeral service and had worn a black suit and a nice sensible *pot* hat. She was somebody's secretary and had one of those nicknames which indicate the somewhat nervous patronage of employers—Jonesy, was it? Or no, he had it now, Pinky, short for Pinkerton.

Presently, as he had said nothing, she started to tell him about himself in a helpful way, as though he had forgotten his own name or where he was. He thought at first that she was only refreshing her own memory, or airing it, rather, to show him how splendidly efficient she was, but after a moment or so he realized that he had misjudged her and she was merely taking the opportunity to straighten out some of her facts.

"You like to be known as Mr. Albert Campion," she said, and although her tone was arch she spoiled any ingratiating effect by keeping her eyes on a really dirty little rosebud which did not care to be detached from its wiry bed. "And you've been on holiday at the Mill House with your wife and little son for nearly a fortnight while Miss Huntingforest who lives at the mill is in America. Miss Huntingforest is a New Englander."

Mr. Campion made an affirmative noise, or the beginning of one, but she forestalled him.

"I do like to get everything tidy," she explained, starting on a solid cross of red carnations. "I know you both knew the village long ago when your wife lived here with Miss Huntingforest, and you were mixed up in all that romantic business when her brother regained the title. But Lady Amanda refers to Harriet Huntingforest as her aunt, and yet Lady Amanda is not an American."

"Er—no," said Mr. Campion.

"But you both called Mr. Faraday Uncle William," Miss Pinkerton continued, fixing him suddenly with very clear and intelligent hazel eyes and tapping on the grave with her scissors as if William Faraday was actually visible. "He has been living here at The Beckoning Lady with the Cassands for the past twelve years and Minnie Cassands is half an American."

The tall thin man with the very smooth yellow-white hair and the blank expression met her gaze with deceptive mildness.

"Quite," he agreed.

She was misled into sharpness. "Quite?"

"Quite half. Minnie Cassands' father was Daniel St. George Straw, who was the second most famous American painter of the Victorian-Edwardian golden age. His great-great-grandmother, so he always said, was Princess Pocahontas, and she was as American as the Eagle."

"Was she indeed?" Either she was not interested or she did not believe him. Her mind was still on the family. "Yet Mr. Faraday was no relation?"

"No."

"Nor of yours either."

"No."

"I see." It was evident that she gave up for the time being and she continued her work on the flowers. "Eighty-two and he drank, didn't he?" she remarked just as Campion was turning away. "What a very happy release for everybody."

Before this monstrous epitaph Mr. Campion paused aghast. He was no graveyard man by nature and the *pompes funèbres* had little charm for him; but Uncle William had been Uncle William and he was quite prepared to see him sitting up suddenly among the petals, looking like the mannequin from the cover of *Esquire* and "dotting," as he would have described it, this ministering female with the half-bottle which was doubtless in his shroud.

Mr. Campion turned back. "Forgive me," he said with the gentleness of studied attack, "but who *are* you?"

She was not put out, merely amazed. "Oh dear!" she exclaimed, conveying he *was* a silly man, wasn't he, "how odd you must have thought me. I'm Pinky." And then, since he still looked vague, "Mr. Genappe, you know. I'm his secretary, or one of them. I've been with him for nineteen years." The slight bridling movement, the bursting pride, and the drop in the voice put him in the picture and explained the "wholly more important than thou" approach. Here was the loyalty of the devotee, the reverence of the acolyte. He realized that the *mystique* must be money and not the man. She could hardly feel that way about poor old Fanny Genappe, who had not that sort of personality. Goodness knows where he was, poor beast. Sitting on his little rock in the Hebrides watching a bird, very probably, both of them bored as sin.

Francis Genappe was the most unfortunate of the three last multimillionaires in Europe, for he had inherited not only his family's money but also their reputation for philanthropy, two attributes which, taken in conjunction, approximated as far as Mr. Campion could see to the dubious honour of being the original butter in the mouth of the dog. As Campion recollected him, he was civilized, over-

sensitive, and something of a wit, the last person on earth
to have to encounter his fellow-men almost solely through
the medium of the heartrending hard-luck story. Doubtless
the lady with the scissors was part of his armoured plate.
She seemed to have the right surface. He said aloud:

"I heard he'd bought the farm on the hill. Potter's Hall,
isn't it?"

"Not now," she assured him with a brief kind smile.
"Mr. Genappe has so much of the surrounding land that
it's now called the Pontisbright *Park* Estate, to distinguish
it from the Earl's little holding. He's your brother-in-law,
by the way."

Mr. Campion knew he was, but forebore to comment.
She was still speaking and still snipping.

"Lord Pontisbright only owns the Mill and the wood-
lands, and he lives in South Africa most of the time." She
made it sound a complete explanation. "Potter's Hall has
been utterly transformed now that so much work has been
done on it. If you'd care to see it while you're down here
I'm sure Mr. Genappe wouldn't mind."

"Has *he* seen it?"

"Not since the alterations. Mr. Genappe is out of England, naturally."

Mr. Campion hesitated. This was all very well in its
chatty way, but what exactly the good lady thought she
was doing fiddling about with Uncle William's obsequies
remained obscure. He indicated the expanse of granite and
marble, the ancient crosses, and the modern bird-baths.

"Have you taken over this too?"

She considered him for a full second and decided it was
a joke.

"Not yet," she laughed, entering into the jolly spirit of
the thing. "We merely pay for it, I expect, through the
rates. No, I'm just doing this to help Mrs. Cassands. I
always do what I can for her. I'm sure Mr. Genappe would
approve of it. She's always very busy with her house and
her painting, so I'm saving her the walk. I'm like that,
everyone's dogsbody." She shook her neat head. "I can't
think why Mrs. Cassands works so hard at her pictures,

but with that extraordinary husband never there I suppose—''

''She's an A.R.A.,'' protested Mr. Campion mildly, giving the institution its due.

''Oh I know. And Mr. Genappe not only likes her work but has been assured by experts that it's quite sound and may even appreciate. We've bought several canvases as a matter of fact, from Fang's in Bond Street, but I do think it's very hard work for her. She never scamps anything. Frankly I wonder that Mr. Cassands doesn't live more at home instead of flitting in and out wasting his time on idiotic things. That so-called musical instrument of his— well really!''

The thin man chuckled reminiscently, as did most people now that the brief scarifying popularity of the inspired noisemaker which Tonker Cassands had achieved had faded decently into the shadow of jokes-over. The name was so beautiful. *"Tum tee tee, tum tee tum—ON my Glü-bal-ü-bal-um!"*

''Don't!'' Miss Pinkerton dropped her scissors and clapped her hands over her ears. ''Please don't. You know what happens. One goes on humming it all day and it's so *silly*. Really, that winter when everyone was doing it drove me nearly mad. Horrid vulgar thing! It looked so dreadful.''

''I don't know.'' Campion wondered idly if there was anything else she could mention which would inspire him immediately to defend it. ''One has to put an arm through many of the wind instruments. In this, one merely had to add a leg, that was all.''

''It wasn't only that.'' She was fluttering with irritation. ''There was all that transparent plastic showing the different sized bladders inside. Frightful! And the noise! How he got paid for such a stupid thing I do not know.''

''Yet it raked in quite a packet, and it's having quite a vogue in Bongoland now, I believe.'' It seemed as good an exit line as any and Campion was wandering away when she recalled him once more.

''They tell me your visitor has returned.''

Since he merely stared she made it easier for him.

''The Chief Inspector, tall, quite good-looking. He's

been at the Mill for some little time, recovering from the wounds he got in the Caroline Street raid. He left just before the funeral.''

"So he did.''

"But now he's come back?''

"Yes.''

There was a pause while she regarded him severely. "I hope you don't think I'm inquisitive.''

"Good heavens no, that's the last thing I should think about you," said Mr. Campion, and he hurried off out of the churchyard and down the road to the heath.

CHAPTER II

Love and Money

I

Whilst taking on the whole a poorish view of Miss Pinkerton and her efficiency, Mr. Campion was forced to admit that she had placed her finger on quite a problem. As he stepped off the harebells and white violets which covered the pocket-sized heath and made for the Mill he was considering it himself.

Divisional Detective Chief Inspector Charles Luke, with whom he had collaborated in several adventures, was at a turning-point in a career which had promised to be remarkable. He had attained his present rank at an astonishingly early age, and now, after the great shuffle in the C.I.D., seemed almost certain to achieve one of the great prizes and become head of the Flying Squad. The Caroline Street raid in February, which had been as messy a business as Campion could remember, had threatened at first to be a major disaster for Luke but had turned out gloriously. Surgery had saved his left arm, the four flesh wounds had healed more quickly than anybody had expected, and he had emerged from hospital with generous sick leave and a recommendation for the coveted Police Medal, a decoration which is never given by accident. Less than a month ago everything had seemed set-fair for his future.

Mr. Campion shook his head as he turned in to the path which led to the wooden water-mill and the house beside it. He thought he had never been more dismayed in all his

life than on the night before, when he had seen Luke
return. Yet the situation had arisen innocently. Charlie
Luke's release from Guy's Hospital had coincided with
Aunt Hatt's departure for Connecticut, and since Amanda
and the family could not get down to Pontisbright immediately it had seemed only reasonable for Luke and Mr.
Lugg, Campion's friend and knave, to come on ahead for
a week or so. Luke was to convalesce and Lugg to nurse
himself over the first revolting paroxysms of the sentimental nostalgia to be expected on his rediscovery of his
favourite place. Campion had thought it impossible that
anything irremediable could happen to the two of them in
the interval, but the moment he had stepped out of his own
car and was experiencing once again the first shock of
surprised delight which the sight of the old house always
gave him, he had been aware of trouble. Luke had lost his
unnatural fragility and was obviously mending fast, but
there was something not at all right with him.

In the normal way the D.D.C.I. was a considerable
personality. He looked like a gangster and was a tough. He
was six-foot-two and appeared shorter because of the width
of his chest and shoulders, and his dark face with the
narrow eyes under brows which were like circumflex ac-
cents was alive and exciting. He possessed the Londoner's
good temper, which is also ferocious, and a quality of
suppressed force was apparent in everything he did. Mr.
Campion liked him enormously.

On that first evening of their joint holiday ten days ago
Luke had done his best to appear much as usual when he
had welcomed his host on the banks of the mill-race, but
Campion was not deceived. He knew panic when he saw
it. For some hours afterwards there had seemed to be no
conceivable explanation. The village of Pontisbright, strag-
gling round the little green, had appeared as blandly vege-
table as ever and a good deal more innocent than Mr.
Campion had known it in his time. But on the following
morning the mystery had solved itself bluntly. At eleven
o'clock the Hon. Victoria Prunella Editha Scroop-Dory

had wandered down from the new rectory, where she lived
with her mother, widow of the final Baron Glebe, and her
mother's cousin, the Reverend Sam Jones-Jones, who was
called "The Revver" by everybody, and had sat down by
the porch. A few minutes later, after a struggle which was
very nearly visible, the wretched Luke had taken the chair
opposite her. There had been no conversation.

Campion had been so startled by this unforeseen misfor-
tune that he had not even brought himself to mention the
matter to Amanda, who affected to be ignorant of it, and
so a whole uncomfortable week had passed with Luke in
misery, Campion feeling for him but thoroughly alarmed,
and the young woman strolling in each day.

The sudden death of Uncle William over at The Beckoning Lady, which had saddened them all, had seemed to
give Luke sudden resolution. On the day before the funeral
he had announced his intention of intruding on their kindness no more, had fetched out his tidy little sports car, and
without making any more bones about it bolted for his life.
Campion had seen him go with heartfelt relief.

But on the evening of the day after the funeral, while he
was still congratulating himself on a serious danger past,
without warning Luke returned. In the soft yellow light,
while the sound of the mill-race and the songs of the birds
were making the ancient conception of paradise appear
both likely and sensible, the familiar car had swung on to
the flags before the house and a grim yet hangdog figure
had stepped out of it to face him. Luke had, he said,
woodenly, a few more days' leave.

So today, taking it all in all, it was quite understandable
that as Mr. Campion strode homewards he was almost
afraid to turn the corner. For a blessed moment he thought
she was not there. He could see the back of Luke's close-
cropped head above a deck-chair in the covey of them set
out on the ancient paving-stones. It was a civilized scene.
There were morning papers on the ground and the gleam
of hospitable pewter in the dark doorway, and behind, the
low half-timbered façade windowed like a galleon and

graceful as if it were at sea. Mr. Campion took a step forward and paused. Prune was present after all. She was sitting quietly in the shadows on one of the settles in the porch, and as the wind stirred the limes beside the house a shaft of sunlight flickered over her.

To modern eyes she was, he thought, as odd a looking girl as one could wish to see. She was very tall, with narrow bones, a white skin, yellow-brown hair, and her family's distinctive features. Throughout the centuries the Glebe face has had its ups and downs. The young Queen Victoria is said to have observed somewhat brutally that it was "particularly becoming in effigy," but since that time it has not been in fashion. Mr. Campion found it sad.

Prune's beauty, he thought, had been bred to express an ideal which was literally medieval. Piety, docility, quiet, might have suited it well enough, but any attempt to invest it with the modern *gamin* touch was ruinous. The girl was not a brilliant brain but she had grasped that much and at twenty-six had given up trying, only to fall back on precepts which had come down to her with, as it were, the outfit. She kept the nails on her narrow hands short, avoided ornament, and dabbed herself half-heartedly with the kind of lipstick which does not really show.

This morning Mr. Campion regarded her with helpless irritation. It seemed to him that anyone who had ever had time to think about her must have despaired. The wars had wiped out the Glebe line and the attendant revolutions the last of their fortune. Somewhere in the middle, all the great purposes for which they had bred themselves so carefully appeared to have gone too. Poor wretched girl, she had been born too late, and had arrived, meticulously turned out, for a party which had been over for some time. He understood from The Revver that as a somewhat desperate measure she had been given five years in the W.R.N.S. but had emerged from the experience just exactly the same as when she had enlisted. Looking at her, Mr. Campion was no more surprised than if he had heard that two seasons with the Pytchley foxhounds had left an

Afghan practically unchanged. He did not like the present
situation at all. Its futility exasperated and alarmed him. In
his view, Luke was a fine and useful man, far too valuable
to have his progress hindered and his emotional balance
endangered by any hopelessly unhappy experience of this
sort. He joined them and sat down a little more firmly
than was his custom.

Luke glanced at him but did not speak. He looked quiet
and watchful and a good deal less than his age, and Mr.
Campion reflected with wry satisfaction that at least he
was retaining his capacity to do everything in the most
thorough-going way possible. Campion hated it. He had
seen Luke with young women before, teasing them, pa-
tronizing them, showing off like a whole pigeon-loft. This
was an entirely new departure. This might do a man harm
for life. He regarded Prune with cold anger.

She met his gaze with a clear blue stare and returned to
Luke. She was sitting on a little stool, her long arms round
her knees, waiting. She had no coquetry, no subterfuge,
no skill; she just thought he was wonderful. Mr. Campion
was left to thank his stars that she could be relied on not to
say so outright.

He had no doubt at all that it would pass and that in a
week or a month or a year that clear-eyed stare would be
directed elsewhere, equally hopelessly. The fact had got to
be faced. Prune as a present-day product was uneconomic.
In present circumstances she was a menace. At last he
cleared his throat.

"Did you—er—bring any message . . . or anything?"
he demanded.

She blinked thoughtfully, considering him apparently
for the first time.

"Oh yes, I did as a matter of fact." Her languid voice,
which was a caricature of all such voices and belonged to a
much slower world, came softly through the summer air.
"Minnie and Tonker are dropping in to see you on their
way to Kepesake station this morning. Tonker is having a
second-class white burgundy week and will bring some

with him. He may be late so will you please have some
glasses at the ready?''

"Oh yes." Mr. Campion brightened despite his apprehension. "Tonker is still here, is he? I thought he'd gone up.
Where did you hear all this?"

"Minnie phoned The Revver this morning." Prune
seemed disposed to answer questions if she could still look
at Charlie Luke. "Just to thank him for getting the funeral
safely over, you know." The remark trailed into silence
and Campion grunted.

"No loose ends?" he suggested helpfully.

"Well, some parsons are frightfully inefficient. The
Revver does get things reasonably tied up. He's not mental, even if he is my uncle." The Glebe mouth, which
Vandyke captured so well and Gainsborough muffed so
badly, drooped with faint self-disparagement. "He was
tremendously relieved. He thought they were still quarrel-
ling when she didn't turn up at the service. The postman
told him that it was because she'd got a black eye, but he
didn't believe that, naturally. But he is pleased she phoned
because they haven't spoken for weeks.''

"Why?" Mr. Campion found himself determined to
divert her attention, if he had to shout at her.

Prune raised brows which were high enough already.
"Oh, just one of their things. The Revver is terrified that
she might go religious. It's all those pictures her father
painted, I think, lions and lambs and saints and rather nice
interiors. But that's only in his subconscious. He says
she's all alone down there except for the menagerie and
that women often go a bit peculiar about that sort of thing
at her age.''

"Does he say this to her?" inquired Mr. Campion with
interest.

"Of course he does." The drawl went on lazily but her
eyes scarcely stirred from the dark brooding face opposite.
"He's always begging people not to be religious. The Bip
had to warn him to use caution lest by sheer inadvertence
he emptied the church. The Revver says you can be as pi

as you like privately, but you mustn't think too much
about it or you may forget yourself and mention it. He was
explaining this to Minnie one day in the winter, when she
was rather miserable and he'd ploughed down there through
the snow to take her the parish magazine, and she said that
what he meant, she supposed, was that a Christian gentleman must never run the risk of degenerating into a vulgar
Christian. He said that was exactly what he did mean. And
she said he was a damned old British humbug.''

"British?"

"Yes, that's what hurt him. He's Welsh. But she was
having one of her American days. Sometimes she's one
and sometimes the other; you never know. And so she
went on to mention that in her opinion, speaking as at least
half a good American, one had only got to consider the
tenets laid down for the English gent to realize exactly
what sort of raging brute the animal must be by nature to
make such a fuss about conforming to them. Not trampling
on old women, and not being cruel to children, and so on.
That was the quarrel.''

She paused and turned slowly to look at him at last.

"It's a good thing it's over," she droned on seriously,
"because Minnie's really getting more and more peculiar.
The village says it's not religion, it's blackmail. They
know most things but they get it a bit wrong usually.''

Mr. Campion grinned at her. "You just hear it on the
drums, I suppose?"

"No." Prune was undisturbed. "I listen. I can't make
friends with the village and I'm no good at bossing them,
but I stick around and after a while they just forget I'm
there and talk. Are you going to get the glasses for Tonker,
or do you want me to do it?''

Before he could reply there was a crisp rustle behind
them and a utility brake, driven with distinction, came to a
silent halt on the exact edge of the gravel. Instantly the
landscape became full of excitement.

A somewhat dishevelled Amanda, who looked so like
herself at seventeen that Mr. Campion discovered that he

was thinking absent-mindedly what a silly young fool he
was himself, slid out, waved to them briefly to stay where
they were, and released a fine mixed bag from the body of
the van. A small boy shot out first, followed by a fat,
Victorian-looking collie, and finally, amid a shower of
lemons, Mr. Magersfontein Lugg himself, garbed taste-
fully *pour le sport*.

Both Amanda and her son wore well-washed boiler-suits
whose original rust colour had faded to a pinkish tan. The
Pontisbright hair, which can be mistaken for fire when
seen under Suffolk skies, flamed on them both, Amanda's
a thought darker now but the boy's a true ruby shouting in
the sun. At that distance they looked absurdly alike, two
skinny figures superintending the descent of the others.
Apart from the fact that the dog dismounted head foremost
and Mr. Lugg did not, the two performances were curiously alike, each operation involving much hesitation and
manoeuvre.

The animal belonged to Aunt Hatt and was a black and
white long-haired shepherd dog. He was marked like a
Panda and now in middle age was of enormous size and
almost indistinguishable from one. The crofter from
Inverness-shire who had sold him as a puppy to the New
England lady had told her distinctly that his name was
"Choc," and, disliking diminutives, she had had it en-
graved in full upon his collar—"Choc-ice." He was frighteningly intelligent and assumed he was the party's sole
host. On the other hand, from the way he was dressed Mr.
Lugg appeared to infer that he considered himself the sole
guest. Taking each garment in order of its first appearance,
he wore tennis shoes, a pair of black dress trousers which
he was using up, a white linen coat as a badge of office,
an open-neck shirt to show his independence, and a hard
black hat to make it clear to the natives that he came from
a civilized city.

As soon as he reached the ground, he stretched himself
gingerly, hitched his trousers, and began to shout at the
boy Rupert. His rich voice, thick as the lubricant of his
latter years, mingled with the chatter of the mill-race.

"Leave them lemons and come 'ere. Bottle o' beer's gone over in the back. Save the fags or they'll be as wet as a Brewer's Calamity. Buck up. Waste not want not. Where d'you think you are? In the Army? We've got to do more than *sign* for this lot."

Amanda left them to it and came over to take the chair Campion pulled out for her beside his own. She was brown and dusty and her honey-coloured eyes were dancing. She spread out her oil-stained hands and her heart-shaped face was alive with laughter.

"Twenty years doesn't count, apparently," she said, her high clear voice sounding suitably gratified. "I'm having the resident mechanic's return. I took down Honesty Bull's electric pump this morning. He's still landlord of The Gauntlett and sent you his best respects. I also saw Scatty Williams who used to work for us. He said I could take his television to bits seeing as how I'd designed an aeroplane! Oh I am having a lovely time."

"So am I," said Mr. Campion. "Been to see a grave. There was a ghoul there." He felt a brute as her smile faded and he patted her apologetically. "Tonker's coming," he said to cheer her.

"Oh but he's not." It was her turn to be sorry for him. "We met them in the village. They're late for the train. They can't make it this morning but Minnie wants us to go over after lunch, if you don't mind awfully working very hard. They're getting ready for the party on Saturday. Hallo Prune."

"Hallo." Prune's eyes were like a Siamese cat's in colour and she turned them reluctantly from the unnervingly silent figure of the Chief Inspector and settled herself to behave.

"It's still on, is it, the party?" she inquired dreamily. "The Revver thought that Minnie was sounding him about it, to see if it was decent to have it so soon after the funeral, I mean, but he couldn't be sure. She's not too happy about it, is she?"

Amanda appeared to consider the question with great seriousness.

"I don't know," she said at last. "She's a little bit odd, and she's hurt her eye or something. But Tonker has no doubts at all. He says it's been laid on for six months and that his old friend Uncle William would burst like a subterranean magnum at the thought of being the cause, however innocent, of delaying the just consumption of alcohol. He also says that he's no idea who he's asked anyway, and so there's no question of putting anyone off. He's going to have the party." She glanced at Campion. "It's a Perception and Company Limited do. Tonker and Wally have laid it on and the Augusts are coming."

Prune stirred. "Last time the Augusts came to one of Tonker's parties it was clowns *v.* kids all over the estate, and there was an awful row because somebody's child got kidnapped and turned up inside the big drum at the grand finale of 'Socks and Shoes' at the Hippodrome."

Amanda nodded gravely. "I heard about that. I heard a lot of peculiar things in the village. Is Minnie all right, Prune?"

"I think so." The observation did not sound convincing. "I haven't seen her for ages, and anyway I expect she's rather upset about Uncle William. She was very fond of him and he did die very suddenly, and it was only last Friday midnight."

"How were they today?" Mr. Campion sounded wistful and a grin split Amanda's triangular mouth.

"To be honest, they looked like a seaside picture-post-card," she said, laughing. "They were wedged in the tub cart together, with the donkey in front looking very knock-kneed. Minnie had her John hat on her grey bob and Tonker was all dressed up for London, and they were roaring with laughter over a game they'd invented. Some woman had written to this morning's paper to say that her cat was so clever that she always had to spell things in front of it. Tonker was chanting 'the m-o-k-e-s-t-i-n— . . .' and Minnie was trying to shut him up because they were passing the Miss Farrows, and giggling so that the tears were streaming down her nose, you know how they do."

Mr. Campion sighed. "They sound all right. Why does Minnie maintain that ass? Exercise?"

Prune gazed into the middle distance. "She says a car is out of the question." She paused and added inconsequentially, "There are fourteen gold frames still in packing-cases in the granary behind the barn."

In the silence which greeted this news, vaguely ominous in a countryside which can boast the highest percentage of rare lunatics in the world, Rupert, who had come up unobserved on springing feet, laid a bunch of wilted greenery on his father's knees.

"For you," he said politely.

"Kind," conceded Mr. Campion, "and thoughtful. A curious collection. Who sent it?"

The boy was at the ballet age. He raised his thin arms and danced a little, whilst thinking no doubt of duller means of expression.

"A man," he said at last and waved vaguely towards the heath.

"Rupert went off on his own whilst Lugg was in the Post Office talking to Scatty, and when he turned up again he had these with him. He says someone gave them to him to give to you," Amanda explained as she leant forward to take one spray from the bunch. "We thought it could be a message, but this is the only one I know—cypress. That means—" she hesitated, "—oh, something silly and unlikely. Death, I think."

"Mourning," a voice at her elbow corrected her, and Charlie Luke sat up suddenly, surprising everybody. For a moment he looked magnificent, poetic even, like the hero in the painting casting aside the restraining garlands of the nymphs. And then the cheerful roar of his personality emerged, starting up like the sudden sound of traffic in a radio programme. "Just a moment, chum, this is right in my manor."

His long hand closed over the bunch of leaves and his bright black eyes glanced round the group as he included Prune gently into the party.

"When I was a kid in south-east London I had a botany
mistress," he announced, sketching her in in silhouette
with his free hand. "She was the first woman I ever
noticed wasn't straight all the way up. We all had a crush
on her and I used to carry her books." He favoured them
with a smug adenoidal smile, crossed his eyes slightly, and
sucked in his breath. "We used to bring her flowers, pinch
them out of the park when the keepers weren't looking.
She never knew, poor girl. She was most respectable, and
a little bit soft, I think, looking back. Well, she had a book
about the language of flowers, and I, being smart as paint,
got the name of it and borrowed another copy from the
public library." His teeth shone for a second in his dark
face. "*That* ended in tears," he said. "Well now, what
have we here? Rhododendrons. I don't know what that is.
Monk's-hood. God knows what that means either. Wait a
minute. Escoltzia. That's more like it. That means 'do not
refuse me.' I always had a bit of that in. And pink. Pink."
He looked up. "A pink means 'makes haste.' Mourning?
Do not refuse me? Make haste? Sounds like the same old
story, guv'nor. Someone is broke again and unusually
restrained about it. That's my translation."

Amanda rose and went into the house and a minute later
leant out of the casement beneath which they sat. She had
a white book lettered in gold and very tattered, in her
outstretched hand.

"I knew we had one long ago," she said. "Aunt Hatt is
amazing. Everything is just where it always was. Look it
up, Albert."

Mr. Campion took the volume obediently and pushed up
his spectacles.

"*The Language and Sentiment of Flowers,*" he read.
"Published by Messrs. Ballantyne and Hanson, London
and Edinburgh, 1863, price sixpence. Rhododendron: danger, beware." He looked up. "Eh? Where's the other
one?" He took the final wilted stalk on which a few purple
buds were just observable. "That's Monk's-hood, is it,
Charles?"

"Was when I went to school. What does it say? 'The bums are in'?"

Mr. Campion turned the pages among which the pressed flowers of earlier heart-throbs lay brown and sad.

"Monk's-hood," he said at last. "Well well. 'A deadly foe is here.' "

Behind him Amanda laughed. "Again?" she said.

Charlie Luke was frowning. He seemed mildly affronted.

"Mourning—danger—do not refuse me," he repeated. "That's a smashing welcome home. Who gave it to you, son?"

Rupert, who had been standing before them throughout the incident, had lost interest in the proceedings. He was making a line on the stones with the rubber heel of his sandal. He liked the Chief Inspector, but the particular way his brows went up to points in the middle reminded him of one certain clown in the circus at Christmas who had seemed to him to have a face so exquisitely humorous that he could not think of it without laughing until his midriff hurt. As he had put the question Luke's brows had shot up, and the mischief was done. Rupert could think of nothing else. He laughed and laughed until he slid under the chair on which Luke sat and was extricated and shaken and sat up still laughing, crimson in the face and hysterical.

"A man," was all he could gasp, "just an ordinary man."

Meanwhile Luke's face had grown dark and he became very quiet. So far he had diagnosed a family joke but was not at all sure at whose expense it had been made. Mr. Campion remained thoughtful. Presently he took out a pencil and made a note of the flowers and their meaning on the back of an envelope. As he glanced up he caught sight of the D.D.C.I.'s expression, and became instantly apologetic.

"My dear chap," he said, "you must think we're round the bend."

Luke turned his head. Amanda had withdrawn and Prune, exhibiting unexpected resource in the matter, had dealt firmly with young Rupert, swinging him up under her arm and carrying him into the house. The two men were alone in the garden.

"You and who else?" Luke inquired suspiciously.

"Me and my chum." Mr. Campion appeared embarrassed. "My correspondent. The lad with the affected handwriting."

Luke thrust his hands in his pockets, jangling the coins there. He was standing with his feet wide apart, rising slightly on his toes; the great weight of his shoulders was apparent and his chin was thrust forward aggressively.

"There's something terrifying about this place," he said abruptly. "It's so beautiful that you don't notice for a bit that it's sent you barmy. I feel drunk. All that greengrocery's quite clear to you, is it? It's just laid on with the sunshine and the nice voices and the barrel in the cellar, I suppose? Just one of the things you happen to have."

Mr. Campion looked more and more unhappy. He was looking at the stones at his feet and retracing with his own toe the line that Rupert had drawn. After a while he looked up.

"Have you ever thought I was a bit redundant?" he inquired unexpectedly. "My job, I mean. Don't get this wrong. I don't mean anything sociological. I'm merely talking of work. Has it ever occurred to you that I don't do anything that the police couldn't handle rather better?"

Luke coloured. He was laughing, and his eyes and the gleam of his teeth were very bright.

"No," he protested, "no, of course not. You're not a Private Eye and you're not an amateur. I expect we look on you as an Expert, a chap we call in like a pathologist."

"Ye-es." The pale eyes behind Mr. Campion's spectacles were hard and surprisingly shrewd. "That's all very nice of you, but it's not the whole truth, you know. I have an extensive private practice."

"And that green stuff is part of it?"

"It could be." Campion was still hesitant. He put his arm through Luke's and they strolled down the path together, with the Mill on one side and Aunt Hatt's flower garden on the other. "All policemen aim to be discreet," he continued at last, "but discretion isn't a virtue, it's a gift. I think you have it. Even so I'm not going to make any startling revelations. But because I don't want you to think that we're *(a)* laughing at you or *(b)* assing about in fairyland, I'll explain how my mind is working. First of all I know no more than you do what that message means or where it comes from."

"But you think it is one?"

"It strikes me as a bit much as a coincidence."

"Oh, so it does me. It's a joke."

"Ah," Mr. Campion paused to survey the multi-coloured garden dancing in the restless sunlight. "That's the likeliest possibility except that the only man I can think of who would play it couldn't possibly have done it."

"Oh. Who's that?"

"You."

"Me?" Luke was scandalized. "Don't be silly. Besides I've been here all the morning."

"I know." Campion's grip on his arm tightened. "If it were you, there would have to be a confederate. I don't think you have one. That leaves me with a straight message from one who knows me well enough to suppose that its inference would reach me."

Luke scratched his shorn curls hopelessly. "It's cockeyed," he said, "out of this world. Who on earth . . . ?"

Campion sighed. "Exactly." He sounded satisfied. "That is just what I thought. The one person who might conceivably have sent me a little dig in the ribs like that is not quite on earth. The reverse, in fact."

Luke regarded him blankly. He had gathered a straw from his wanderings and had been fiddling with it for some time. Now he stuck it idly in his hair by way of comment.

Campion frowned at him. "Come come," he said. "Use the outfit, Chief. Start her up. It's not as bad as that. Haven't you ever had a business letter from a man who

was almost too coy to send it? Something which begins
with 'Private and Confidential, Secret and Without Prejudice,' and continues 'Burn before Reading' or words
to that effect in the margin of every paragraph? Of course
you have. In my experience, those letters always say the
same thing. Someone who wishes to be kept right out of
the affair has observed something which he feels it may be
to his interest for you to know. This message strikes me as
being the same sort of thing, but more so. It's a business
letter which in fact is so discreet that it doesn't exist.''

Luke began to grumble. ''Damned subtle stuff.''

''Of course it is. That's my line,'' said Albert Campion.
After a pause he turned back to the house. ''Mourning,''
he remarked. ''This afternoon I'm going over to the only
house in the place which is technically in mourning. Coming with me?''

Luke hesitated. He was staring across the border at a
clump of Russell lupins, tall, narrow blossoms, cream
fading to yellow fading to brown; odd, formal flowers, but
beautiful and very unusual. Beyond them the river wound
through the water-meadows to a grey distance which was
streaked with gold where the woods began. He spoke
reluctantly, but although there was apology in his voice
there was no indecision there, rather a sort of resigned
finality.

''I'm booked to go that way this afternoon,'' he said,
nodding upstream. ''There's otter there, they say. I've
never seen one.''

Mr. Campion opened his mouth to object that an otter is
a creature of the dusk, but he changed his mind and said
nothing. He recollected an axiom of his grandfather's: ''A
treed cat, a man in love, and the French. God help the fool
who tries to rescue any one of them.''

They walked back to the house in silence, but before
they went in the D.D.C.I. spoke again. The withered
posy lying on the stones caught his eye and he stopped to
pick it up and tidy it away under the bushes by the door.

''I don't pretend to know much about it, but I'd say that
if you're right there was only one thing in the world as shy

as this lot suggests," he remarked seriously, "and that's Money."

"Yes," said Mr. Campion casually, "that's what I thought."

II

"Speakin" as a sentimental ole fool," announced Mr. Lugg, breathing heavily from his climb up the embankment, "there's nothink so loverly as a loverly drop o' Nachure."

"That's only nachure, I suppose," said Campion, who was just ahead of him with Amanda.

Lugg dropped on to the grass with a grunt. "Sarc won't get you nowhere," he said ominously. "Tittle and tattle, rattle and natter, fritter away your life with it. Whatever you say, you won't better this—always supposin' the lady we're a-visitin' ain't teetotal or otherwise vicious. Sit down, carn't yer? Them two is all right." He shook his festoon of chins towards the remainder of the party, Choc and Rupert, who were scrambling down the bank towards the path below where an oak tree shed deep shadows over a stile and a rustic bridge. The boy went first and the fat dog followed more cautiously, his great plume waving over the remarkable white petticoat breeches which he appeared to be wearing.

Amanda sat down and Campion dropped beside her. "It's the best view of all of the house, I think," she said. "It always pulled me up, even as a child. You can see how the place got its name."

They were looking down into a hidden valley, part natural and part created by the bank on which they sat. In a hollow, lying beside the stream, which at that point was wide and shallow, was a little estate. It was all alone. There was no other building in sight, and all around it the deep meadows and the fenlands, where the cricket-bat willows look like egret feathers, were tucked about it like a pile of green cushions. At that distance it appeared toy-sized and unreal in the very bright light which simplified all the shapes and colours until one could believe that one saw a miniature in a paperweight. There was the house, which was fifteenth-century and gabled like the Mill, the barn which was thatched and enormous, one of the famous tithe barns of the east country, a small cottage, a boat house, even a white dog kennel, very vivid and neat by a yard pump with a hat over it, all scintillating in the dazzling glare. There were white fences and little white gates about, and everywhere a mass of flowers which outrivalled Aunt Hatt's own.

"The Beckoning Lady," said Mr. Campion. "How came a pub there, down at the end of such a lane? It isn't even on a through road."

"It was never a pub." Amanda spoke without taking her eyes from the scene. "It's just the local name for the house, which got into the deeds at some point. No one knows why it's called that, except that as far back as anyone can trace it has been owned by a woman, and there's always been trouble over it because it is said that as soon as a man sees it he tries to get hold of it to do it in. It has an extraordinary history. There have been dozens of lawsuits over it. This bank we're sitting on is the beginnings of a railway. There was an awful row about that last century, but it got stopped in the end at enormous cost. Then Minnie's mother had it, and her father the painter fell for it, and when she wouldn't sell it he stayed on and married her."

"Determined chap," suggested her husband.

"Oh, I think he fell for the lady too, but the house started it. He was a widower and she wasn't a girl. It's a queer place, though. People do go silly about it."

"I know why," Lugg said thickly. "It's got the ole come-'ither. Look at 'er. 'Come 'ere and be 'appy, dear,' that's what she's sayin'. I should say so! 'Come 'ere and rest, duck. Wot's an ole death-watch beetle among frens? And if we lie a bit low, damp won't 'urt a great strong bloke like you.' You can see it in every line of 'er. Lumme," he added, sitting up as abruptly as his bulk would allow, "wot's that? Indians?"

He pointed across the glistening landscape to one of the wilder enclosures where, amid stones and huge clumps of bramble, there were two or three unmistakable wigwams.

"Kids," said Amanda. "Minnie's father instituted that camp. In those days we had to have some excuse for going about half-naked. Whenever there are enough children down there it gets revived. Minnie collects kids, especially when Tonker has a party. They like it and it makes it fun for her. Her niece and nephew are there, of course, the American ones. The Bernadines, and I think some of their school friends. They *give* the party."

Mr. Lugg was interested. "Do they 'ave charge of the booze?"

"I think so. Who better? They don't like it."

A smile of ineffable sentimentality crept into Lugg's rheumy eyes.

"Bless their little 'earts," he said piously. " 'Ullo, now wot?"

The sheep-dog's bark, than which there is nothing more misleadingly offensive, was shattering the sunlit peace. They could see him distinctly standing in the ditch at the side of the bridge which was not overgrown. His fluffy bulk almost filled the dark opening under the platform as his tail flashed from side to side like a flag. He was barking as collies do, with apparent rage, making a beastly raucous sound and producing more of it than would seem possible from one animal. Rupert was trying to pull him out without success. The petticoat breeches nudged the child back whenever he advanced, and the noise continued.

"Orl right orl right, I'll go." Lugg lumbered to his feet and stumbled on down the slope, grumbling. "Can't sit down now without you yappin'. Shut up, I'm coming! Shut up for Gord's sake! Leave the pore cat alone."

The others left him to it. Amanda glanced back at the house once more and spoke without looking at Albert.

"In the village they say that everything's going to be cleared away down here to make room for a dog track, and the railway to be built after all these years. Fanny Genappe's new house is to be a hotel, and the Forty Angels are

moving in. It's not open talk yet, but I've had it whispered
to me three or four times."

"The Forty Angels?" said Mr. Campion. "That's something out of our childhood."

She smiled, her triangular mouth curling as he liked to
see it best.

"Oh well, they always say that. It just means no name,
no pack drill, and always speak well of them as has money
to sue. But it's crazy, isn't it? I mean, a dog track here,
miles from anywhere."

Mr. Campion's face was as blank as a plate. "Sounds
wrong somehow."

"Somehow?"

He nodded at her. "Somehow. Got any other choice bits
of misinformation?"

She considered. Lugg had reached the bottom of the
slope and was preparing to descend into the ditch.

"They say that Minnie doesn't want to part with the
place but that she's being driven round the bend by a
blackmailer."

"Oh yes?" Campion was inclined to be entertained.
"This always was a lively spot. What is her guilty secret?
Tonker? That's a lie. Not only did I dance at their wed-
ding; I swung from a chandelier."

"No, seriously. They don't know what she's hiding, but
they insist it's blackmail and it's gone on for at least six
years."

"Six—? Oh nonsense."

"They say so. They'd know too. It's no time at all by
their standards."

Mr. Campion shook his head. "Great man fails to con-
nect," he said seriously. "No. No answering buzz whatever. It's happened again, something I don't know. Tell
me Amanda, without prejudice, would you leave me for an
otter?"

She laughed and her hair glowed like fire in the sun.

"You can't stop *that*," she said. "I don't see how you
can expect to. That's got to take its natural course. People
in Pontisbright are born knowing that. Oh dear, here comes

Rupert. Lugg's got stuck, I suppose. I do wish he wouldn't wedge himself into such impossible places.''

"Cat-burglar blood," said Campion absently as the small boy, bright-eyed and important, came scrambling towards him. "What's the damage, Captain?''

"Lugg says please will you go down without me and Mother, because he has something to show you private.''

"Private to show me, has he? All right, you two sit here.''

He went off down the steep slope, his long legs swinging loosely and easily as ever. Amanda watched him with affection and made room for her son beside her. Rupert lay back in the grass and looked up at the sky. Presently he said:

"There's a man asleep down there.'' Watching her slyly out of the corner of his eye, he saw that she was suitably startled.

"Really?'' she said at last. "How do you know?''

"Because I saw him when I looked under the bridge. I couldn't get near because Choc kept pushing me out. He is an enormous dog, soft but enormous.''

"Yes," she agreed absently. Her light-brown eyes were worried, and she stared down at the two men who were now both in the ditch by the bridge, peering at something.

Rupert continued to contemplate the infinity of the sky. The blue had turned into a million colours, he noticed, like hundreds and thousands.

"Uncle William went to sleep," he said distinctly.

He was the first child she had known well, and Amanda was taken aback. She turned right round to him, which was the reaction he had in mind.

"Who told you that?''

"Lugg. He said 'He's gone to sleep, pore old perisher.' '' Rupert sighed. "And so they buried him," he said with great matter-of-factness.

Amanda felt the need to assert herself. "Look here,'' she said, "you think you know a lot, but you needn't hold out on me. Who gave you those old flowers this morning?''

Rupert screwed up his face and made a great effort at concentration.

''He did,'' he said at last.

"Who?"

"The man who is asleep down there."

A cloud so small and white that it seemed to have no substance passed over the sun and its shadow raced towards them over the grass, gave them a chill kiss, and was gone.

"Are you sure?"

Rupert decided to come clean. "No dear," he said, "not truly sure. But you know, I do really think so. He was much the same."

CHAPTER III

At The Beckoning Lady

Mr. Campion, telephoning from a seat on the bed in the room over the kitchen at The Beckoning Lady, thought he had never had such difficulty in persuading authority to notice a corpse before.

His old friend Sir Leo Pursuivant, the Chief Constable at Kepesake, wanted to talk about everything else; his well-remembered voice came crackling over the wire.

"Campion. My dear fellow. Couldn't be more pleased. Heard you were down. For Tonker's party, I suppose? I said to Poppy, hope to goodness we see something of them. We shall all be there on Saturday. Poppy's going to run the bar. Minnie kindly asked her. She's been prinking herself up all this week. Not enough of that sort of jollification these days down here. Money tight and life dull. I pulled a tendon in my foot so I'm stuck at the desk, but I shall be there on the day, please God. Amanda all right? And the boy? Poor William, eh? I didn't come over. He wouldn't have wanted it. Would have wanted to slip off quietly without casting a blight. What was it? Anno Domini? Ah, gets us all in the end. Seems a pity. What's your news, my boy? Still turning up interesting things?"

"I don't know." The caller got a word in at last and proceeded to explain.

"A body? Dead man?"

Mr. Campion could envisage the mottled hand feeling first for the pen and then for the pince-nez on the thick black cord. "Found it yourself, did you? God bless my soul, Campion, what an extraordinary feller you are! You're at Harriet's mill, are you?"

"No sir. The Beckoning Lady. We found the corpse just now, coming along. Lugg went back to report it to the bobby and I came on here to the phone."

"Ah. Unfortunate just at this time. It's not actually on The Beckoning Lady land, I hope, is it?"

"I don't know. I haven't seen a soul to ask. I came straight up to the telephone. It's in a ditch by the side of the footpath. Do you know the country?"

"Shot over it all my life. There's an old embankment, full of birds in winter. Start from there."

"That's it. Just there. There's a stile . . ."

"With a bridge by it. I know. Just in there, is it? Thank goodness for that. That's not Minnie's. Very well, my boy, we'll see to that for you. Keep the young people out of the way and give us a couple of hours. No need to alarm the women."

An involuntary smile twisted Mr. Campion's wide mouth. "It may not be quite as simple as that," he said cautiously. "I didn't like to disturb anything so I can't tell you much, but he's very dead, he doesn't look like a local product, and he's got a tremendous hole in his head. Death must have been instantaneous."

There was a brief silence.

"Not natural causes?"

"No. Blunt instrument. Perhaps not quite so blunt."

"Very well." There was a note of resignation in the pleasant voice. "The Superintendent will come down at once. Pussy's gone, you know, but we've got a new fellow called Fred South. He's been in the Urban area for years and is finishing his time with us. He's very intelligent and uncommonly quick by our standards. Where will he find you? Still with Minnie?"

Mr. Campion hesitated. "I was going to ask you about that," he said. "Lugg actually found the body. I am on holiday—er—technically, and I wondered if I need be called as a witness?"

The Chief grunted. "That's the most suspicious thing I

ever heard you say. Still, Lugg will do. Tell him to stick to his story.''

"Chief Inspector Charles Luke is staying with us," Mr. Campion suggested diffidently. "I don't suppose for a moment that you'll want to call in the Yard, but if you do I thought you'd care to know that there's a good man already here."

Leo showed unexpected interest. "Luke? I want to meet him, he's a brave chap, Campion. I read about it. A gallant officer. Nice type too, eh? Good. Well, I'll get South's report and if it warrants it I'll telephone London. I've been thinking. You know what this will turn out to be? Motorists."

Mr. Campion's bewildered expression faded. "As opposed to local people who drive cars?" he suggested.

"Eh? Yes, that's what I said. Motorists. Terrible fellers from God knows where. Depend upon it, one of those has run down some poor feller, carted him for twenty miles or so, and then got rid of him. That's about it. What did you say?"

"I said it'd be a long way to carry him. He's lying half a mile from the road."

"Is he?" Leo sounded unimpressed. "All the same, the Yard are the best people to deal with a killer of that kind. They've got the machinery, they know the type. Good-bye my boy. I hope we meet on Saturday. Good Lord yes, Poppy would never forgive me if anything happened to stop that."

Mr. Campion sent his love to that plump and smiling lady who had once been the darling of the musical-comedy stage and had married Leo late in his widowerhood. He also took the opportunity to ask after Janet, Leo's daughter by his first wife. She had married a sort of friend of Campion's own, one Gilbert Whippet, now Chairman of the Mutual Ordered Life Endowment Insurance Company— "the Mole," in the vernacular—and he heard with gratification that they too could be expected at the party. It promised to be quite a gathering.

As he hung up he glanced about him curiously. He

found the entire room surprising, inasmuch as it appeared
to be his hostess's own. At any rate, the painted four-
poster which he remembered from the studio in Clerkenwell
quite twenty years before had been moved in here from the
great sunlit chamber in the front of the house which she
and Tonker had shared in the early days of her return to
the country. All round the walls were treasures peculiarly
Minnie's own. There was her father's head of a cherub,
the exquisite Rushbury water-colour and Edmund Blampied's
superb drawing of a farm horse, with "For Minnie on her
birthday" inscribed under the signature. Campion looked
for the famous caricature which Tom Chambers gave them,
and found it on the other side of the bed. He went round to
look at it again: *"The Eternal Charleston, Minnie and
Tonker, 1928."*

The drawing made him laugh now as it had then; Minnie, shown as more than half a mule with her long nose
and wicked eye, was wearing a dress of the period, its
short skirt made of the Union Jack and the long-waisted
blouse of the Stars and Stripes. On her head was a brave's
full head-dress, with paint brushes dripping where feathers
should have been. It was wickedly like her, yet the master-
piece was Tonker. Tom had drawn Tiger Tim as he had
appeared in the weekly comic paper of that name, and had
apparently lifted the animal completely. There was the
jaunty back, the overstuffed paws, and the waving tail, yet
every line of the figure was also irrefutably Tonker himself, truculent, sandy, and thinking of something dangerous to do. They were dancing, or fighting, and the dust
rose in clouds from under their feet.

Mr. Campion was still contemplating it when the door
was kicked open and a small woman came pattering in.
She did not see him immediately because she was carrying
a newly-pressed dress on a hanger high in front of her, in
an attempt to save its trailing hem, but as he swung round
she heard him and peered across the bed. He saw it was
Emma Bernadine.

Emma was a handmaid of the arts. When he had first
met her she was painting children's white wood tuck-boxes

to look like pirate chests. In those days she had been a
sly-eyed little party, much younger than the crowd which
had grown up with Minnie, but she had strung along with
them and, when Jake Bernadine's first wife had given up
in despair, had married and mothered him, enjoyed his
strange pictures, and had children by him. Just before the
arrival of the twins they had borrowed the cottage on The
Beckoning Lady estate for a summer holiday and, since
the landlord of their Putney studio had taken that opportunity to distrain upon their goods, had not yet gone away
again.

It was some years since Campion had set eyes on her
and he saw with interest that she had become a type in the
interim, stocky and cheerful and quite happy in the exhausted fashion of the times.

She was wearing a bright blue dress of coloured sheet-
ing, embroidered across the shoulders with huge hand-
worked flowers, a black sateen peasant apron, and rope-soled
shoes, while her head was wrapped in a dinner napkin,
cunningly creased as long ago in good houses they used to
serve bread.

"Hullo," she said, "why aren't you working?"

"I suppose people really do say things like that." Mr.
Campion sat down on the bed, since there was no chair.

"Get up, don't make a mess, be careful, look out." She
shooed him away as she spread the dress on the counter-
pane, and he looked at it dubiously. It was a minute print,
grey on white, and seemed to be very plain.

"Minnie's, for the party. I made it. We hunted everywhere for the material and found it at last at the village
shop. It must have been there in one of the stock drawers
for seventy years. Ninepence a yard and we starched it.
Isn't it very nice?"

"Very," he agreed and hunted for a word, "restrained."

She screwed up her eyes and stood looking at it. "Oh
not bad, it will look odd, you know, and rather good."
She pulled a seam out carefully and stood back. "Jake is
painting mine," she remarked. "I sized a piece of calico
and ran it up, and he's doing his damnedest. I must get

back before he decides it's too good to wear and cuts the
skirt up to frame. Isn't it fun, but isn't it exhausting! My
feet . . ."

Mr. Campion looked dismayed. "You make me feel
elderly," he said. "Is it still worth it?"

"Oh yes," she assured him, her round face packed with
earnestness. "It's our only chance of seeing anyone at all.
It's *killing* while it lasts and the clearing up takes months,
but at least one's alive for a few hours. You don't know
what it's like down here in the winter, sweetie. Not a
sound. Not a voice. Only you and the radio. I exist from
one of Tonker's parties to the next."

The conversation threatened to become emotional.

"I haven't seen Minnie yet," he said, hastily. "I wanted
to phone and someone in the kitchen sent me up here. I'm
in her bedroom, I suppose?"

"You are. The telephone's here, you see. It's the only
one. There's a bell in the front hall and when it rings you
have to run like stink before the caller gives up. Perfectly
insane but there you are! Have you seen the rooms I've
redecorated for Minnie?"

She took his sleeve to hurry him and he found himself
dragged first into Minnie's old bedroom and then into the
smaller one beside it, where there had been a transformation. His first impression revisiting the old house had been
that it was shabby in the pleasant way in which old homes
crumble, but in the two bedrooms now so proudly displayed a start had been made. They were a little arty in
their sprigged chintz petticoats, even a little dated, but
they looked comfortable and the beds were plump and
new, and there was running water.

Emma looked round her and sighed. "Oh lovely," she
said earnestly.

"Pleasant," he agreed. "Who sleeps here?"

"Just exactly who you'd think!" said Emma. "Nobody
at all, of course. What a life, eh? So far round the bend we
meet ourselves coming back. Run along. See you later.
I'm dying to talk but I haven't got time. Look up old Jake.
He's doing some very new stuff. Ask about it. Don't just
look."

"I will." He tried to sound enthusiastic and went off down the staircase. On the first landing there was a magnificent leaded window overlooking a flower garden and he paused to glance out at the blazing mass of colour. The drive was a little shaggy he had noticed coming along, and the kitchen garden was a wilderness. But here there was a display which would have done credit to a Dutch bulb-grower's catalogue. The effect was blinding; arches and trellises, vines and crawling roses, massed one on top of the other in ordered glory. The wide river, shallow as a ford, was almost obscured by the show. One small opening draped with clematis and lace-vine had been left, however, and as his eye was drawn towards it he saw Rupert pass by on the other side. He blinked. Unless he had been utterly deceived, the item clutched to his boiler-suited bosom had been a magnum of champagne. Campion saw the gleam of the gold paper distinctly. Before he had had time to clear his mind, another child passed the archway. She was a fat little person clad solely in yellow pants, and a squaw's single feather. She too carried a gaudy bottle. Behind her came a boy two or three years older, and behind him a girl in her early teens. They were all vaguely Red Indian in costume, and were all laden with the same sensational freight, which they carried with earnest concentration. The operation appeared to be secret and of a military character.

Campion was turning away when he saw two more laden children go by. A trifle dazed, he went on down the stairs. The door of the room which had been Minnie's mother's drawing-room was directly in front of him and he could not resist putting his head in to see the Cotman again. The white-panelled room was much as he remembered it, but the picture had gone. There was a flower-piece of Minnie's own in its place, but the magic water-colour, so passionate under its placidity, had vanished for ever. Saddened, he pushed open the door of the old front kitchen which was now, it seemed, the family dining-room. There was a Swedish cooking-stove in place of the old range, a tiled floor, and an elm farm table scrubbed white and

surrounded by innumerable stools. It was all very tidy and
spartan and pleasant, and he passed on into the back
kitchen where nothing, as far as he could see, had changed
since the house was built. It was a dim, whitewashed shell
of a place, very large, with a worn stone floor and a flat
stone sink with a hand pump over it. Two doors, one
leading into the garden and one into the yard, stood wide
open, letting in the sunny air.

At work at the sink was the woman he had seen briefly
before in his search for the telephone, and as he came
drifting in she turned to give him a wide china smile.

"Found it, duck?" Her accent was as riotously cockney
as Lugg's own, and as Campion glanced at her he thought
she could have sprung from no other place. She was a
mighty woman, tall as he was, and built on aggressive
lines, like a battle ship, with a square squat head to which
the iron-grey hair was bound as tight as possible in an
intricate mystery of tiny plaits. He guessed that she was in
the sixties but she was powerful still, and hearty, with a
merry eye and clear fresh shining skin. Her pinafore under
the tweed apron, cut lightheartedly at some time from a
pair of trousers, was gay to the point of silliness, and
earrings as big as curtain rings, with a tin bird perching on
each, brushed her plump shoulders where a wisp or two of
hair which had escaped the plaits hung free.

The general effect was sobered a little by a black band
suspiciously like the top of a woollen stocking, which was
pinned to the short sleeve above an arm as thick and
powerful as a navvy's. He suspected that she had been
talking to herself, for as he appeared she went straight on,
merely raising her voice to include him into the party.
"It's not right, is it?" she was saying—" 'Im 'ardly in 'is
grave yet, poor old dear. We know 'e was old but then
that's a thing we've all got to come to. Surely you can put
the Londoners' outin' off, dear, for a week or ten days? I
said. No I can't, she said, and that's flat. You don't
understand. We can't back out of it now. Can't? I said,
there's no can't about it. Oh shut up! Dinah, she said.
They call me Dinah, though me name's Diane. Miss Diane

Varley. I've never bin married. But Mrs. Cassands *was* upset. I could see it, though some people couldn't. Well, she would be. 'E was like a father to 'er and me. We was just 'is girls to 'im. I'm speaking of 'er uncle, Mr. William that was, a saint on earth except for 'is bottle."

Mr. Campion, whose face had been growing more and more blank, took himself in hand. One item in the harangue stood out as an insult to his intelligence. He knew for a fact that this sterling example of a type which was as familiar to him as the city itself, could never have escaped matrimony. Glancing at her left hand he saw at once the bone-deep crease of the wedding ring. Fortunately she was wiping her eyes with the corner of the tweed apron and did not notice his stare.

"Oh I miss 'im," she said brokenly. "I've cried meself sick every night. Bleary old nuisance, 'e was, and I've told 'im so until I was sick of it. I know 'e was lucky to be took so quick. Sometimes they lie and lie. But all the same it was sudden. Old Harry was here, and we was sitting up. We 'adn't gorn 'ome because Mr. Will seemed queer and I didn't like to leave 'im to Mrs. Cassands while Mr. Tonker was down. She doesn't 'ave a lot of time with 'im. Just before twelve I said to Harry—that's my friend—I said, 'I'll take 'im some of this 'ere tea, because 'e may wake up and then 'e'll want it.' So I did, and I went in talking like I always do. 'There you are, you old lump of love,' I said, 'nice and 'ot,' and I turned up the light and then of course I dropped the cup."

The thin man was gratifyingly interested.

"Mr. Farraday was only ill for a day, was he?"

" 'E wasn't ill at all," she protested. "You'd 'ave soon 'eard about it if he was ill. If 'e was poorly 'is little bell rang night and day. 'E was only sleeping. They do. Old people sleep and sleep until you wonder why they bother to wake up."

"What did the doctor say?"

"What could 'e say? Said 'e was dead. I could 'ave told 'im that. 'Is poor old jaw was tied up by the time the doctor saw 'im."

She returned to her pail of soapsuds.

" 'E agreed it was sudden. Told us 'ow lucky we was. Said 'is 'eart 'adn't seemed so bad, but at 'is age and with 'is 'istory we couldn't be surprised at anything, and signed the doings. But we *was* surprised. The old chap 'isself wouldn't 'ave believed it if 'e 'adn't 'ad to."

"He wanted to live, did he?" Mr. Campion had seen his old friend for a few minutes the week before his death, and had seen then that he was very tired. He was happy enough, but weary, and like some crumpled baby seemed anxious to get his head down to sleep.

"Come Gumper," said Miss Diane unexpectedly. " 'E'd made up 'is mind to live till Gumper night. 'E told me so."

Mr. Campion blinked at her and she laughed.

"That's what they call it down 'ere," she explained. "Gumper treason and plot. Guy Fawkes night to us Londoners, bonfire night. My old love said 'e was goin' to live till then. 'That's right,' I said, 'go to 'eaven on a rocket, so you shall.' But 'e didn't. Midsummer night, more like. That's what Saturday is, Mr. Tonker's party. Midsummer night, and William lyin' out there missin' all the bubbly."

She rubbed soap in her eyes and distracted herself, and at that moment there was a shrill shout from Emma somewhere in the house.

"Four o'clock, Dinah!"

"Four o'clock!" echoed Miss Diane and rushed to put her head out of the garden door. "Four o'clock, Spurgeon!"

"Four o'clock!" an answering bellow resounded from the border, and Mr. Campion, who was taken off guard, was just in time to see a man in a straw hat fling down his hoe among the lilies and sprint towards the house. He diagnosed some domestic emergency, but it seemed to be merely a matter of fetching coke from the shed to the kitchens. The operation was conducted at the double and was followed by a headlong dash with the garbage pails to the incinerator, after which the man strode away upstream from where, for some time past, there had come the sound of hammering.

The whole incident was mildly lunatic and Campion was still astonished by it when a voice he recognized floated in from the yard, and Minnie with a boy of about sixteen came in, carrying a load of stacked zinc baths between them.

Visitors from easy-going New York, which will suffer parading Irish and piping Scots without a qualm, were sometimes taken aback by a first sight of Minnie on her own home ground. Latter-day Rip Van Winkles had been known to pour themselves drinks with shaking hands, whilst under the impression that the classic adventure had somehow overtaken them in reverse. Minnie's America had been handed down to her by her father, who had left that country in 1902 and had not then been considered an advanced member of his generation. Like most painters, he was a simple and direct personality of strong affections, and his favourite authors were those of his childhood: Mark Twain, Fenimore Cooper, and Louisa Alcott. Minnie visited the country and kept up with her relatives there, but neither experience had succeeded in modernizing her view. She too was a simple obstinate person with the memory of an elephant, who wore strange clothes. In her youth she had adopted the Mother-Hubbard as the perfect garment to suit her angularity and the eagle's beak nose of the Straws. She always worked with a stout apron for painting, and now, after twenty-five years, these had become as normal a part of her appearance as her John bob and piercing grey eyes. Since The Beckoning Lady was the kind of place where a covered wagon might easily be standing just round the corner, the effect at times was disconcerting. At the moment she looked tired and a trifle harassed but it was clear that she was enjoying herself and in command of a complex situation.

The boy was very like her and was almost as tall. His hair was a corn-coloured mat and the laughter-wrinkles were already deep across his forehead and round his eyes. They planted the baths on the stones with a clatter and Minnie held out her hand.

"Albert, how nice of you. Amanda told us you were

here. There's a frightful lot to do still. You haven't met
Westy, have you? Isn't it a blessed miracle? He's in
quarantine for mumps. Sent home from school last night.
The angels do take care of us. Now, this is Westinghouse
Straw, my grandnephew. My father married twice, you
know." She had a slow deep voice, very English in
intonation.

The youngster shook hands. "After that you just have to
work it out," he said with a hint of apology, which
reminded Campion of Leo mopping up after one of Poppy's clangers. "My sister and I are the children of the
painter's eldest son. Our parents wanted us educated over
here, and so we just moved in on Minnie. Annabelle is
over at the boat house, keeping an eye on the chain-gang,
or at least we hope so. Aunt Hatt's dog is minding the
cellar, and at least we know he'll raise the roof if anything
happens."

Minnie sat down at the table and sagged a little.

"Wouldn't it be awful if they started opening them?"
she said. "That would shake old Tonker."

Westy shot a horrified glance at her. "They might," he
said. "You don't seem to know how young they are."

"They're all right." Minnie spoke with complete conviction. "They've got an orange-juice bar they're running
down there, and they're all going over to the cottage for
tea in a minute."

"I didn't think they'd drink it," said Westy with dignity, "but they might pull the wires off to hear the bang."

"Nonsense, they're not fools." She had the sublime
faith of her type of matriarch. "I *never* have *stupid* children here. Now." She fished in the pocket of her skirt and
brought out a bundle of crumpled lists fastened with a
safety-pin. "That's done the baths. You'll clean them,
Dinah, will you? They're only dusty. Then, when you've
finished, write Ice with this bit of chalk on the two best,
and leave them all here. Albert, would you like to catch
the donkey?"

"Frankly," said Mr. Campion, who had met the beast,
"no."

"I agree," put in Westy hastily. "That's a job for Jake, Minnie. He likes it."

"Well, will you see he does? Then you can harness the tub, and the baths and the six boxes of glasses can all go down together. Don't forget to get yourself some tea. This goes on for days and you'll get utterly exhausted and hate it if you don't eat. Have a lump of cake now."

"Okay ma'am, I'll get it as I go by. Any message for the cottage?"

She examined the list carefully. "No—unless . . . 'Tell Jake about stomach' . . . Westy, I wonder if that wouldn't come better from you."

"What's that?"

"Well—" she hesitated and her fierce eyes were deeply serious, "—no one minds how a man dresses nowadays, and all that sort of rubbish has gone for good, but sometimes when people haven't seen one before and they're new to the place they get sort of embarrassed. Do you see what I mean?"

Westy began to laugh. He had just reached the age when the full rich absurdity of his elders had burst upon him in glorious treasure-trove.

"In other words, if Jake won't shave and doesn't have a hair cut, he must do up his shirt?" he suggested.

Minnie's laughter, which always seemed to take her unawares, burst from her famous nose in a snort.

"Well, the bottom buttons anyway," she said, "*if* he does up the neck. It's the great bow-tie and hairy belly effect which gives strangers a start. Do you think you could put it to him really tactfully? Be careful. He's a funny boy. You know what happened once."

"When someone tipped him?"

"Yes, well, that was utterly unforeseen. It's so unusual nowadays. The poor man was a Jewish box manufacturer and one of Wally's best clients. He had a Rolls and Jake liked the lines of it, so he showed him how to get it in without scratching it. The man gave him half a dollar and, oh dear!"

The boy was sympathetically serious. "He hit him, didn't he?" he said gravely.

"Hit him!" Minnie was indignant. "Not only did he throw him down so that he was stunned, but he took *all* his money, about thirty pounds. He sent ten pounds of it to the Artists' Benevolent Fund right away that afternoon, and threw the rest in the pond. My God, there was a row!"

"What happened?" Mr. Campion was forced to ask the question in spite of himself.

Minnie went back to her list. "Oh, Tonker squared it," she said indifferently. "The man was awfully decent about it. They all came to stay afterwards. Nice noisy people. I painted the daughter. A name like Potter-Higham. Oh Westy, the chairs from the village hall."

He nodded. "I'll talk to Scat. He's up here working on the Wherry. That's going to be whacky. Be seeing you." He padded off, calling in at the pantry on his way.

"Sent by God," said Minnie casually. "What on earth would happen without them all? I can't go tearing about like a two-year-old. Painting the house nearly killed me."

"Landscape? That's a new departure." Campion was interested and she grinned at him.

"Don't be a clot. I mean the house. We colour-washed it, Dinah and I, in April. Didn't you notice?"

Mr. Campion regarded her with astonishment. "I thought it looked very nice," he said.

"It bleary well ought to," remarked Diane from the sink. "She did the top and I did the bottom. Gord we was in a mess! And stiff—blimey!"

"But why?"

"Because it looked like death," said Minnie frankly. "We concreted Will's little terrace as well, and now he'll never use it. Oh dear, I do miss the old pet, Albert. I keep thinking I hear his little bell. He used to ring when he wanted anything."

"And when you took your 'ands out of the water and dried 'em and got in there, 'e'd forgotten what it was," added Diane, laughing.

"You saw the room we made him out of the old dairy, did you?" Minnie hoisted herself to her feet. "Come and look. It made it possible. Once he was bedridden we couldn't manage the stairs. It's very pleasant. Scat—that's Scatty Williams' son, you remember—knocked a south window in for me so that he could see the river.''

As she spoke she led him out into the garden and along a bricked path to the disused dairy. The door was locked but she produced the key from her pocket and they went in. It had made a charming room which as yet was much as its owner had left it, and all the homeliness and sharp realism of old age was there. There was no design and no pretence, but great comfort and an airiness unusual in such apartments. The new window reached from floor to ceiling and outside there was a little concrete platform just big enough for the high hospital bed to be wheeled out upon it.

Minnie sat down in the rocking-chair before the window. "I used to sit here and mend, and shout at the old villain," she said. "He was quite happy, you know, Albert," she said. "He used to sleep all day and nearly all night, but he wasn't bored and he wasn't a fool."

Mr. Campion was wandering about the room. The pathetic medicines were still on the mantelshelf: talc and old-fashioned pills and a small white box labelled "The tablets."

"How did he get here in the first place?" Campion said presently, taking up the box and eyeing its contents through one lens of his glasses. "Did he get left over at a party, or did Tonker bring him to you as a birthday present or something?"

"No." She seemed to be wondering about it herself. "Oh, I remember. Of course. He was evacuated. They bombed London."

"So they did," he agreed. "And he drifted down here, then, did he, and just settled?"

"I suppose he did," she admitted. "We'd known him for ages before that. He was a good old boy, Albert."

"I liked him," said Campion. "He had such stupendous innocence. What are these things in here?"

"Those?" She edged round to look at the box he held out to her. "Pluminal, I think. He used to have one a night, sometimes two in the latter part of the time. The

doctor gave it to us. He used to take it with his last
drink.''

Mr. Campion put the box back and moved on to the
chest of drawers where, in lonely glory, stood Uncle William's tantalus. The centre bottle had still a quarter-inch of
Scotch in it, and from the little drawer below an orange
envelope of a kind now familiar in Britain peeped out
unblushingly.

"Football pools?" he inquired. "Did he still do those?"

"Rather! And he still had a bit on a horse. One of the
last things he did was to pay his bookie. Old Solly L., you
know. He's coming to the party. It was a whacking great
bill, I'm afraid, but Will paid it and it left him pretty well
broke. Solly was overcome. He came down to see him.
They had a glorious session. I thought he'd given Will a
new lease of life. I filled the pools in, of course. They're a
must, aren't they?''

Mr. Campion considered querying this remarkable statement but changed his mind. At the moment, Uncle William's death was his chief concern. So he said instead:

"I suppose that window was kept wide all day?"

"Not lately," she said sadly. "He'd started getting so
cold.''

Mr. Campion crossed the room to stand beside her, and
looked down over the flowers at the stream.

"Was he insured?" he inquired with uncharacteristic
bluntness.

Minnie glanced at him oddly. "No dear, he wasn't. He
was too old before he thought of it and besides—'' she
hesitated and finally laughed. "He'd given most of his
money to me you know—made it over to me four and a
half years ago. That's why he wanted to live to November.
The five-year gift period ended then and there wouldn't
have been death duties to pay. I don't think it was wrong
of me to take it in the first place, do you? I was in a jam
and he hadn't a soul in the world.''

"I know he hadn't and, even so, my dear girl, he
couldn't have bought this kind of care for any money on
earth.''

"That's what I thought." She sighed. "Oh my dear, I can't bear it, let's go out of here and look at some pictures."

Mr. Campion was sealing an envelope he had taken from his pocket, and he tucked it away before moving.

"Doctor sensible?" he inquired casually.

Minnie rose. "Very young," she said, "but quite all right. I think he felt we were making a lot of fuss over a foregone conclusion."

The tall man smiled at her. "All the same, he wasn't surprised when it happened."

"Well he *was*, rather, oddly enough." Minnie was fastening the window. "So were Gordon Greene and Sir Frederick Hughes. They came down to give the old darling a complete check-up last spring, and they said then he ought to be good for a couple of years. However, go he did, poor pet, so it couldn't be helped. Well, there it is. Come along."

She led him out and relocked the door after them. "I just want to leave it exactly as it was for a bit," she said.

Mr. Campion spoke on impulse. The matter had been in his mind for some time, but his curiosity brought it to a head.

"I was going to approach you professionally, Miranda Straw," he began. "I was wondering if we ought not to have a portrait of Amanda while her hair is still red."

Minnie appeared interested but embarrassed.

"The full treatment?" she inquired. "I'm afraid it would have to go through Fang's."

"So I should hope. None genuine without," he agreed lightly as she paused to look at him, her head on one side.

"I'd love it. There's something there to put down. I could fit it in too, I think, but it'll cost you a pretty penny, my lad."

He was undisturbed. "I thought it might. But Rupert will bless us later on. I'll talk to Copley of Fang's."

"If you do, I'll do my damnedest to get it in this year. I've got to start on an Australian beauty next month, but the rest can move back one."

"Right. I'll hold you to it. Things are booming, are they? Did I see something about the Boston Art Gallery?"

Her strange fierce face glowed. "You did, thank God," she said. "It's marvellous. Four. Two flower-pieces, Mrs. Emmerson, and Westy. It's a queer mixture, isn't it, flowers and women and kids? And yet I suppose you can't really photograph any of them without either sentimentality or brutality, and mine's an essentially realistic approach, even if it is a bit individual. Remind me to show you something."

They were back in the kitchen again when he put his last question.

"Have you seen a stranger near here lately, Minnie?" he inquired. "About eight or nine days ago; a man in a raincoat?"

He got no further. Behind him there was a crash like the end of the world as Miss Diane dropped a zinc bath on the flagstones. In the instant before he swung round he saw that Minnie's expression of mild curiosity had not changed. However, there was still sensation to come. As if the clatter had been a roll on the drums, a shadow fell over the bright doorway to the yard and Mr. Lugg, breathing like a porpoise, and indeed looking not unlike one, his face dark with exertion, stepped heavily into the room with a limp body in his arms.

" 'Ere's another," he gasped as he planted it on the table, where it stirred and moaned. "Cut 'er stay lace. She ain't 'arf 'ad a shock." He turned to Miss Diane by instinct.

"Give us a drink, duck. Anything but water. I 'ad to carry 'er the last few yards."

Mr. Campion's horrified stare left Lugg for the sufferer on the table and he saw to his astonishment that it was his grave-tending friend of the morning, the secretary to the bird-watching Fanny Genappe, Miss Pinkerton of the Pontisbright Park Estate.

CHAPTER IV

Clots in Clover

I

When Miss Pinkerton regained command of herself, she became very angry, as people who feel they have been trapped unfairly into a show of weakness often do. Her sensible face was patched red and white, and her nose and mouth were pinched.

"Thank you, Mrs. Cassands. Thank you, Mr. Campion. I'm perfectly all right, perfectly." She sounded outraged. "Just leave me alone. I shall lie down for a moment. I don't want to give any trouble. Just throw me into Mr. William's old room. I shall be quite myself in a moment. It was coming on it suddenly like that. Really, the police should have warned me. So very, very revolting and unpleasant."

"What is it? What's happened? Pinky, you look like death." Minnie took her arm firmly and led her into the body of the house. "Come upstairs. You'll be all right in a moment. What on earth is it?"

Mr. Campion did not follow them but turned to Lugg, who was sitting on the edge of the sink taking a pull at a brown bottle which Miss Diane had miraculously produced from somewhere beneath it.

"Now what?" he demanded.

Mr. Lugg handed the empty vessel back to his benefactress, who was looking at him with a hard incurious stare, and wiped his mouth.

53

"Thank you, mate," he said. "I'll be seeing you again."
Then, heaving himself upright, he winked at his employer
and jerked his chins towards the door before lumbering
out. "Bloomin' woman stuck 'er 'ead right over the corp,"
he said as they paused by the pump, just out of earshot of
the kitchen. Mr. Campion had to screw up his eyes to see
at all after the dimness indoors. Out here the light was like
diamonds, and Lugg's face, vast and slightly mischievous,
loomed against a blaze of green and white. "It wasn't
nobody's fault." The fat man's growl was lowered confi-
dentially. "She came 'opping along the path like an ole
she-'are, sniffin' this way and that. There we all was, me
and the Super and the Sergeant and the bobby and the
doctor 'oo'd just arrived. None of us saw her until she was
right on top of us. I put up me 'and but I might as well
'ave tried to stop an 'en taking sights of a bit o' grub. She
darted round me and give a refined laugh. 'Oo, what's
a-goin' hon 'ere?' " He sniffed. "She fahnd out. Just then
orf come 'is 'at, and lord luvaduck!"

"Did she recognize him?" inquired Mr. Campion with
interest.

"Couldn't say." Lugg was thoughtful. "Might 'ave
done. But just as easy might not. The way 'e was lookin' I
doubt if 'is wife could have took to him."

"Did she scream?"

"More of a whistle, like a train. Then she started to
'eave. The old Super, 'e's no amachoor, give me the sign
to take 'er away and no loiterin'. I supported of 'er in."

He was pleased about something. A fresh masculinity
appeared to have been aroused in that well-bolstered breast,
and his small black eyes turned towards the door. "Pore
ole maid," he said.

"Did you find out anything new about the corpse?"

"Fracture of the occiput. I made that out as I was
supporting of her orf. The bloke was only sayin' the
obvious, you could 'ear that. 'E 'adn't got down to nothing."

A foolish little ditty from his undergraduate days crept
into Mr. Campion's mind and mingled with the hum of the
bees and the bird song.

Sand in his little socks he put
And wopped her on the occiput.

"Any sign of a weapon yet?" he inquired.

"No."

"You'd better get back."

"In a minute." The small eyes had developed porcine indignation. "D'you know what you remind me of? A midwife, knowin' a confinement's goin' on in the next room and can't get at it. For 'eaven's sake! I thought you'd got private business 'ere to see to."

He broke off. A small girl clutching the inevitable bottle to her bosom passed slowly across the end of the yard and vanished into the flower garden. A beatific smile spread over the white countenance.

"Ho," he said, "perhaps you know what you are a-doin' of." He paused, and added "Sir" as an afterthought. "Yus, I see," he went on with new enthusiasm, "this 'ere 'ouse must be pertected. I'll just step back into the kitchen to 'ave a dekko at something I noticed and then I'll get back to the flics. They call rozzers that in France, did you know? I learnt it on the pickchers."

Mr. Campion made no comment but followed him into the cool gloom of the house once more. Minnie and Miss Pinkerton were not visible, but Miss Diane was scrubbing the table, her huge red arms glowing and her earrings shaking until it seemed that the birds upon them must take flight. Mr. Lugg paused at the clean end of the board and leant upon it, his hands placed squarely on the damp surface. Miss Diane promptly ceased her toil to imitate him, so that they faced one another like poised buffalo, heads down for the charge.

"I seen you before," said Lugg without preamble.

"I thought you 'ad," she said woodenly, her clear skin bright in the shadowy room.

The fat man's eyes were lost as he narrowed them in an effort of recollection.

"You was on top of one of those ruddy great railway delivery vans, 'orse-drawn," he said at last. "You was in tight trousers and you 'ad a pinky bow in your 'air, and you was eatin' a bite of bread and Bovril.''

"Marmite," she corrected him, laughing.

"So it was, I dare say," he agreed. "We was 'eld up in the traffic for an hour and an 'arf outside the old Mansion 'Ouse . . .''

"You was in your bus . . ."

"Call it a car, missis." He was affronted. "That was 'is Lordship 'ere's reconditioned second-'and mechanic's snip. I was in me shover's uniform . . .''

"I know you was," she said. "It's years and donkey's years ago. Fancy you rememberin'. I frew you an orange.''

Mr. Lugg raised a hand as large as a Bath Chap. "You frew me a happle, my girl," he said, "and don't you forget it. Well, I got to git on now. Got a spot of trouble on me 'ands. But—" his eyes wandered to the flower garden whence the child had vanished, "—I'll be back, I shouldn't wonder.''

"That's right," she said. "I'm always 'ere except when I'm at 'ome. Cheery-ho. I thought I'd seen you before when you first come in.''

"Cheery-ho ducks," said Mr. Lugg, and smiled at Mr. Campion as they went out together. " 'Er and me is old friends.''

"So I see." Mr. Campion was amazed by the coincidence. "I'm very glad to hear it because she knows something about that corpse.''

"Getaway!"

"I think so. Do you know her well enough to find out what it is?"

Mr. Lugg began to laugh with a skittishness Mr. Campion never remembered seeing in him before.

"I never set eyes on 'er before this afternoon in all me natural, Cock," he said, "but since you arsk, I don't think she'll 'ide much from me.''

Mr. Campion stared at him until the fat man began to fidget.

"Oh all right, all right," he said at last, "I ain't comin' out in leaf. She's rather my type, though. Vi-vacious. This isn't arf a funny place, orf the map but it's got hatmosphere. Let me get 'er down to the local and I'll tell you anythink you want to know. Don't you go shaking her up. The idea is to keep the cops away from this 'ouse, isn't it? Well, I'll get back to these 'ere flickerers. So long. Be good."

He waved a careless hand towards the flower garden.

"Nachure in the spring," he said, and rolled off towards the small white gate to the meadow.

As he vanished behind the barn a strange sound reached the speechless Mr. Campion. Mr. Lugg was singing.

> *"Roll me o-ho-hover*
> *In the clo-ho-ver!"*

II

Old Straw, Minnie's father, had transformed the inside of the tithe barn into a studio in 1905, when he was at the height of his fame and had given his mind and about half his money to the enterprise. As Mr. Campion stepped into it on that brilliant afternoon, when the east doors which could accommodate a loaded haywain were open to the sky, he wondered at it afresh. The original building, which was of solid oak and the same size and shape as the parish church, had always proved too expensive to heat, and after various experiments the painter had retired from the struggle and had constructed in the northern transept a studio within a studio.

This room was built eight feet above the main body of the hall, so that the effect was not unlike a stage-set, with the north window as a drop at the back. A carved balcony, railed and balustered, prevented one from falling from the smaller room to the larger, and turned at one end into an elegant staircase. In winter a partition could be erected behind the rail, leaving a large light room within. It was here that Minnie worked, and as Mr. Campion stood on the red-tiled floor of the main building he could hear Amanda moving tea-cups above. He coughed discreetly.

"He jests at scars," he remarked conversationally, "who never felt a wound. Is that an otter that I see before me?"

There was a moment's silence and then to his gratification a scramble as someone skidded to the balcony.

"Deny thy father and refuse thy name," said a cheerful New England voice forthrightly, "or if thou wilt not, be but sworn by love and I'll no longer be an old Capulet. The otter's wrong."

A thirteen-year-old face, bright as a buttercup and handled like a loving cup with yellow pigtails, beamed at him over the rail.

"Hullo, I'm Annabelle. Your wife's up here. I know nearly all that."

"Nice for you," said Mr. Campion.

"Yes," she said airily, "not bad. Come and have some tea. I'm going to fetch the children. We mean to polish the table." She pointed downwards and he saw for the first time the piece of furniture which was so large that his eye had rejected it. It was a twelve-legged Carolean banqueting board, twenty-five feet long, heavily carved below and smoothly shining above, and it took up half the centre of the main hall.

"That's a nice thing," he said inadequately. "Do you slide on it?"

"No, we put the twins in padded pants and drag them along," she said gravely. "They're over-weight. It's very useful. I'll go and get them."

"Not yet." Amanda spoke firmly from the background. "They're over at the cottage, eating. They've got to keep the ballast right."

"Okay, but it has to be done."

"Later. Have some milk."

"No more, thank you. I think I'd better go along to the wherry. There's only Scat and old Harry Buller there, and it must be constructed properly. Perhaps you'd care to discuss your plans with your husband? He hasn't done a thing yet, not a thing." With which thrust she slid down the stairs, granted Mr. Campion a provocative glance, and darted round him out into the green and gold afternoon.

She was a true Straw, he noted, but had mercifully escaped the nose.

He went upstairs and the smell of turps and tea met him like a wave of nostalgia. The room reminded him of any studio possessed by Minnie and Tonker, a shabby, cluttered place full of toys and packed with pictures in all stages of composition. Amanda was kneeling on the mat by an electric kettle, a tea-tray set with different coloured cups in front of her.

"I knew it wasn't you," he remarked pleasantly, "by the hair."

"Ah, but I knew it was you," said Amanda, patting the battered leather sofa against which she leant, "by the fervour. I say, whatever happens on Saturday, this must be the real party. The children are having a whale of a time and so is Minnie. She must be as strong as a horse."

"Our son is taking to it kindly, I hope?"

"Very. I last spoke to him when he was sitting on the lawn with an even smaller child, polishing a pile of the most expensive-looking plates. He said 'Sorry dear, but I must get on.' "

Mr. Campion sat down. "Interesting," he said seriously. "Minnie must have harnessed the last wasted energy in the world."

His glance fell on the kettle. "Real electricity, eh? That's an innovation. It must have been quite an effort to get it brought down here from the village."

Amanda gave him a thoughtful stare and her honey-coloured eyes were clouded.

"It's laid on in here and in two spare bedrooms and the dining-room they don't use," she observed. "Nowhere else. What's the matter with Minnie?"

"Nothing I noticed. She seems remarkably cheerful. At the moment she's comforting my ghoul friend, Miss Pinkerton from Fanny's outfit. The poor woman stumbled on the police just as they were raising the body."

"Oh dear," Amanda was sympathetic. "People never look away. But seriously, do you really think that Minnie is all right? The whole place seems to be run like an Alice in Wonderland factory—all crazy union rules.''

Mr. Campion resumed his spectacles. ''It must be something to do with officialdom,'' he said. ''Everything in the free world is, today. It'll pass, but at the moment we're in the midst of it. I know. I've lived through the Jazz Age, the Age of Appeasement, the Battle Age. Now it's the Age of the Official. By the law of averages we ought to move on to something more cheerful next time. Meanwhile, my sweet, I fear we have a more immediate problem.'' He hesitated and his eyes grew dark behind his spectacles. ''It's Uncle William. I can't prove anything yet but I'm terribly afraid someone meant him to go when he did.''

''Oh Albert, no!'' Amanda was sitting back on her heels, her intelligent face paling under its tan. ''That's dreadful,'' she said at last. ''Are you sure?''

''Almost. I rather think someone did something very simple and rather horribly off-handedly clever to Uncle William and I take a savage view of that.''

''Does Minnie know?''

''No. It would break her heart I think.''

''Then . . . ?''

''I don't know.'' He raised his head. ''Listen. Footsteps. I say, there's a ferocious draught somewhere.''

Amanda continued to look troubled but she nodded towards the window, and he saw for the first time that one of the large upper panes was splintered. He eyed it curiously.

''Someone has chucked something through that from here inside,'' he said. ''One of Minnie's labour risks, I should say. I wonder young Annabelle didn't instruct me to repair that lot pretty smartly.''

''Who's pretty smart?'' demanded Minnie, striding into the barn. ''Good heavens. Albert, can't you come to tea without finding something awful in the meadows on the way? That poor wretched woman,'' she continued, stamping up the stairs and flinging herself into the worn chair opposite him before he could rise. ''She's been shocked out of her wits. A dead tramp, she says.''

''Tramp?''

"So Pinky says. A lie-about. Poor chap, I do hope he wasn't hungry. We could have given him something. Whatever next? Everything seems to happen at these parties. Tea, darling? Bless you, you're saving my life."

"Where's poor Pinky now?" inquired Mr. Campion solicitously.

"In the drawing-room. Dinah's with her. I phoned Potter's Farm—they called it the Pontisbright Park Estate—and told them to send a car for her. All these efficient people go to pieces when they have a physical shock. She's never seen anything like it before and it's made her sick. I expect old Lugg is a bit of a horror-monger too, isn't he? He told her it had been there for weeks, and that she must have passed it every time she crossed the bridge."

"What was the lady doing here at all?" inquired Mr. Campion.

"She was coming to help." Minnie's high cheekbones were spotted with colour. "I seem to need a lot of it one way and another. Westy's mother sent me most of my food or seemed to until recently. Pinky types. She's employed by Fanny Genappe, but he's lent her to the man who is handling the transformation of the estate. I think she has plenty of time on her hands, and she offered to help me with any secretarial work I needed. She's been most attentive." She shrugged her shoulders, dismissing the subject. "Poor old Fanny," she remarked after a pause, "it is a shame."

Amanda was sitting cross-legged on the mat, her boiler-suit hugging her slenderness. She was still pale but the new subject interested her.

"I don't think Aunt Hatt and I will be exactly fond of him if he exploits the village," she murmured.

"Fanny?" Minnie was indignant. "Oh, you couldn't blame Fanny. That really wouldn't be fair at all. He only bought a little quiet cottage with a few threadbare uplands round it, where the larks nest. That's all he did. He meant to sneak off there and watch them, but then of course all his dreary money people got hold of him and turned him out, and made him buy up all the land near it, tore the place to pieces, and scared away all the larks. It's always happening to Fanny. As soon as he gets anything he wants they have to snatch it away because it isn't economic.''

"But it's his money," objected Amanda. "He gets the money doesn't he?"

"Oh that old stuff," said Minnie. She sat for a moment twisting her thin lips, and her piercing eyes were introspective. "It's not Fanny's fault."

"Then who is to blame?"

Minnie glanced up, she was frowning still. "I rather imagine it's a man called Sidney Simon Smith. Do you know him?"

"Oho!" Mr. Campion sat up. "The S.S.S. man. Is he about?"

"Very much so. He's Pinky's temporary boss. He's transforming the estate for the Genappe interests. I've met him but I wasn't attracted. What a very modern type he is. Tonker calls him the 'palindromic V.I.P.' ''

"Why 'palindromic'?" inquired Amanda.

Minnie laughed. "You're supposed to say 'what!' and then Tonker says ' 's P.I.V.' ''

Mr. Campion's wide mouth twisted. "Sometimes he's called the 'Jack in the Boat,' '' he murmured. "The one who is doing very nicely. Is he coming to the party?"

"I expect so." She seemed to have no feelings in the matter. "Do you remember when there were real parties, Albert?"

"My hat, yes!" he said fervently. "Twenty of us, as tight as owls on our own exuberance. I remember the one you and Tonker gave down here before you were married, when your father was in Spain. There were stuffed relations all over the house to make it respectable. How crackingly respectable we were! There was a dreadful old lady in bed, someone sitting on the stairs, and a very solid-looking person reading *The Times* in the dining-room. But he had a painted balloon for a head, and when a guest opened the door suddenly the draught caught it and it just sailed away. Who *was* that who saw it happen?"

"Someone who didn't know us very well. I shall never

forget his colour. It was the first time I knew the meaning of *eau-de-Nil.*'' Minnie was laughing. "I forget his name. All the same, these new shows are great fun. You never know who's going to arrive, and I do fix it so friends can come too. And then we get to like the new people and they become friends for the next time. It makes the do's a bit big."

"I can see that it might. What is this actually in aid of? Cassands and Co.?"

"No, this is a Tonker special." She was a girl again in her enthusiasm. "It's a combined Perception and Company Limited and Miranda Straw X-annual Publicity Gala and Fête Champêtre. It's all been audited, vetted, sanctioned, and scrutinized, turned inside out and proved to be sound, so our consciences are clear."

"Fully tested," agreed Amanda. "Why X-annual?"

"Because X is the unknown quantity. We never know when we may have it again."

"Eminently reasonable," agreed Mr. Campion approvingly, "but it sounds like a lot of homework. Tonker and Wally are Perception and Company Limited, aren't they? What do they actually do?"

"I think I know that. They're on a job for Alandel at the moment," ventured Amanda, referring to the aeroplane manufacturing concern with which she was associated. "They 'perceive a way,' don't they? They're looking into the sociological aspects of the supersonic bang for us. They're super P.R. boys with vision, isn't that it Minnie?"

The painter leant back in her chair and stretched her long arms above her head.

"They're ideas-men," she said. "A tiny high-powered firm, with no capital to speak of, who have somehow managed to keep independent. They're rather like a small boy walking through the playground sucking a particularly attractive-looking lolly, but so far they've got away with their skins. Obviously they can't advertise directly, so their best way of doing business is to show their clients to each other, and they have to put on a very good show to get them to play."

"Yes, I see that," he said. "Where do you come in?"

"Me? Oh, you remember the old Show Sundays of long ago? Tea, sherry, pictures, and little pink cakes on the Sunday afternoon before sending-in day? Well, this is a modern version of that. I invite everybody who has anything to do with selling my work, some old clients and some prospective ones. I've got Bedger coming from the Lyle, and Van der Hum and oh—dozens of them. There will be a lot of us. Perception has spent the whole of its allotment on champers and I'm doing the rest."

Mr. Campion raised his brows. "Solid champagne?" he inquired.

She nodded. "I know some people don't like it, but it's so easy. And besides—"

"Besides?"

"Well, the silliest official would never credit that you'd take a bottle of champagne privately to bed," she said. "It'd be so difficult, for one thing. But they might be very dubious about gin."

"Official?" he was beginning, but she looked away and he changed the subject. "Has Tonker got any surprises for the party?"

"Dozens." Her face lit up as it always did when she spoke of her husband. "The prize one is absolutely filthy. Have you heard of Tonker's Masks? It's deadly secret, but that doesn't mean much."

"His *masks?*"

"Yes. A man's invented some latex rubber stuff which really is porous. You can breathe through it so it doesn't make your skin hot. It was too soft for most things, so he went to Tonker to think of something to do with it. Tonker immediately invented a mask which is *literally* a beauty mask. He calls it the Old Original Skin Deep and you can, unless you've got a beak like mine or four or five chins, put on a perfectly new face, padded out where yours needs it, smooth where yours is wrinkled. Conks are disguised and bags concealed. It's no thicker, except where you need it, than a good foundation of that powder-base stuff, and isn't so artificial looking. But naturally it's not alive. Isn't it a beastly idea? Any one who steals a kiss promptly faints. Tonker thought they'd be so nice for the theatre."

Her visitors regarded her in undisguised dismay.

"How horrible!" said Campion at last. "Have you really seen these things, Minnie?"

"Of course I have. I helped with the first two. I couldn't spare the time for any more. They were fun to play with." She was lying back in her chair laughing, her eyes watering with amusement. "Tonker and I thought out how to do it, and he got Liz Dean, the beauty woman, to see to the real work. You take a cast of the natural face, you see, and Liz works on it with wax from a sketch of mine. Then you take another cast of that in plaster. Then you make a mould and fill it with the latex, or the inventor does. Then you paint the mask."

Mr. Campion ran a finger round the inside of his collar. "It's got a nasty likely sound," he said. "But if they have to be made for each person individually they'll be expensive, probably mercifully prohibitive. We shan't see many."

A crow escaped Minnie. "Don't you be so sure, my boy. It's the client's material, and Tonker has no copyright in the idea. I don't see why they couldn't be mass-produced. Famous film-star masks, perhaps, made a bit stretchy to fit anyone whose features were roughly suitable. Can't you see them in three sizes on sale in the chain stores and all the little gals parading in them? Very likely they wouldn't fit too well, like those awful bosoms."

"Minnie!"

"I know." She was still laughing. "It's one of Tonker's Frightfuls, like the glübalübalum. He gets them every now and again and they're always winners. Listen, is that the car from Potter's? Albert, you can just see the front door if you peek out of that little window at the side there."

Mr. Campion rose obediently and craned his neck. "Yes," he reported. "A Humber Snipe. Chauffeur-driven, and oh yes indeed, Minnie, your friend the palindromic V.I.P."

"Mr. Smith?" Minnie sat up, looking apprehensive. "Oh dear, I'd better go down. Tonker says the danger with that man is that he may buy up the firm you're working for, keep it long enough to sack you, and sell it just in time to be sitting in the office of the next one which grants you an interview. I think you two had better come with me."

"I think so too," muttered Mr. Campion, who had remained at the window. "Here comes Lugg with something which looks ominously like a Superintendent of Police."

CHAPTER V

Two Alarming People

As soon as Mr. Campion came face to face with Superintendent Fred South he realized that Lugg's estimate of him was very fair. Here indeed was no amateur. He turned out to be a plump elderly man with the face of a comedian, who dressed in highly coloured tweeds which were disarmingly shabby and a good deal too tight for him. His eyes, which might have been designed by Disney, had tufts over them. His walk was buoyant to the point of exaggeration, and as he shook hands he was smiling all over his face.

Beside him Lugg appeared subdued and wore the expression of a gun-dog who, much against his better judgement, has brought in something unfortunate—say a prize rooster.

Mr. Campion met them outside the barn some little distance from the front door and he paused to speak to them while Minnie and Amanda went on ahead.

"Pleased to meet you." The Superintendent's expression was packed with semi-secret entertainment. "The Chief Constable told me to look out for you, so I thought I'd just step across the meadow and touch my cap, so to speak. So to speak," he repeated absently. As he spoke, his bright glance was darting happily in all directions. It was like a small torch beam flickering over a suspicious corner. "Well sir, we've got the nasty thing right out of the way for you. There'll be a few fellows down there taking pictures and scraping up little bits of nonsense for a little while yet, but it'll be all tidy in no time. Not a bit of paper left on the grass."

67

He was making no real pretence at deception. The thickest skinned could not have taken the words seriously. But he was not in the least irritated. His irony was hearty and even friendly, and Mr. Campion, who had by this time a vast experience of policemen, became very cautious indeed.

"What is it, Superintendent?" he inquired gravely. "Murder?"

"You thought so, Mr. Campion, didn't you?" Fred South chuckled, apparently with pleasure. "So did I. But we must wait for the doctor to tell us. There's a hole in the poor bloke's head as big as a house and we can't think what it was done with." He stepped back and his glance ran up and down and round and about where the light was slowly turning to gold, on to the cobbles by the door and back into the barn behind them. On every loose and heavy object, a bootscraper, a spade by the gate, a hoe-head lying in the grass, it paused and rested for a while. "We just can't think at all," he said.

"Any hope of identification?"

Instantly the smiling eyes met his own. "Hope?" South inquired softly. "There's always a hope, Mr. Campion, even though every scrap of paper on the fellow has been taken away by some wicked thieving person. His money wasn't touched. He had two pounds, three shillings, and fivepence on him, but he hadn't a watch and he hadn't a baccy-poke, and there were no shreds of tobacco in the linings of his pockets. I wonder if I could bother you for a cigarette, Mr. Campion?"

The thin man produced his case gravely and offered it to him. "Sailors," he said. "Or I have some Laymans."

South was still grinning, but he was disappointed. "Thank you very much," he said, helping himself. "I usually smoke Blue Zephyrs," he added shamelessly.

"Then you do yourself proud," murmured Mr. Campion, still very seriously. "The telephone number you want, Superintendent, is Whitehall A-B-A-B, extension two hundred. They'll tell you anything you want to know about me. Ask after Jean."

The countryman's grin grew broader and broader and his dancing eyes were merrily abashed.

"That's one little job done then," he said meaningly. "How was I to know? Well now, what do you think that is then, Mr. Campion, that dead feller?"

"I haven't the faintest idea and I can't imagine. To the best of my belief I've never seen him before."

"Ha," said Fred South, "I have." He took off his green pork-pie hat to scratch his thinning crown. "Blow me, I can't think where."

"Will it be possible to take prints?"

He nodded, laughing and twinkling with implied confiding. "Surely. He's nowhere near as far gone as we thought. The doctor says about a week, and he's never very far wrong. Wonderful nose for a corpse, the doctor. But I don't think we shall find this fellow's picture in the library. If I see a wicked man alive or dead, and I ought to know him, I get a kind of pricking here." He held up his solid red thumb. "I don't know why. I had an old granny who could do the same kind of thing. A terrible old woman she was. This chap'll come back to me sooner or later."

"Are you sure you've seen him?"

Fred South nodded again and swayed a little on the balls of his feet. Innuendoes and hidden meanings, each presented with smiles and chuckles, seemed to shoot out of him like sparks. The thin man found him terrifying.

"I've seen the fellow," South said when he had finished giggling. "I've seen him and I've got something against him. Yet I don't think he's a client of ours. I may be wrong, but I don't think so. I'll have him cleaned up and I'll pore over him."

"I wish you luck," said Mr. Campion. "Do you want to see anybody else here?"

"No." The Superintendent was shaking his head in helpless mirth over some joke which he clearly felt they shared. "No, I just wanted to find out if everybody who was here about a week ago is still here and intends to remain here, and I can best do that in the kitchen, I

think." His glance slid to Lugg and he creaked a little as if
he was suppressing roars of laughter. "No need to disturb
the distinguished lady painter, nor the visiting children,
nor the angry artist at the cottage, nor yet his busy missis.
They're all getting ready for a party, I understand. The
Chief Constable has got an invite." He broke off to slap
his thigh. "Perhaps we shall all get one." His smile faded
and he moved his head sharply. "Who's this gentleman
coming along now, sir?"

There had been some little activity before the front door
for some time. Miss Pinkerton, evidently explaining that
she did not want to give any trouble to anybody, had been
helped into the back of the car. Now a sturdy, middle-
sized man in a dark city suit was hurrying over the stones
towards them.

"The name is Smith," murmured Mr. Campion. "He is
visiting the new estate on the hill, is not well known to the
Cassands family, appears to be collecting the secretary
who was sickened by the corpse. Yes," he added aloud
cheerfully, "try the kitchen by all means."

"Campion?" Sidney Simon Smith raised his voice while
still some yards distant. He appeared to be in a tremendous
hurry and certainly wasted no time whatever in ordinary
civilities. They received a fleeting impression of a flat-
tened version of the middle-aged pretty-boy face, complete
wih protuberant blue eyes and corrugated dark brown hair.
His urgent voice was remarkably pleasant and friendly.
"Campion, have you a car down here?" He came no
nearer but hovered, glancing back at the Snipe as if he
feared it might leave without him.

"Not with me." Mr. Campion, who was old fashioned
and whose only previous meeting with the man had been
brief, sounded unusually definite.

"Shame. Has he got one?" The S.S.S. man indicated
the Superintendent, intimating thereby that he was aware
of his existence.

"No. He came by the fields."

"What about you?" Lugg got a dazzling smile, equaliz-
ing, kind.

"That's my batman."

"Oh I see." The smile was taken away from Mr. Lugg, who was amused. Smith was signalling to the chauffeur to remain where he was. "I say Campion, is that red-headed girl the Amanda Fitton of Alandel?"

"Yes."

"She says she's your wife."

"So she is."

The pretty-boy face crumpled angrily. He had still come no nearer.

"Nobody told me that. I didn't know."

"Don't cry about it, mate," Lugg was beginning, but was silenced in time by a look from his employer.

"There aren't any cars then?"

"No."

"I see. And Miranda Straw hasn't one either? Well, wait a minute while I tell the Genappe chauffeur to come back for me. There was no point in him doing the double journey if someone else had a car."

He ran off again and they all looked after him.

"Waste not, want not," said Superintendent South.

The three men resumed their conference.

"This is the only thing I've got to show you at the moment, Mr. Campion. Look, a little bronze bead," South said, opening a matchbox to display it. "It was lying on the body's shirt, just near the collar, quite loose. My Sergeant happened to see it. I can't think where it could have come from."

Mr. Campion stared at it. It was less than a quarter of an inch across, and flat. It reminded him of a beaded footstool which had stood in the spare bedroom at Uncle William's mother's house at Cambridge, when he himself had been a very young man. He handed it back.

"Odd," he murmured.

The Superintendent pocketed the box. "It probably means nothing at all," he remarked, his grin reappearing. "You find the strangest things in fields. I found a fried egg once, an ordinary fresh fried egg, still hot, miles and blessed miles from anywhere. There wasn't a caravan, there wasn't

a fire, there wasn't a soul in acres and acres, and yet there
it was lying in the grass like a daisy. Must have fallen out
of an aeroplane.''

They both looked at him fixedly and he laughed again
all over his face.

"That's what I put on my report, anyway," he said. "I
couldn't think of anything else. I only mention it to explain why I say that open fields are very tricky places.
Now I'll trouble you further, Mr. Lugg, if I may. You and
me will go round to the back door together and you can
introduce me to the help. Here comes the gentleman who
understands the value of time. We'll leave him to you, Mr.
Campion. Good-day.''

They went off together, walking a little way round to
avoid Smith, who was hurrying back, his hands in his
pockets, as the Snipe slid away.

"We're going to see the arrangements for the party," he
announced as soon as he was within earshot. "I'm bringing the Augusts, you know.''

The Imperial Augusts, that celebrated quintet of clowns
who were modelled on the pre-war Parisian Fratellini, had
been a non-stop success in London for so long that Mr.
Campion was surprised at the proprietorial note.

"I didn't know they were one of your ventures.''

"They're not. I passed on the message. Tonker Cassands
told me to tell them there was a party, and I did.'' He
smiled briefly and his flat baby face was mildly amused.
"I think your wife's amazingly clever," he added, and
turning to Amanda, with whom they had now caught up,
said, "I've been telling your good husband I think you're
amazingly clever.''

"That will please us both," said Amanda gravely and
slid her arm through Minnie's.

The S.S.S. man's attention was recalled to the business
in hand.

"We're to arrive here for lunch, aren't we? Or was it
four o'clock?''

"Four," said Minnie with a firmness which startled her
older friends. "Come earlier and you'll have a long dull

patch with nothing but tea to drink and probably children dancing on the lawn. The Augusts aren't coming until five when they're going to arrive as a group of artisans in 1890 going down the Thames on a wherry with their girls on a beanfeast. Or that was the programme when last I heard it."

They had crossed the lawn to the river's bank as she spoke and Smith looked into the shallow water trickling over gravel bright as boiled sweets.

"You'll never get a wherry down here," he protested with instant suspicion.

"Not a real wherry," she explained earnestly, "but a raft disguised. We shall have more water too. There are sluice gates down there in the fen meadows. We let it out in the ordinary way so no one can fall in and we can get across by the stones. On Saturday the boat house is to be the pub which the beanfeasters are making for—The Prospect of Dunstable, or something. A lot of exciting people are coming, I believe, and certainly all the people I'm fond of are, so it ought to be all right."

"Wait a minute," he said curiously. "Is this river which you let run out *our* river up at the Estate?"

"You own the river bank and the stream to midway across," said Minnie with the same unexpected authority. "If you want to keep it deep up there you can build your own sluices."

"Then you wouldn't have any water here." He sounded rather pleased at the prospect.

"If I didn't have any, you'd have too much," she said promptly. "There's quite enough for everybody. And if you contaminate it, you're fined. Now, we eat over there in the barn."

He nodded gravely, as if he were getting it off by heart, but the word had made him dubious.

"It's a real studio inside," she explained hastily. "My father, who was a well-known painter, had it properly converted."

"So it's done rather well, is it?"

"I think so."

"I see. That'll be all right then." He turned his attention to the boat house on the opposite bank. "I want to see that," he announced. "I've heard about that."

The building, which was made of weatherboard and tiled, had been used on so many occasions as a play-room that it had gradually acquired a very definite character, quite different from its original purpose. For one thing, a small balcony running across the front was approached by an outside staircase, which made the building look as if it possessed two storeys. Under this there was a wide door with windows on either side, and the whole façade was much like one of those utility sets so much in vogue with repertory companies. Indeed, the balcony had been used in its time as a stage by performers as diverse as Tutti and Ben Burp.

Today, a newly painted inn sign, "The Half Nelson," had been framed between the two mock windows of the upper storey, and the rail was hung with little flags.

Minnie led the way across the river and Smith followed her closely, his polished heels looking odd against the slippery granite. He made something of a to-do about helping Amanda up on the other side, but left her at once while he peered in through a window as Minnie got the door open. Then he stepped closely after her into the light dry room within. Here, the walls were made of varnished match-boarding reminiscent of a waterside hostelry, and were hung with Tonker's lifelong collection of old playbills and bar trophies. There was no furniture at all save for a bench running round the walls, and the matting over the floorboards was worn, but the effect was pleasant and even sensational, for the entire back wall apart from the window, which overlooked the meadows, was lined with shelves and protected by a shop counter, and the children, unhampered by any false notions concerning the vulgarity of display, had presented the whole of Perception's contribution to the feast, all fourteen dozen of it, unstrawed and unshrouded on the shelves, bottles above and glasses below. It was an impressive sight, only mitigated by one small item. In the centre of the ten-foot counter top, collected by the thoughtful Westy and arranged by him in a neat row, were the four assorted corkscrews the house possessed.

Minnie laughed and collected them. "Children are such realists," she said. "Dear oh dear, it looks a little much put out like that, but welcoming, don't you think? That's rather sweet." She pointed to the darker end of the counter where two sticky bottles of orange cordial and one glass had been carefully preserved against a rainy day. The only other items on the board were a siphon, a used tumbler, and a screw of lead foil from the top of a bottle. Minnie's eagle glance rested on these, at first casually and then with fixed astonishment. She picked up the glass, sniffed it, and handed it to Campion.

"What's that?"

"Scotch."

"That's what I thought." She looked about her in bewilderment. "How extraordinary! We haven't any in the house. Where's the bottle, anyway?"

They looked under the counter and round the empty room, but apart from the dazzling display upon the shelves there was no sign of alcohol of any kind. It was a ridiculous incident, reminding Mr. Campion irresistibly of the Superintendent's fried egg. Minnie was puzzled and finally her gaze came to rest, firmly and suspiciously, on what she clearly felt to be the one dubious entity in the vicinity. The S.S.S. man, however, was unaware of her scrutiny. At the sight of the corkscrews his own black suspicions had been aroused. His eyes had moved as Minnie had gathered them up, and now he went round behind the counter and began to read the labels.

"Hibou 'forty-seven," he said at last, taking a bottle down and turning to her in surprise. "But that ought to be excellent. Almost too good for a party. That's Veuve Genet's second cru imported by White and Brook."

"I think it's all right," she agreed in astonishment. "Wally and Tonker know quite a lot about that sort of thing. The children put the corkscrews there by mistake."

It became evident that he did not believe her. He did not

believe her. He did not say so, but his expression remained inquisitive. It was a slightly embarrassing exchange, so that no one was looking at him, and his next move took them all by surprise. His fingers, which had been fidgeting with the bottle, moved deftly. The wine was up from its recent handling, but he eased the cork out softly and with a swift and even graceful movement whipped a glass from the shelf behind him just in time.

"Four of us," he said, his eyes intent on the frothing neck. "Just right."

He poured the awkward liquid with the skill of a *sommelier*, pushed the glasses towards them, and looked up. Mr. Campion's face was completely blank. Amanda's was not so discreet. And Minnie promptly collared the bottle. There was no doubt whatever about the reception of the move, and the man was forced to exert himself. A sheepish expression appeared upon his crushed face and he smiled disarmingly.

"Perhaps I should have waited to be asked," he said, his pleasant voice charming them by sheer physical sound. "I think I ought, you know. I know I ought. But I'm so damned greedy that my hand moved instinctively. We drink to the Inland Revenue, don't we, Mrs. Cassands? Our hosts and masters."

"Oh no we don't," said Minnie without animosity. "The party hasn't started yet. This is on me. We drink to old friends. I always drink to old friends. Tonker says it's corny as a toast, but I think we're so frightened of a bit of corn these days that the children are being brought up on husks. Here's to you, my dears."

Mr. Campion raised his glass to her and the party proceeded.

"A beautiful wine," announced Sidney Simon Smith, reassured and pleased about it. "When it's chilled it will be excellent. You are able to get ice, are you?" He eyed the zinc baths thoughtfully. "What about the smoked salmon? Do you go to Bernard for that?"

"Yes."

"Oh well, that's perfect. You have an old house, expensive to run I'm afraid, but it's very delightful. I do congratulate you. If only you could get this playroom lit by electricity, especially outside. I've heard that before and I see how right it is. You could do that, surely, couldn't you?"

It was a request rather than a query, and Minnie, who, on half a glass of warm champagne, was becoming more eagle-eyed than ever, put her head on one side.

"You know, you're behaving as if you were thinking of asking me if you can bring someone to this party," she remarked devastatingly. "Who is it?"

He looked as injured as if she had struck him suddenly.

"Unfair!" The unspoken protest, shrill and shocked, was almost audible. Minnie appeared to hear it distinctly.

"Nonsense," she said. "Out with it."

"Oh well." He looked a little sulky, but the speech had been prepared in his mind and he gave it in its entirety. "I happen to be having some old friends for lunch that day. They are charming people, you will like them. And Lady Amanda will be particularly interested in one of them, Barry Pettington."

Amanda was not playing. She was still polite but she was taking no part and her eyes said as much.

"He's a director of the firm of Gloagge," the S.S.S. man persisted, sounding as if he were Santa Claus producing a prize from the sack. "Your firm will know him. They manufacture ball-bearings. And he has," he added, throwing in a small token for Campion, "a most beautiful wife."

"Who else?" demanded Minnie inexorably.

His eyes met hers with faint exasperation. "Tony Burt and Jack Hare may join us," he conceded grudgingly. "I don't know yet."

"Burke and Hare!" Minnie looked astounded and Mr. Campion decided to intervene.

"Burt, not Burke. You're thinking of the earlier model," he murmured, and added casually as he turned to the visitor, "it's quite a comment on our civilization, don't you think, that nearly all the new fortunes are founded on scrap?''

The S.S.S. man laughed. ''That's amusing,'' he said, and after a pause, ''and true too. Now, Mrs. Cassands—do you like that better than Miranda Straw?—if they should be with me, will it be all right if I bring them in for a drink? They'll have their wives with them, of course, just to see my friends the Augusts. I told you I was sending them down, didn't I? They're very good, you know, and quite unobtainable for parties as a rule.''

''The Augusts are coming as friends of Tonker's,'' said Minnie. ''I know them, and this is the first time I've let them come back after that frightful business with little Bill Pitt. Poor child! They might have killed him in that drum. Actually he loved it, little beast, and has lived on it at school ever since, but it was very wrong of them. Yes, of course, bring who you like, but if you can't find room to sit down at dinner you *must* give way to the others, because they've been properly invited. I'm quite ruthless. I shall make you.''

''That is so kind.'' He sounded completely genuine and indeed obviously was so. ''Thank you. I wonder if my car has come yet? I mustn't keep it waiting.'' He finished his drink and went over to the door.

Minnie followed him—''There, it is,'' she said. ''You've got to go, have you?''

''I think I will.'' He seemed slightly more ordinary and natural for the encounter, and much of his relentless force had deserted him. ''Good-bye then, until the party. You are really most kind. Do try to get that electric light on. It will make such a lot of difference.'' He raised a hand to the others and escaped. ''I can get over here alone,'' he said, waving at the river.

''Good,'' said Minnie, ''that's right.''

She came back into the room looking tired. ''I'm sorry you got let in for that,'' she remarked, eyeing them guiltily. ''Or were you entertained? I was. I'd never really met him properly but I'd heard of him such a lot. I suppose he is a spiv, but I should call him a clown.''

"I thought him a shocker," said Amanda. "I can imagine him being called anything."

"Why a clown?" inquired Mr. Campion.

"Because clowns are children without innocence." Minnie spoke with casual authority. "That's why they're so awful, truly awful, I mean, and why only children and people in childish mood think they're funny. I found him rather refreshing. There's nothing there to clear away first, is there? You see the worst at once. He came to see if the party was going to be good enough for him to bring someone who might be useful to him to it. If young Rupert had had the horrid sophistication to want to do such a thing, he couldn't have set about it more simply."

"He'll then enter it on his own expense account, no doubt," said Amanda.

"Oh no, surely not!" Minnie was horrified. "That would be dishonest."

"My dear Minnie, whatever makes you think he isn't?" Amanda was laughing.

"I think Minnie's right." Mr. Campion spoke slowly. "We're not talking of ethics, of course, but in a strict legal sense I really doubt if that man ever does anything dishonest."

"Then why," demanded Amanda peremptorily, "does he want to bring those very peculiar people to Minnie's party? The only thing I know about Burt and Hare is what everybody says about them. Alan calls them rag-and-bone men on the biggest possible scale. He says they tip the housemaids at the back door to give away the family's old clothes."

"Good old Alan!" Campion was laughing. "I think they'd take that as a compliment. That's charitable."

"Why should Smith want to bring them here?"

Mr. Campion put a hand on her slender shoulder bone. "I don't know, yet," he said, "but do you know, I find the question absolutely fascinating. When I find out that I shall be even happier than I am now."

Minnie was still thinking about the S.S.S. man. "Such a strange face," she remarked as she gathered up the dirty glasses. "Like a kid's, but squashed. I wonder, do you think he could have been overlaid? I mean, it would account for how he got that way, mentally and everything."

It occurred to Mr. Campion that she was probably the first and last person in the world to worry about why Sidney Simon Smith saw life entirely and solely from the angle of his own desires. Most people devoted themselves to the problem of how he was getting away with it.

"I think that must be it, you know." She sounded satisfied. "It would have bent his face like that, and it would have got it into his head that he *must* look after himself." Her snorting laugh escaped her. "I don't think he's so awfully clever. He told me one thing he didn't mean to. He is the client Findahome keeps writing me about. I thought so."

They turned to look at her. "They're estate agents," she said, "and he told me this house was 'old and expensive to run,' and that's the term they use."

"Why Minnie!" Amanda was appalled. "You're not trying to sell?"

"No, they're trying to buy. That's why I noticed it."

Mr. Campion removed his spectacles. "Do they just write and say your house is old and expensive to run, and so sell it to us?" he inquired.

"That's what it amounts to," Minnie was frowning. "That's why I suspected they really wanted it. When strange people come up and say what a rotten old place it is, they usually do."

Mr. Campion remained silent as he fitted this new piece of information into the jigsaw in his mind. Minnie hesitated.

"I'm not really being as bright as that," she said, as if it was a confession. "I had another clue. Just before he went abroad Fanny Genappe came to say good-bye, and after he'd told me how fed up he was about his little farm and the larks, he looked round at my house and said 'Sting 'em, Minnie. Don't say I said so but you sting 'em when the time comes.' I hadn't heard from Findahome then, but when I did I suppose it was obvious, but I didn't know who exactly was behind it. Now I see, it's that 'S-P-I-V.'"

"But isn't he merely acting for Genappe?" Amanda demanded. "Won't it be Genappe's money?"

"That's almost right." Minnie put the empty bottle under the bar counter. "That's why poor Fanny looked so guilty. He felt he was being wicked. Fanny has his own loyalty. He doesn't sin against money as a rule."

"It's no good," said Amanda, "I don't see it, and I don't like it."

"You're just cross." Minnie shook her head at her. "You think Fanny's going to spoil the village and that alarms you. Whereas the truth is that old Fanny has simply got so much money that it has become a commodity, and that means it must be used or it becomes so much dangerous waste. His experts have discovered that his toy is too expensive and must be made to earn, so they've got in this man Smith to see to it, in much the same way as the latex rubber man called in Tonker to invent the masks. What I just cannot conceive is what the S.S.S. man has thought of. I can't think what he could do with Potter's. Make it something awful, like a leper colony, perhaps. The village says a dog track, but that's wishful thinking. What *has* he thought of, Albert? Do you know?"

Mr. Campion met her eyes and looked away. "I'm not sure," he said, "not sure at all. Are you thinking of selling?"

"My dear boy," Minnie's laugh was infectious, "I'm concentrating very hard indeed on not selling. Where should I go? What a silly life it is, isn't it? The trouble I have just to live quietly and paint a few pictures!"

Having tidied the bar, she took her sheaf of notes from her pocket and began to scribble on one of them. Campion looked over her shoulder. "One bot. champers—No!" she had written, and he touched her arm.

"I ordered a portrait today," he said. "I'll stand the brute that one."

"Of course! I can query that." She scored out the exclamation point and added a question mark. "Albert, how clever of you."

"Not at all," he said laughing. "I merely insist on my

rights in the new order. And while we're on the subject, forgive me if I'm interfering but I do hope you've got a really good professional accountant? There are good and bad practitioners and a really good one can make the difference between reasonable peace and sheer unadulterated hell in this unenlightened age. Let me put you on to my chap. Aubrey is . . .''

"Oh no dear.'' She waved the whole matter away as too difficult. "I haven't got the temperament. I just do what they tell me and then I know I'm doing right. I don't mind about that side of it.''

He stood looking at her, his head tilted and his pale eyes inquisitive. "Is there another side?'' he asked at last.

Minnie grinned. "There was,'' she said. "And very alarming too. But that's all right now. We've seen to that. Now where was I? Oh yes, the Palindromic V.I.P. I do wish he hadn't come here. He's started me worrying about those wretched lights.''

"For this place?'' inquired Amanda with interest.

"Yes. We really ought to have something. The subject crops up whenever Tonker has a party. We can have lanterns inside but the outside presents a problem. It'll be worse this time because the river will be up. We're going to use the wherry raft as a bridge, but it won't be terribly safe, especially with the Augusts about.''

"It sounds terrifying,'' said Campion sincerely. "How deep will the river be?''

Minnie considered. "Not quite two foot just here,'' she said. "Not serious, but—well—''

"Wet,'' suggested Mr. Campion.

"As anything,'' she agreed. "Once when we did it before, we drove a car on to the lawn and turned the headlights on, and let the battery down and the people had to stay all night.''

Amanda turned to the doorway. "I'll fix you some lights,'' she said. "I saw Scatty's son working on the wherry. He and I could get you quite a blaze.''

"Could you!'' Minnie had the layman's attitude towards electricity which confuses it with magic.

"Of course we could." The prospect of a glorious potter about was too much for Amanda. "I'll just go and sound him and see what he's got in the way of flex. Would you care for your name in lights, or The Lady Beckoning? Keep an eye on Rupert, Albert. He'll have to go to bed soon. I'll hurry, Minnie. We shall have to rout round the village, I expect."

She went off and the older woman looked after her. "That hair with that boiler-suit!" she said. "Isn't she wonderful! And these 'S-P-I-V's Albert, aren't *they* extraordinary? However furious one is with them one always finds oneself going to enormous lengths to get them what they want."

Mr. Campion laughed and his glance fell on the tumbler which was still on the bar.

"What about this?"

She took it up and sniffed it again. "That's more peculiar than you think," she said. "It really is. Jake doesn't drink spirits and neither does Emma. The children would hardly have a bottle of whisky, and I haven't any. The siphon belongs to the orange squash, and so does the glass I suppose. It does look as though someone came in, opened a bottle he'd brought, and poured a drink."

"Could anybody walk into the place and out again without being seen?"

"Oh yes." She spoke without any doubt whatever. "It's the country, you know. I often find people wandering about looking for me. If the policeman comes to see if I've paid my dog licence, the chances are I find him on the stairs . . . which reminds me, Albert, that poor tramp. I saw you with the detective. What's he like? I had a very soft spot for the old Superintendent but this man is new. What do you think of him?"

Mr. Campion considered Fred South. "Rather an impressive item," he said at last.

"Thank God for that." Minnie showed her weariness. "Come on," she said, "children first, and then, at last, pictures. He can be relied upon to see to all that, then, can he?"

"Who?"

"This man South."

"Oh yes," said Mr. Campion slowly, a considerable shadow passing over his affable face. "Oh yes, he'll see to everything. He's that sort of chap."

CHAPTER VI

The Master of the House

It was moonlight when Mr. Campion sat in the yard with his arm round Amanda and wondered if the scene was quite true. It was one of those nights which only a capricious climate can achieve, and then only occasionally. The soft sweet-scented wind stirred the fresh leaves without noise, and the silver highlights on barn and tree were liquid and still warm with the day's gold. Behind them the kitchen, lit by oil-lamps, looked like a Dutch painting. Minnie sat at the table having a final conference with her henchmen, Westy and the friend he had brought from school, who were laying in stores apparently for a night's camping.

Supper was over, the dishes were dried, the younger children sorted out and restored some to their parents who had called for them, and some to the cottage. Mr. Campion had indulged in a mild flirtation with the twins, whose names were so far as he knew Yellow Drawers and Blue Drawers, and had been gratified to discover that they were Emma Bernadine's contingent. Annabelle the beautiful was in her bed and Rupert, with Choc on the floor beside him, had been put to sleep on Minnie's. Amanda was waiting for her new ally, Scat, son of her old henchman Scatty Williams. He had slipped down the village on silent sneaker-shod feet to post a letter for Mr. Campion, to pick up a plug, and to fetch the station wagon from the Mill.

"You say you rang and rang the Mill and there was no

reply?'' murmured Mr. Campion at last. ''Luke's still out then, the old . . . otter hunter.''

Amanda closed the clasp knife she was holding and thrust it into a pocket.

''That was hours ago,'' she objected reasonably. ''It was still sunny when we put Rupert on the bed in Minnie's room. I've not telephoned since for fear of waking him. He must have passed out quite peacefully. There hasn't been a sound from him. Anyway, I've told Scat that if he sees a light in the Mill house he's to knock. I think Charlie Luke will feed himself. Don't be so jealous.''

Mr. Campion stiffened. ''I'll chuck you in the river for that. What a monstrous thing to say.''

''All right,'' said Amanda with dignity, ''but it's a perfectly sensible reaction. It's always jolly frightening when one's friends fall in that sort of love.''

''Why?''

''Well, they're never the same again, are they? A fusion of metals and all that. I mean, love isn't a cement, it's a solvent. Look at Minnie and Tonker.''

Her own peculiar quality of inspired common sense comforted him and surprised him, as it always did.

''The only thing is,'' she went on, ''that like any other Act of God it can't be helped.''

Mr. Campion looked at the barn in the moonlight. ''It's such a pity. He's such a good chap, so sound. If it had been any other girl in the world, almost, it might have been the making of him. But this can only mean an upset at a time when he's due to make a great effort, and a chip on his shoulder for the rest of his life.''

Amanda remained silent for a moment or so and all the little stirrings in the garden became audible in the night.

''Prune is a strange girl,'' she said at last. ''It's only that incipient inferiority complex—the other-people-think-so-even-if-I-do line—which I find depressing.''

''Prune,'' Mr. Campion was uncharacteristically savage, ''is about as useless as a gasogene.''

''A what?''

"Well then, useless as any elaborate thing evolved for a specific purpose which no longer exists. A sedan chair, if you like. Prune has been bred, not merely brought up, to be a suitable wife for a man who is no longer produced. She can't be altered and she can't be camouflaged. Besides—" he ground his heel into the stones irritably, "—her mother is a Gallantry, and therefore mad, of course, as they all are. Poor silly old thing, taking refuge in strange religions. At a guess, Prune has about one hundred and eighty pounds a year, less tax, to live on, and there's no sort of job in which she would be at all suitable. She makes me miserable whenever I think of her."

"Charlie Luke has a mum too, hasn't he?"

"So he says." In the darkness Mr. Campion grinned. "A power in his life by all accounts. According to him, she's a C.I.D. Sergeant's daughter, a Superintendent's widow, is two jam-pots high, and can smell breath over the telephone. I can't see her being sympathetic. Oh no, Amanda, I see bother there. Trouble. Tight lips. Broken hearts and God knows what. That sort of chap is liable to have mighty soul-shattering passions. That wretched girl is no darned good to him at all."

Amanda sighed and the June moths floated by. "Poor Prune," she murmured. "I hope they saw the otter. I say Albert, what about Lugg?"

"Lugg is a witness in this scarifying murder inquiry which everybody is taking a darned sight too calmly. I imagine he's still with the police."

"I'm glad to hear that," said Amanda, "because I heard he was in The Gauntlett with someone else's old woman. His Knees up Mother Brown is said to be a sight worth drinking Honesty Bull's dreary beer for."

Mr. Campion's eyes grew wide behind his spectacles and it occurred to him that he had not seen Miss Diane all the evening. He turned to the crisp head so near his own.

"Dognosed anything else, lieutenant?"

"Not much. I am in the process of collecting data. The old man whose old woman has been appropriated by Lugg is called rather ominously Old Harry. He's been working up here on the wherry but he sheered off at six o'clock and Scat told me why. He's gone with them.''

"Always the best way."

Mr. Campion sounded considerably relieved. ''What's he like? I thought his name was Buller.''

"So it is. Old Harry Buller. He's one of those tough little country chaps who have pink cheeks and a way of spreading their eyelids modestly downwards, which means they're not going to tell you anything they don't intend to. He's 'retired,' and that means he does anything he's a mind to. He cures rabbit-skins, cuts the odd hedge for favoured customers, helps Minnie shift things about. There's a lot of shifting about on this estate, there always was. And he's the only man in the entire county, including the Borough Surveyor, who knows how the Pontisbright sewer is laid. He's also the bird-catcher. Scat says he's practically a dog.''

"Eh?" said Mr. Campion, taken aback.

Amanda chuckled. She was as gay as he had ever known her.

"He goes by instinct," she explained. "Smells things out. He knew Lugg had designs on his girl friend merely by seeing the top of his head over a hedge. It's all a little indelicate. They must all be in the sixties, if not more.''

"I don't know what the old are coming to," Mr. Campion spoke lightly. "It's telling them they've got to work until they drop, I suppose. Puts ideas in their heads. Anything more about the possible future of the Pontisbright Park Estate?''

"No. I was on that when you came along, worrying about Luke and wanting your letter posted. You sent something to Pritchard, I saw. What has got to be analysed?''

Mr. Campion glanced at her in the moonlight. ''A small white tablet which I stole from Uncle William's room.''

"I see," she said softly. "And you called the death of the tramp, or whoever he was, scarifying. Does that mean you think he must have something to do with this house?''

Mr. Campion bowed his head over his loosely clasped hands.

"I don't know anything, yet," he said, "but I just can't believe that two mysterious killings, taking place within half a mile of each other at approximately the same time, are completely unrelated. Can you?"

Amanda surveyed the graceful silhouette of The Beckoning Lady against the depthless sky.

"I can't believe in murders here at all," she said. "Everyone is so happy. The party seems to be the only thing that matters. I hate it, Albert. It's all wrong here."

"That's what I thought," said Mr. Campion. "But the man Choc found wasn't a tramp by any means. Quite the contrary. A natty figure in his own way. He was certainly murdered, coshed by something quite extraordinarily powerful. I'm finding the whole thing nerve-racking, because by being over-cautious I've placed myself neatly outside the inquiry. It will look most unfortunately pointed if I go barging in now."

"Of course. That leaves you at the mercy of the local man." Amanda spoke thoughtfully. "What's he like?"

"Nemesis," said Mr. Campion briefly. "Is this the wagon?"

Amanda rose to meet the car and there was a hasty consultation in the darkness before she came hurrying back.

"We've got the plug. I'll just go and fit it and superintend the final items. Then we'll have a preview and go home, shall we?"

"All right. What about Luke?"

"The house is dark, but his car has gone. Perhaps he's run away again."

Mr. Campion brightened. "There's always that possibility," he said, and wandered across the yard to the kitchen. He had expected to find Minnie and the boys engrossed in their plans for the party, which even to his inexperienced ears had begun to sound a formidable undertaking, but they had finished with that for the day and had got on to Art in capitals, with murder further away than the stars.

"I have the greatest possible sympathy with the idea," Westy was saying as he leant his lean weight on the bulging haversack on the table, "and George Meredith here will concede that economy is always a good thing. But I tell you, Minnie, I just don't think that guy can paint at all." He shook his yellow thatch and his eyes were grieved. "I find that very disturbing because I like him."

George Meredith, Westy's friend from school, who lived overseas and had therefore been brought home as a matter of course, was a saturnine child, dark browed and silent. He sat across a stool and stared with a fixed expression, either of boredom or bewilderment, straight in front of him, and it occurred to Mr. Campion that the only young people whom their elders invariably find incomprehensible are those brought home by their own offspring. Minnie was talking.

"Nothing on the canvas at all, you say?" she demanded. "Oh come in, Albert. We're talking about Jake. He's showing one or two things with mine in the barn on Saturday, but just lately he's taken to painting so very small. I did want him to show one decent-sized canvas and he promised he would. I left a space and he's hung it. But now Westy says there's nothing on it."

The boy seemed as worried as she was. "It's a plain grey background, just as smooth as he could get it."

"And nothing else?" Mr. Campion inquired, interested.

"Only the snail-shell, stuck on the left-hand corner about two inches from the bottom. He says it's very important where it goes."

"Yes, well, I dare say it is," said Minnie. "I mean, the whole point of . . . oh dear!" She dabbed her eyes, but her tears were not of laughter. "That boy's exasperating," she said with sudden anger, "because he's got something to say. You're quite right, Westy, he can't paint. He can't even draw. I never met such a kack-handed jackass in all my born days. But that doesn't matter. The world is full of people who can paint and draw like angels, and who have nothing to say but boring old clichés. Jake really has a sound emotional idea, and if he'd only stick it down with the tail of his donkey someone else could make an effort and share. It's just pride. It's not even shyness, not even embarrassment over his lack of skill. It's just straight wicked pride which won't let him share.''

There was silence after she had spoken, broken only by an inarticulate squeak from George Meredith, who smothered it hastily, coloured up to the roots of his hair, and resumed his deathless contemplation.

"I guess George agrees with you, Minnie," said Westy, exhibiting clairvoyance, "and certainly so do I. But what are we going to do? Because, as it stands, that canvas appears to me as looking kind of uncivil.''

"Of course it does." Minnie was angry and her nose had grown sharper. "It's such a pity," she went on with exactly the same intonation as Campion had used about Luke. "I saw that snail about a week ago when he started. It had a sort of design about it and the idea was there. But he's simplified and simplified, saying in effect 'I shan't tell 'em this, I shan't tell 'em that,' till he's painted out the whole thing. Oh he is a trying chap. Besides,'' she added seriously, "you never know, someone might have bought it, and they could do with the money. Emma's been working for me like a black all through the year, but she hasn't earned very much. They wouldn't stand for it.''

"Who is 'they'?" murmured Mr. Campion involuntarily.

Minnie looked at him. "Oh, people," she said vaguely. "Well boys, it's another long day tomorrow. You must hit the hay. They're sleeping in the Indian camp," she explained to Campion. "It's jolly comfortable up there and not so stuffy as the house. Besides, we're so short of bedrooms. Ready now?''

"All set.''

Westy kissed her good night, and so did George Meredith, much to her astonishment, making a thorough job of it so that her cheek showed a white circle after the caress.

He said nothing, however, but strode off after his friend into the glittering night.

"They're done," said Minnie, laughing. "I wonder if that boy's any relation?"

"To reality?" inquired Mr. Campion with interest. "It does speak, I suppose?"

"Oh, I imagine so, or Westy would have told me. He's a very thoughtful child. That boy is getting used to us. He's rather nice and very intelligent. Not everyone of that age would have grasped all that about Jake. So often people just sneer as if the man was mad." She stood up. "Well now, let's creep up and peep at Rupert. I do want to slip over to the studio, and he'll be alone in the house except for Annabelle and Choc."

She was leading him through the dark rooms as she spoke and lowered her voice to a whisper as they gained the stairs, but as they reached the landing she paused abruptly. The door of her room showed slivers of light round the frame.

"Mercy on the child, he's lit a candle," she ejaculated, and hurried in, Campion behind her.

The soft light spread feebly over the small room, making the bed a pool of colour in the dark surround. On it, stretched diagonally across its wide expanse, in an attitude of utter comfort and content, was a sleeping sandy man. His compact and powerful body was fully clad save for his jacket, and his cheek was cradled against his shirt-clad arm. He had removed his shoes, and his feet, in discreetly checkered socks, were folded over one another on Minnie's print dress for the party.

"Tonker!" Minnie stood staring at the apparition. "When did you come back? Tonker, wake up."

He opened one eye, as blue as a sugar bag, and smiled with singular sweetness.

"Hullo, Minnie darling. I'm having a zizz."

"Tonker! What have you done with the child? Where is he? Tonker, wake up."

A delighted giggle behind them settled the main prob-

lem. Rupert, with Choc behind him, came in from the
larger room whose fresh decorations Emma had displayed
so proudly earlier in the day. As soon as he saw that
Tonker was still asleep he put his own head down on the
edge of the bed and closed his eyes. Choc sat down
heavily and began to pant. Minnie picked up her dress,
shook it out, and hung it round the post.

"How silly of Emma to leave it on the bed," she said
unreasonably. "Wake up, Tonker, here's Albert."

"Where?"

He sat straight up out of sleep and looked about him.
"Hallo Campion. How are you? Sorry I couldn't get in
this morning, but that moke of Minnie's is worse than
useless. No idea of pressing on at all. Well, this is good,
eh?" He slid off the bed, found his shoes and jacket, and
paused for a moment to look down at Rupert, who by this
time was lacing his own shoes.

"Good morning," he said.

"Many happy reorientations," said Rupert unexpectedly, and they both roared with laughter.

"Our thought for the day," said Tonker. "Well now,
supper, eh Minnie?"

She looked at him and laughed, her eyes dancing with
amusement.

"We've had ours, you old cad. What would you like?"

Tonker turned to Rupert. "It's up to you, really, old
boy," he said. "What would you like? It's late, so we'd
better have something light. They do omelettes very well
here. We'll start with melon, Minnie, then an omelette,
and I shall be quite content with a touch of cheese."

"A touch of cheese is all you deserve," she said firmly.
"Where's the whisky?"

"That's right." Tonker appreciated the reminder. "With
great forethought, and aware that we might have guests, I
procured a single bot. Where is it? There's only one drink
gone. Boy!"

"Many happy reorientations," said Rupert.

"Save it," roared Tonker. "Wait till we get another

punter. Meanwhile, did you observe, you silly little chump, what I did with the whisky?''

"You took it under the bed," said Rupert.

"So I did." Tonker retrieved it and handed it to him. "You carry that, and remember that the whole success of the evening depends on the care you take of it." He turned to Campion. "Get 'em used to handling the bottle young," he said, "then the feel of it doesn't drive 'em MAD later on.''

"Rupert is Albert's son," Minnie murmured.

"Well of course he is," Tonker said without a tremor. "He told me his name and I knew he wasn't a brother. Too young. Supper now, eh?''

"Tonker," demanded Mr. Campion, "why did you take the whisky under the bed?''

"Because . . ." his famous bronchial laugh which invariably ended in a dangerous high-pitched wheeze, escaped him, "I feel a fool! I came home, looked about and saw you, Minnie, and Amanda entertaining the dreariest man bar none that I have ever met. And so I came up here to have a quiet zizz, nap, or buzz-session, until he went away. I was awakened by twitterings on the landing and, not wishing to enter into a lot of laborious explanations, I slid quietly under the bed, having the forethought to take the bottle I had so kindly brought for you all with me. The next thing I knew was that your wife and mine had bunged this nice but redundant child in my place, and there was a ruddy great dog sniffing at me under the hangings.''

"So you turned Rupert out and got back on the bed." Minnie sounded less horrified than she meant to. "You told me you weren't coming back until the party. You are disgusting. You're so selfish, Tonker, I'm ashamed of you.''

"Not at all." He was outraged. "I made the child supremely comfortable, with rich pillows and eiderdowns, upon one bed, and did the same for the dog on the other. I shared my thought for the day with them, and I showed them where the electric light switch was, an item which, I may add, I am not permitted to possess myself. Then I left them and we all three appear to have had a very pleasant and refreshing zizz. Unfortunately we are now all starving.''

"Oh all right, get on," she conceded, "but what you think you're doing, coming home unexpectedly and crawling under the bed, I do not know, or what Albert will think.''

"Good God," said Tonker, "if a man can't crawl under his wife's bed, where can he crawl? And as to what Albert may think, it is nothing to me.''

He had reached the inner kitchen by this time and now sat down at the head of the scrubbed table, motioning the father and son to stools on either side of him. He still looked remarkably like the caricature in the bedroom, Mr. Campion noted; powerful, sand-coloured, compact, and truculent. A waving striped tail would have been surprising but not extraordinary.

Minnie, who had been looking weary, seemed to have been injected with new life by his arrival.

"Put the bottle on the table, dear, very carefully," she said to Rupert. "The glasses are here and the plates are there, and I'll get the water and the frying-pan. No Albert, stay where you are and talk. I shan't be a moment.''

The bustle was considerable. The two zizzers made it clear that for them at any rate the evening was only beginning.

"Seen the pictures?" Tonker demanded.

"Not yet." Mr. Campion found he was apologizing.

"Splendid, I'll show 'em to you. You must see the secret stuff, too. I think the woman's got something." He was pouring the drinks carefully. "For boys, water," he said to Rupert. "In ten years' time come to me and I'll initiate you into a very important mystery. Until then, stick to water, or milk if you must, so that your palate remains virgin for the ceremony. Above all, never touch green sherbet. Green sherbet is death to the taste-buds.''

"You be quiet, Tonker," said Minnie, "and eat this." She had produced an omelette, apparently by conjury, and now gave Rupert a small one also. "How about you, Albert?"

"My dear, I've just eaten."

"I should make the effort, Campion," Cassands advised earnestly. "It's going to be a long night. Minnie, about the blow-out on Saturday, have you got any glübalübali?"

"Oh, Tonker, those awful things again . . . are you going to revive them?" She was standing by the stove, her hands on her hips, her coarse apron hanging in stiff folds over the printed gown.

"The Augusts want them. Keep one back, because we shall never see them again. Are there any, anywhere?"

"I think there's six in the granary, gold-painted. They'll be a bit black by now."

"That doesn't matter." He turned to Rupert. "You get them out tomorrow, old boy, and dust 'em up a bit."

"How can he?" Minnie's exasperation was vigorous. "They're bigger than he is."

Tonker did not turn his head from the child. "Your father will help you, no doubt," he continued, buttering a slice for him. "He always was an idle fellow, even at school, but keep at him and the job will be done with reasonable efficiency."

"You wicked little man." Minnie shut the lid of the stove with a bang. "You bully and trick everybody into working for you."

"I do resent that." Tonker spoke without heat. "What happens when less intelligent people arrange a social gathering such as we are about to have on Saturday night? There is fuss, nerve-strain, hysteria, exhaustion, and a profusion of useless, hired servants who listen in to private conversations, pester the unwary guests for largesse, and secrete unfinished bottles in unlicensed receptacles. The way I do it no one is bored, no one is tired, there is enough to go round, and every man has the supreme satisfaction of looking after himself. Albert and Rupert have honoured me by accepting an invitation to the party, so they shall have the honour of unearthing the glübalübali. It's not much to ask."

"Remarkably little," agreed Mr. Campion, who in common with all Tonker's friends had no illusions about him. "I shall sacrifice myself for the child, who should see the things while still of an age to appreciate them. What a riot that idea was, and how utterly insane! How did you arrive at it, Tonker?"

The sandy man laid down his fork and blew a kiss to his wife. He was beaming.

"Oh, fortuitously, you know," he said airily. "I was mucking about, waiting to be demobbed. Wally was still in Germany, and we hadn't decided if to team up again. Minnie was broke—no one bought pictures during the war, and she'd lost that whole exhibition when the *Polchester* went down—and I thought I'd better get cracking. Alan Dell sent me a chap who had been making plastic windscreens for him. The contracts had been cancelled as the war ended, and he had tons of this stuff in sheets on his hands."

"So you just looked at him and said, I know, let's make glübalübali?"

Tonker laughed. "It wasn't unlike that," he admitted. "We were having a drink at The Howdah and there was a cabaret in the restaurant, which one can just see from the bar. I was trying to get from the oaf what *could* be made with his stuff. He said anything: stamp it out and bend it up, the bigger the better. Just then a fellow came on in the cabaret playing a sousaphone. I looked at it and thought what a nice thing it was, and how I'd like to have one, and what a pity it was it wasn't even bigger, and I said to my chap, could we make that? He screwed up his eyes and considered it and said, 'We could make something that looked like that. It wouldn't play, of course.' So I said, give me a pencil, and the thing was born."

"But I thought it had an arrangement of bladders in it?" said Mr. Campion.

"So it had, in the end." Tonker was laughing again and Minnie, despite her disapproval, was grinning. "Bokko and I thought of that. It had to make some sort of satisfactory noise, you see, and with some little manoeuvring we got a scale. We sprayed the thing outside in various colours, but left the innards clear. It looked a bit crude, but not too crude, and we got Teddy Silkworm and his Band to put it over. I don't know why it was such a zinger, unless it was that it was very big and very cheap, and there hadn't been anything big and cheap for years and years. It appealed to the mood of the moment, and of course there was Bokko's inspired tune . . .''

"Yes indeed." Mr. Campion spoke hastily. "Someone mentioned it this morning and I've been humming it all day. Tum-tee-tee, tum-tee-tum, on my glübalübalum. Good Lord Tonker, you say you've got six of these things?"

"Five. Leave one for the files."

"I read somewhere that the Solomon Islanders are buying them in quantities. Is that true?"

Tonker shrugged his shoulders. "It may well be. It touches some deep human chord, old boy. I don't know what's happening to it now. We sold out at the peak of the boom and split the profits." He scowled with sudden ferocity, but soon after began to laugh in the half-crestfallen, half-villainous way typical of him. "I got seventeen thousand quid, kept two, and in a fine burst of careless generosity gave the rest to Minnie, who was broke, as I told you. Like the mug she is, the poor benighted gal paid all our debts with it, including all the arrears of income-tax, and so at a single stroke I sold her into bondage for the rest of her life. Didn't I, Minnie?"

His wife shut the stove with a bang. "Never mind," she said. "I've forgiven you . . . almost."

"I haven't." Tonker's self-criticism was unusually sincere. "You see, my old and valued friend," he continued, returning to Campion, "by an unfortunate oversight I had omitted to observe that, due to the increased business done in my absence by that notable band of brothers, the Inland Revenue Department, the entire item when taken in conjunction with my own and Minnie's hard-won earnings in an exceptional year, amounted in total value to the splendid sum of six hundred and fifty-three pounds, two thousand of which I had already expended re-establishing myself in civilian life. Since we did not discover the damage for the best part of two years, you will readily understand that the gift, as a gift, was a failure. A donation, in fact, with all the charm of a financial time-bomb. Pure sulphuretted hydrogen. Minnie has never seen the full humour of it.''

"It was a stinker, all right," said Minnie, obstinately unamused. "And now, Tonker, you've got to wash up."

"Never." He conveyed that they could carry him kicking and screaming to the sink before he would hear of it. "Listen. Someone outside."

"Rubbish. That's a very old trick. Come on, Tonker, you're showing off. Rupert, show him how to do it. Come along, Tonker, or I'll tell about you and the poor wretched County Councillor."

Since it was but a matter of four plates, three glasses, and a mixing bowl, the operation was accomplished without much difficulty. Minnie washed, Mr. Campion wiped, and Rupert put away. Tonker dried one fork very carefully and showed Rupert how to turn it into a jew's harp.

When they had finished making a noise, and Minnie had rinsed her hands, she pulled open the drawer of the table and took out the local weekly newspaper.

"There you are," she said, "it only came this evening. Read the worst."

Her husband felt for his glasses and drew out his cigarette case with them. He handed it to Campion, who took one and examined it curiously before lighting it.

"Blue Zephyrs," he observed. "Someone was talking of these today. How long have you been smoking them?"

"Ever since they announced that cigarettes were death." Tonker did not look up from the paper. "I thought I'd commit suicide with a jewel-handled knife. They get them for me at the village shop here and at Herbert's in town. Why?"

"Nothing, except that it's odd."

"Not so odd as this is." Tonker was scowling at the

page. "Local Government election result. Out on one of his great red ears, my poor chum is." He lifted his face to Campion and gave him one of his seraphic smiles. "Sometimes, my old and valued friend, I wonder if I am entirely sane," he said seriously. "Dear good chap and brilliant reasoner though I am, I sometimes try to help my pals in the silliest ways it is possible for the human mind to conceive."

"The trouble with that particular idea," announced Minnie, who was tidying up before going over to the studio, "is that you were so keen on making it work that you forgot what it was for."

"What *was* it for?" Mr. Campion insisted. "I can hardly wait."

Tonker's wheezing laugh, much ashamed but still secretly tickled, echoed hollowly among the whitewashed beams.

"It was . . . well, it was . . . sort of . . . it was *euthanasia*, Campion. Euthanasia by the County Council of the New Useless. That was the bit you couldn't leave out, kick it about as much as you liked. The Councillor ought to have seen it, silly fathead. He would have done if he hadn't gone straight from the lunch to the Council Meeting."

Mr. Campion stood staring at his old friend.

"This wasn't put up in any seriousness by you, I take it?"

"No, no, of course not." Tonker was not entirely convincing. "Old Ted Fenner, our solicitor, started it," he explained cheerfully. "He came for lunch one day and depressed us both by telling us that ours was going to be the generation which would die of want and neglect because the young would be too over-worked to look after us, and no one would have any money anyway. I started thinking round, as I always do when presented with a problem, and I wondered what the blazes they *would* do with us, snarling and whining about the place. I thought, good Lord! they'll have to put us down, and I started working out in an idle fashion how they could sell the idea to us, because we shall still have a vote presumably.'' He paused and grinned. ''You have to be a teeny-weeny bit tight to put this idea over.''

''So I should hope.'' Mr. Campion was shocked but entertained in spite of himself. ''What exactly did you envisage, my little man?''

''A beautiful white van,'' said Tonker promptly. ''Very elegant, and very charming, with the County arms on it, done very modern in black—something really choice, by Ashley perhaps—and a nice jolly attendant who got out after a bit and sat with the driver while the carbon monoxide drifted slowly in.'' He scratched his hair, which was the colour of a new jute doormat. ''That was the mischief,'' he went on. ''I got this blessed van absolutely vivid in my mind and I sat next to this poor bloke I've been talking about at a luncheon at The Bull. I quite forgot he owned one of the last coach-building businesses in the East country. We had a good few drinks together and I couldn't think why he was lapping it up. I got him absolutely sold on the idea of the vehicle. He must have gone straight into the meeting, got up on his hind legs, and started talking about it with awful fuddled earnestness.''

Minnie stood leaning against the doorpost, her arm held high, her hand on the lintel.

''I see them all drawn by Daumier,'' she remarked. ''Solid, mountainous men, sitting very still like basking bulls, and just their eyes, little pools of shiny dark, slowly moving until they were all watching him quietly, thoughtfully, mercilessly. They'd all be fairly old themselves, you see.''

''*Ha-ow*, Councillor, would this here van of yours be *a*-used?'' bellowed Tonker suddenly in very broad Suffolk, his dark blue eyes opened wide as full realization descended upon him. ''Oh Lord, what a black egg! What a shower of bad taste! Silly Tonker. Silly drunken Tonker. Tonker disgraced. Let's take the bot and go in the studio.''

''I don't know.'' Minnie sounded practical. ''I find it rather comforting as an idea.''

Mr. Campion grinned at her. "On the principle that there'll always be a County Council, no doubt?" he suggested.

She flashed a smile at him. "No, I just felt that Tonker would be sure to think of *something*. Yet it's very unfortunate, because the neighbours are always asking what exactly it is that Tonker does, and this is the first of his ideas which will be threshed out by them in its entirety. There may have to be a few explanations."

At this point Rupert, who had been listening to the conversation much as if it had taken place in French, took a long shot.

"Many happy reorientations," he announced suddenly and brought the house down.

CHAPTER VII

The Lion and the Unicorn

"The illuminations," said Tonker to Amanda, as at last they all trooped into the studio, "are bang-on. We've always wanted them and couldn't manage it, somehow. What have you got? Miles of cable?"

"No." There was a hint of triumph in the mechanic's voice which made her husband glance at her sharply. "No, just a dry battery . . . out of a big car. It'll last a long time."

"Amanda." Mr. Campion had become acutely aware that his wife was back in her home country where humours matched her own. "Where did you get it?"

Honey-coloured eyes, candid as Rupert's, met his own. "Scat has had it to charge up for someone. We're just borrowing it for the time being."

He continued to look at her. "It's the S.S.S. man's battery, I suppose?"

"Well, he was the one who wanted the lights," said Amanda. "Always see the right visitor pays. We're rather good at that in Pontisbright. As Scat says, he won't mind if he don't never know."

"Now isn't that nice." Minnie sounded pleased. "Just like the country."

"Where everyone is his own Robin Goodfellow," mumured Mr. Campion cheerfully. "What a shocker that fellow Smith is, Tonker."

"Oh, a depressant." The sandy man spoke with feeling. "Why did he call, Minnie? To quote us for the empties?"

"He wanted to bring six people to the party."

"Indeed? Did you let him?"

"Wasn't that right?"

Tonker shrugged his shoulders. He was scarlet in the face and the famous lightning temper, which had earned him his nickname, flared for an instant.

"I don't care," he said bitterly. "Fill the place with curly-conked coyotes if you want to. It's your house. It only happens to be my party. He asked me the same thing a fortnight ago and I told him then that I was sorry, but the show was booked solid. But cancel all that if you want to. It only makes me look a fool."

The attack was so unfair that everyone was a little startled, save Minnie, who sailed into battle with all guns, pennants flying.

"You miserable good-for-nothing, how you dare!" she thundered. "He's *your* friend."

"That," said Tonker through his teeth, "is an insult I shall never forgive. Did he bother to tell you what he was bringing to your half of my party?"

"Two people who make ball-bearings, man and wife."

"They were the two I refused to have." He was biting off his words and sounded so like his father, the Headmaster of Totham School in Mr. Campion's youth, that the phrase "Sandy in a bait" came back unbidden.

"And two grave-diggers, I mean robbers," continued Minnie defiantly, her eyes flashing.

"Who?"

"Burke and Hare."

"*Burt* and Hare? The body-snatchers? Really? Both of them?" Tonker began to laugh, his fury evaporating. "Oh what a lark. Oh, all the better. Yes indeed, he didn't tell me that. Oh dear me, Minnie, you little know what a clever old duck you are." He jerked her apron-strings undone and she put a long arm round his neck in a wrestler's hold.

"You are a silly man," she said.

"Huh," said Tonker, disengaging himself. "With luck this is going to be a very, very satisfactory story. I don't like Smith. Campion doesn't like Smith. We will proceed to deal with Smith. Smith is about to be done."

"I think Minnie should be preserved from Smith," remarked Amanda. "He treated her exactly as if she was letting rooms."

Minnie laughed. "I enjoyed him," she said sincerely. "He's the new style gate-crasher, the one who won't take pot-luck. Kindly notice the electric lights over my pictures."

To be taken round a show by the painter is not always the easiest way of enjoying pictures, but Mr. Campion possessed the advantage of having followed the career of Miranda Straw since they had been young together, so that he could pick up the story, as it were, and perceive at once what she was about. In this collection pride of place had been given to the portrait of Westy. She had painted him full length, standing against the arch of the drawing-room fireplace. He was smiling and a thought shy, and his young leanness was brilliantly suggested, despite the formality of his first tailored suit.

"Oh my God," said Minnie without impiety, "that dreadful suit. He wanted it so much. We don't go in for custom tailoring for boys over there, you know, but he'd set his heart on it so I pulled up my socks and made a job of it. Its come off, hasn't it?"

"It has indeed." Mr. Campion was looking at the picture, his eyes narrowed. "Is that for Boston?"

"Yes. I wanted it to go to Belinda, but it can't be helped. I'll do him again later. Goodness aren't they ugly, though, these modern clothes?"

"Wait till you see my party raiment," murmured Tonker. "That's the gal I like, Campion. Minnie's made something of her, hasn't she?"

They went on down the line and the history of long industrious and sometimes exalted days was gradually unfolded. Tonker was very proud of Minnie. His delight was almost touching at times, and she basked in it. They were supremely happy. But just before they reached the end of the room she turned to him.

"If you got one of those glübs out of the granary, Tonker, you could show Rupert exactly what you want. There isn't much more here."

"Very well," he agreed obligingly. "But I want to see Jake's stuff. And they must, repeat must, see the secret."

He went off taking Rupert with him, and the others went on.

"What is that?" demanded Amanda suddenly. "Is that one of your father's paintings, Minnie?" She had been brought to a standstill by a small portrait which was quite different from anything else in the show even to its frame, which was uncompromisingly Edwardian baroque. It was the head of a man, set against a background of crumpled paper. The face was not particularly distinguished inasmuch as it was a typical twentieth-century mask, close cropped and shaven. The chin was obstinate and the small pursed mouth was smiling in a faintly pitying way which was disconcerting. But the outstanding quality of the work was the ruthless masculine venom with which it was executed. Mr. Campion stared at it. He felt he knew the man, and it occurred to him that it must be one of old Straw's more famous pieces. Minnie stood looking at it thoughtfully.

"Horrid, isn't it?" she said at last. "I did that."

"But who is it?" Amanda was as puzzled as Albert and in exactly the same way.

"A model." Minnie made it clear that she was not going to be more specific. "He owns it and he's delighted with it. He lent it to me to show. It's some years old now." Her snorting laugh took her by surprise again. "There really is nothing like creative work to get that kind of thing out of your system," she observed unexpectedly and swept off across the room to the opposite wall, where a second row of hooded lights displayed Jake Bernadine's pictures, half a dozen very small canvases and one medium-sized one.

Mr. Campion lingered and was still frowning in an effort of recollection when he joined the others some seconds later. Minnie and Amanda were looking at the small canvases when he came up. They were very, very small, some of them postcard size, and were painted with myopic thoroughness all over, in every corner and, one felt uneasily, possibly round the back. The larger picture was exactly as Westy had reported it save that the grey background was not paint at all.

"That's lino." Minnie touched it gingerly with an experimental forefinger. "That's a mercy. I was afraid he'd been painting out. If his original canvas is in existence I can get hold of it, or Emma can. Dear me, I hope that poor snail was dead . . . Why, Tonker!" Her final exclamation was in response to a ferocious tearing sound which had been released just behind her and was accompanied by delighted squeals from Rupert. The three swung round to find themselves confronted by the creator of the glübalübalum and his instrument.

There have been many attempts to describe the glübalübalum and even the one submitted to the Patents Office was not particularly successful. As Tonker had pointed out, it was very large. It was also very simple, being in effect a very long tube with an immense horn at one end and a cork at the other. In between there were, so to speak, digressions. The newspaper which is called by its detractors the *Daily Bibful* had once employed a psychiatrist to explain to its readers the mechanics of their own reactions to it, but the articles were not convincing. It was only at Oxford that it was noted that the position of a person playing the glübalübalum approximated very closely to the attitude of the central figure of the Laocoön. Children, on the other hand, observed at once that its true charm was that it had obviously got out of hand.

At the moment all three adults were laughing and Rupert was hysterical. Tonker was peering out at them from a monstrous embrace.

"Two bladders gone," he said. "E flat and an A. We'll have to make up with spares from the others."

Mr. Campion was drawn forward. "How do you blow it?" he demanded.

"You don't." Tonker was slightly breathless. "You pump it up first, see?" He turned sideways to reveal a window in the tube and by its side a slot in which nestled a perfectly ordinary bicycle pump. Through the window, a line of bladders, now a trifle flabby, were plainly visible. "Listen." Tonker seized the mouthgrip. "Tum-ti-tee, tum-ti-squish, on my glü-bal-ü-bal-squish. Not quite good enough, is it? Don't be silly, you ape, you've heard it before."

Mr. Campion pulled himself together. "It's horrible," he said. "A pornograph, Tonker."

"Not at all," said Amanda seriously. "It's very remarkable, and as far as I can see an entirely original mechanical principle. Could we take it to bits?"

"We'll have to," he assured her earnestly, "tomorrow, to get the repairs done." He paused and eyed Rupert. "Boy," he demanded suddenly, "do you realize that if I had been your father you would have been this?"

Rupert smiled politely but moved over to Mr. Campion, and Tonker was turning away when he caught sight of the snail picture and edged himself closer to peer at it.

"My God, Minnie!" His explosion was sincerely furious. The hampering coils of his invention were entirely forgotten. His face became scarlet and his eyes blazed. "Yes, well, that's simply a damned insult." He spoke with a suppressed hatred. "I suppose you realize that, Minnie? I suppose you're not going to subject our helpless guests. . . ?"

"If you got out of that thing," said Minnie with equal venom, "you could strike me. I hope you burst another bladder."

"Oh, all right." Tonker tore himself out of the contraption and caught sight of Mr. Campion's expression. "Well," he said sheepishly, "they're both damn silly things. Take the picture down, Minnie dear. Dear Minnie, will you?"

"Of course I must," she said, patting him and his glübalübalum. "Jake doesn't want to show at all, that's his difficulty."

"I do." Tonker spoke with sudden enthusiasm, all his anger gone. "Get the secret picture, Minnie. See what they think."

"I'm going to." She went off at once and they moved up to the other end of the giant table, which shone like the slide the children had made of it. The lights went on in the inner studio, and presently she reappeared carrying a canvas.

"Now," she said, coming down the stairs, her long gown accenting her angularity, "I'll have that easel, Tonker."

He pulled it out for her and together they adjusted its position to the light. It occurred to Mr. Campion that he had always seen them like this, their heads together, up to something. At last Minnie stood back.

"Mind you," she said, "this is an experiment."

The visitors stood looking at the picture for a long time. After the first shock of surprise the eye lingered. It was a sort of meticulously executed doodle enclosed in a formal vase shape. Presumably it was a portrait of Annabelle, since the child appeared within it many times. The effect was strangely stimulating and in an indefinable way joyous. After a while Minnie laughed and took it away.

"It's not very commercial, is it?" she said. "But it was something I felt I wanted to say about her that I couldn't express in any other way. It's a purely personal picture of my own mind. Can you see at all what I meant?"

"I can." Mr. Campion felt oddly elated. "I don't know why. Leave it here for a bit."

"No, my dear, I mustn't." Minnie was already half-way up the staircase. "I shall only get keen on it and that really would be fatal. It's not permitted just now. A pity, but there it is."

"Who won't permit it?" demanded Mr. Campion.

"Circumstances." Minnie ran up the stairs and vanished into the smaller studio behind the balcony.

"Circumstances, my boot!" said Tonker. "It's my fault again." He was sitting in the shabby armchair which he had pulled out from the wall the better to admire the canvas. The glübalübalum was beside him, standing upside down on the rim of the horn looking like some embarrassing optical illusion. Rupert was sprawled behind it, trying to get a trapdoor, which he had found in it, undone.

"My boot," Tonker repeated, cocking an eye at the balcony.

There was no response from Minnie, who had taken her secret into some further fastness, and after a pause he cast a thoughtful glance at his old friends. "It's all part of the same silly business," he said with uncharacteristic bitterness. "All part of the same seven-year-old row. I think Minnie's mad and she thinks I'm dishonest, and we're both explosive personalities. They'll do what they're setting out to do, you know. They'll split us."

"Who is this?"

Tonker considered and finally decided to confide. "Minnie's horrible chums, the tax-gatherers. I told you the start of it in the other room. I made a fearsome blob over my glüb money and Minnie lost confidence in me in a big way." He sighed. "We're neither of us great financial brains, let's face it. When the bad news broke we had the first real dust-up of our lives. It was a rotten present to receive, but it was also a highly irritating present to have *given*. Minnie didn't altogether appreciate that point."

"What happened about it?" Mr. Campion sounded apprehensive. "You've been paying up ever since, I suppose?"

"Minnie has," said Tonker. "I don't come into it. I'm a salaried worker and I keep just under sur-tax, so they filch my bit at source without my even stroking it. Minnie does the rest. Since the glüb fiasco she won't have any interference from me. It's a bit complicated because we don't live together, you see. Never have."

Mr. Campion laughed. "You have in the legal sense, you idiot."

"We haven't in the literal sense." Tonker spoke with unanswerable logic. "That's the whole tragedy. Before we were married, over twenty-five years ago, Minnie and I, being astute youngsters—we were both nineteen—perceived that all the difficulties, partings, and troubles in married life arose directly—*directly*, mark you—from nothing more nor less than money and housekeeping. How right we were. We decided, very reasonably that we wouldn't have any. We were both able to keep ourselves then and we have ever since. When we were young we lived near each other, and as we grew older we visited one another frequently. We've each got our own work to do and we don't ask any more of marriage than the tie itself. We've had plenty of fights but never any real bitterness until now. And why has it happened at all? Because some silly official first decides that we're the same person for income-tax, and then starts trying to split us because even he can see that we're not. We don't conform to the blue-print, so we've got to be altered. And they're doing it, too. Minnie's off her head, you know."

Mr. Campion glanced towards Amanda and saw that she had wandered away and was looking at the pictures again. He returned to Tonker.

"In what way?"

The sandy man studied the toes of his wide shoes. "Haven't you noticed it?" he inquired at last. "She's given herself over to them. She's let them into her life, so that her existence is a lunatic farce. There are only two good bedrooms in this house and she's not allowed to sleep in either of them. She employs a gardener but he's not allowed to grow vegetables because she only paints flowers. She hates champers but she's not allowed to drink anything else, and then only when some dreary customer is present. She has to account for all her clothes. My word, I get savage!" He grunted. "Then of course I say things, and so does she." He frowned and cast a sidelong glance of reproach at his stupendous invention. "Normally I curb myself," he went on presently, "but sometimes there's too much provocation, and this last business seemed to me to be the end. I may have overstepped the mark. They've had everything the woman could lay her hands on, Campion: William's bit, the silver, the Cotman, and God knows what else. And now if you please they want *me*. She says they want us to divorce. I did kick at that. It's not civilized."

The thin man stared at him in amazement. "That's absurd," he said. "Not true. Minnie's made a mistake."

"She hasn't, y'know." Tonker shot him a bleak glance. "That's the devil of it. Minnie's mistake seems to have

been in trying to remedy my glüb error by stepping up
production. That appears to be fatal. Once you do that the
problem behaves like wages chasing prices, round and
round and up and up until the bell rings and we all fall
down. That's the trouble. Minnie having had the wind-up
and made a superhuman effort has now reached the stage
where she can't humanly hope to earn any more in a single
year than she does now, and as time goes on she's pretty
certain to earn less. They see this, I suppose, and since
they only want to keep their books straight—I mean,
they're not bluing the cash happily in private somewhere
in a way one could almost forgive—they've pointed out to
her that if she was single she could call a halt to the dash
up the spout. That's the frightful thing, old boy; she's not
got it wrong. She trotted up to London and took Counsel's
opinion."

"Minnie did?" Mr. Campion was amazed.

"Fact." Tonker's eyes opened to their widest. "Without telling me. It shook me. She's never done such a thing
in her life before. She's half American, of course. Those
gals take action. They don't sit down and wait for it. I
didn't hear a thing about it until she'd got it all thrashed
out. One night she put it to me. I was taken by surprise.
That's why I reacted as I did, I suppose. Must excuse
myself somehow."

"No Counsel advised divorce," declared Mr. Campion
with conviction.

"The lad didn't *advise* it." Tonker was unnaturally
gentle. "He simply explained the position. If Minnie sacked
me she could get out of the spiral which I and my glüb got
us into. And," he added with growing wrath, "it's got to
be a real split. No cheating by divorcing and living in sin
afterwards. These Inland Revenue chaps have discretion,
someone told me, to assess a man and woman living in sin
as if they *are* married, so I don't suppose I'd be allowed to
see the old gal at all. Might take her out to tea, perhaps, if
we had a bloke with O.H.M.S. on his hat sitting with us."
His anger boiled up and he bounced in his chair. "I've
never liked officials," he announced, "and now by God I
know why."

"Oh Tonker, how could you!" Dame Sybil Thorndike could hardly have delivered the line with greater intensity. Minnie had appeared on the balcony like Minerva in a prologue. "You promised never to mention it again. You gave your word, you brute. No American husband . . ."

"I am not a brute," hissed Tonker with smothered savagery, "and don't talk to me about America. There a wife is an income-tax asset. A fellow can count half his income as hers, not all hers as his. That's something else they're more sane about than we are. I don't want to hear any more about America. I hate America and all Americans."

"Tonker!" Minnie was sidetracked and reproachful. "What about Paul? What about Ken, and Milton, and Isabelle? And Laura, and Mackie, and Ruth and Ned, and Lavinia? And Robbie and Howard and Mollie? And . . ."

"They're all right." Tonker sounded ashamed of himself.

"Well then." Minnie seemed in danger of falling over the balcony. "What about Tillie, and Mary, and John? And. . . ?"

"And Wendell," put in Tonker, who had become interested in the recital. "And Ollie, and Irving."

"Irving?" Minnie had become dubious. *"Irving?"*

"I like Irving," said Tonker with dignity. "Irving is a phenomenon. Irving hasn't merely got hollow legs. The ground beneath Irving . . ." He broke off abruptly and glanced round at Rupert. "Oh, got the bladders out, have you? That's good. Put 'em in a row. Don't stick your fingers through them, you little chump. That's it. It's not such a bad toy, is it?"

Rupert looked up at him in worship. "It's a zinger," he murmured, trying out the new word cautiously. "I love it."

Tonker was surprised into a flush of pleasure. "There you are, Minnie," he said, "he likes it."

Her smile came out like sunshine. "So do I, Tonker," she said. "Honestly, so do I."

For the rest of the visit they talked of nothing but the party, and when Tonker helped his guests into the station-wagon he had got back to the body-snatchers. "Burt was one of Sheikh Ben-Sabah's influential young friends, Campion," he remarked. "Did you know that?"

A white light of comprehension, as vivid as a star-shell, hit the thin man squarely between the eyes and arrested him half-way into the driving seat as he saw the probable answer to the question which had brought him down to Pontisbright on the pretence of holiday-making, and had made him so chary of becoming unnecessarily involved in any other inquiry. He could hardly trust himself to speak.

"Was *he* in that racket?"

"Of course he was. It was the foundation of his fortune." Tonker's voice was contemptuous in the darkness. "I was one of the few who spotted him. However, he's coming to our party. That should be good. See you tomorrow. Dog in? Good. God bless."

"Good night, my dears." Minnie slid her arm through her husband's and they stood together, waving after the departing car.

Amanda laughed softly as the wagon crept up the lane where moonlight dropped from the hanging grasses and the air was breathless with the scent of blossom. "They adore one another, don't they?" she said. "Life is one long friendly fight. A permanent exhibition bout. They look a bit like the lion and the unicorn. I say, Minnie must either have a most peculiar tax-gatherer, or she's got the whole thing upside down. She's just wrong, I suppose?"

"I sincerely hope so, or the country's going to the dogs." Mr. Campion spoke fervently.

"Tonker's rather odd, don't you think?"

"You noticed that, did you? I wondered. He's unnaturally subdued. Shaken, I fancy. No wonder. It's an alarming story. Poor old Tonker and his frightful present."

Amanda was not satisfied. "I think it's something else," she said. "Something he's ashamed of. Something recent."

"It could be." Campion spoke lightly. "Tonker does do things. He's an uncertain animal. I don't quite see why he came dashing home, do you? Why did he go to the boat house and not walk in on the family?"

"Uncle Tonker came home to telephone some clowns,"

said Rupert unexpectedly. "He told me so when he asked me if he could have the room, when he came out from under the bed."

"Goodness," Amanda's arms tightened about him. "I thought you were asleep."

"So I am." Rupert was ecstatically happy. "Wouldn't it be wonderful if Uncle Tonker *was* a clown? He is a zinger. I like him."

"I do too," said Mr. Campion. "A prince among fatheads. And if he did commit the glübalübalum his punishment seems to be on the heavy side."

He set them down at the door of the dark house, helped Choc to follow them, and drove on to the garage. As he walked back a vast black shape disengaged itself from the shadows of an arbour and the unmistakable odour of malt was mingled with the dizzy scent of stocks and tobacco flowers.

"Wot yer." Mr. Lugg's voice was little more than a growl. "I've worn meself out for yer. Pore Charles 'as just come in. I didn't speak to 'im. 'E's preoccupied. We can count 'im out. I picked up something, though. My friends aren't spilling everythink they know, but they let somethink drop. They know 'oo the corp is."

"Really?"

"Yus. It ain't discovered yet though it won't 'arf be in the mornin'. The corp, cock, is an official of the ole Inland Rev. In other words, chum, 'e's the Income Tax man."

Mr. Campion stood transfixed, the hairs tingling in his scalp. He knew now what it was that had worried him about the portrait in Minnie's studio and why he had recognized it. The face had been the dead face in the ditch, and the crumpled paper behind its head had been forms, hundreds and hundreds of screwed-up buff forms.

"Hell!" said the mildest of men.

CHAPTER VIII

Love and the Police

The country round the Mill at Pontisbright at five o'clock on a June morning was of itself a spell. The near distance was dizzy with haze, the dew beads were thick on the grass, the waters were limpid and ringing, the birds sang with idiotic abandon, the air was scented with animals and a thousand flowers.

For Charlie Luke, the Londoner, who was wrestling with a whole assault of a force of unfamiliar furies most cruelly released within him, it was a merciless fairyland.

By five he had swum in the pool, been for a walk, examined his car, looked at the telephone, set his watch wrong by the grandfather clock, and made himself a daisy-chain. By six he had repeated the entire performance, save for the chain, which he had had to bury in case anyone found it, and by seven he was hungry, exhausted, and resolute.

He was just going in to start getting breakfast himself, if Lugg did not appear, when he found a small bird's nest made of green moss and grey lichen. Its fragile valiance astounded him and immediately a wave of terrifying softness passed over him and frightened him out of his wits. Within five seconds he was standing looking at the telephone again. As he looked it began to ring.

Instantly, now that the living companionship which he had both craved and dreaded was, to put it mildly, superfluous, Lugg and Rupert appeared on the stairs and Choc, apparently assuming that sound constituted breaking and entering, rushed at the instrument barking like a house dog. By the time Luke could hear anything at all over the wire, he was in such a pitiable state of nervous irritation that it took him some seconds to grasp that the call was from London to himself, and that the C.I.D. Commander was speaking, presumably from his home. He sounded bright, fatherly, and explicit.

" . . . so since you are on the spot you can take over immediately," he was saying. "Here is the outline."

Luke's training did not let him down, but although the essential notes appeared under his hand on the telephone-pad, someone new within himself stared at them with dismayed surprise.

" . . . photographs. P.M. this a.m. Identification established. Friend of deceased subsequently interviewed."

"Charles . . . ?"

"Yes, sir."

"You see what has happened. The victim was a minor official of the Inland Revenue local collector's office. That fact must narrow the field considerably. It's unlikely that you'll run into much mystery, but, since all these little rural places are much alike, I imagine the Chief Constable is appealing to us so as not to embarrass either himself or his own men rather than from any other reason. Do you see what I mean?"

"Not exactly, sir." Luke's voice was wooden but he had gone white round the eye-sockets.

"You will, Chief, you will." There was amusement in the voice of authority. "You're staying with Campion, aren't you?"

"Yes sir."

"That accounts for it. He seems to have told Pursuivant that you were there and the old gentleman has jumped at the hint. That must mean that they want somebody who has absolutely no personal interest in the place, someone with no local friends, a whipping-boy, in fact, who can shoulder any odium which may be accruing. Now do you see?"

"Yes sir."

"You sound very quiet. Are you all right? Good, I think you may find that the whole thing is an open-and-shut case, but if I don't hear from you by four this afternoon I'll send you an assistant."

Luke's brain began to work with a jolt like a truck starting up.

"Meantime, might I have Mr. Campion as an immediate associate, sir?"

"Campion? I don't see how I could justify that."

"He speaks the language, sir."

There was a laugh far away in London. "Oh, it's like that, is it? I've heard it's very primitive and near the soil."

"There's something disconcerting about the place, sir." Luke spoke with a dry mouth. "Will you have a word with Mr. Campion now, sir? I should appreciate it very much." He put his hand over the mouthpiece and swung round on Rupert. "Cut up and tell your father that the house is on fire," he commanded through his teeth.

"Is it?" inquired Rupert with delighted interest.

"It will be," muttered Luke with suppressed ferocity, "if he's not down here in ten seconds from now."

Twenty minutes later, while Charlie Luke was listening to Superintendent Fred South, to whom a previous call to Sir Leo had directed him, the rest of the family was at breakfast.

"If you're going to stay with Charles, Rupert and I will take Lugg, if you can spare him, and go down to The Beckoning Lady at once, don't you think?" said Amanda. Her brown face was troubled and her eyes watchful. "There's still a great deal to do, and people are inclined to stay away from that sort of trouble. They can't possibly put the party off, you see, and at the best of times it's a rather fantastic operation. Minnie seems to do it with one old woman and a pack of kids."

Mr. Campion hesitated. "You think that now is the time to rally, do you?" he murmured. "Perhaps so. What about those chums of yours, Lugg? Do they really know anything?''

Mr. Lugg, who was standing by the window drinking a cup of coffee, thus epitomizing his chosen position as servitor and friend, scratched his bald head thoughtfully.

"Old Harry knoo more than 'e let on," he said. " 'E's a funny sort of bloke. Likes a secret, that's about the size of it. I reckon 'e knoo the stiff was there for some days, and quite likely 'e's 'ad a look at it, mucking up all the clues. 'E don't know 'ow it got there, that I'll take me affydavey.''

"Why wouldn't he report it?" inquired Mr. Campion.

" 'Oo can say?" Lugg shrugged his vast shoulders with urbane sophistication. "Didn't want to be mixed up in nothing so unrefined, per'aps.''

"In that case he either knew the man or knew someone else who did." Amanda spoke with the authority of one who knows the terrain. "If he didn't report it the first time he saw it, he thought that the man could be traced to have had some association with himself or with someone fairly near him. The connexion may have been very slight.''

Mr. Lugg sighed. "That narrers it down to Miss Diane, because old 'Arry ain't got no relations. 'E told me that 'imself. That's about wot. Miss D. knoo the chap and was frightened of 'im, 'avin seen 'im about, and didn't tell 'Arry why. When 'Arry found 'im dead 'e pinched 'is papers to find out 'oo 'e was.''

Mr. Campion blinked before this stream of reasoning.

"Why did he take them away? Why not read them and put them back?''

Mr. Lugg regarded him coldly. "Some people like to make a proper job o' readin'," he observed. "Not a quick skim-over like a perishin' show-off flippin' through *The Times* noospaper." An ignoble smile spread over his white moon-face. "She's a lovely woman," he remarked. " 'Er 'eart's as big as the barrel she keeps it in. I'd better go down to the 'ouse with the young 'uns and make myself useful.''

While the meal continued, Charlie Luke remained in

the hall at the telephone. When at last the local Superintendent had rung off, he had been able to put through the call which had been on his mind for so long. His powerful body with its heavy shoulders and narrow hips was arched like a cat's over the instrument, his dark face eager, and his eyes in their odd-shaped sockets tragic. His voice, naked in its disappointment, poured out his explanation and apology.

"And so you see," he finished helplessly, "I cannot drive you."

"That's all right." Prune's ridiculous drawl sounded so cool and remote that an icy drop congealed and fell within him. "Think of me at three o'clock."

The final request turned his heart over and the colour rushed into his face and up to his close-cut hair.

"Then you'll go without me?"

"Of course I shall," said Prune.

"I'll see you," he began, but she had gone. He heard the far-off click as she hung up.

He wiped the sweat off his forehead as he went in to join the others, but he was exalted. The buoyancy of his step had returned and the black tomcat effect, which was always apparent when he was happy, had reappeared in the lines of his neck and head. His very white teeth were showing when he sat down at the table.

"If it's dirty, if it stinks, if not even a mum could love it, send for a cop," he announced, smiling at Campion ferociously, "and that includes you."

Campion nodded. His pale face was very serious. "Thank you," he said gravely, "thank you for fixing that. I had no idea how I was going to get back on the band wagon. What have they got so far?"

Luke gave him a long searching stare. "Are your pals involved?"

"I hope not."

"So do I, guv. We're supposed to be the men come about the bracelets."

"Good Lord, have they got as much evidence as that already?"

"No." Without thinking, Luke was eating as if he had never eaten before. "No, to me it didn't sound as if they'd got enough to shop pussy. But they seemed quietly confident. They've got an identification and a statement from a friend, who seems to have opened his mouth even wider than a friend usually does, which is saying a deal. The Super, whose name is South, is meeting us at the local Copper Shop in twenty minutes. He says you can tell me the preliminaries. Can you tell me about *him*?"

Mr. Campion rose from the table and pottered round the room, looking for cigarettes.

"He's finishing his time quietly in the country, which would indicate that someone hasn't liked him," he said slowly, "and he's one of the I'm-your-pal contingent."

Luke grimaced. "Smile—smile—got yer!" he remarked, illustrating the phrase with a graphic movement of his long hands. "One of the Central Office's older models, like Sailor Harris I suppose. I hate those chaps. They get us clean boys a bad name."

"South," said Mr. Campion seriously, "makes Sailor look like a cricketer."

"Christmas!" Luke crossed his fingers. "Let's hope all our chums are nice innocent people. Who are also deaf mutes," he added as an afterthought. "We'll get going in my car, shall we?"

He came back a moment or so later with a request to Lugg.

"I wonder if you'd send this wire to my mum for me," he said, placing a sheet from the telephone-pad and three shillings on the table. "It's her birthday, and she likes a card. So long."

Lugg took up the message and pocketed the coin. "Sentimental lot these cops," he remarked affably to Amanda as the door closed behind the Chief Inspector. " 'Luke, twenty-four Linden Lea, London S.W. thirty-three.' Listen to this. 'I have got my eye on you, Nipper.' That should bring a lump to the old lady's larynx. I'll send this over the phone and then we'll get straight down there, shall we?"

Amanda said nothing. She was looking at a piece of paper which she had found in an empty milk bottle by the kitchen step. The handwriting was round and schoolboyish in the tradition of the new education, and the message was in the form of a question.

"Why was the P.C. up all night looking on the Battus Dump without his uniform?"

There was no signature, but the oily smudge on the paper was sufficient to suggest that Scat, son of Scatty, was following the family tradition. Amanda looked across at her own son, who was stacking plates without being asked.

"When is a policeman not a policeman?" she inquired.

"When he takes his clothes off," said Rupert, licking the marmalade spoon. "Then he's just an ordinary silly old man."

CHAPTER IX

The Helpful Official

A silent group of men climbed out of the two cars in the drive of The Beckoning Lady shortly after half past ten. Mr. Campion and Luke, who had followed behind the police car, were in anxious moods and Luke particularly was wary. Superintendent Fred South alone was smiling happily. His horrible hat was worn well on the back of his head, his tight sports coat was open and he looked the kindest and jolliest of countrymen.

"I'll leave my chaps here, Chief," he suggested, his eyes full of merry unspoken hints. "No need to frighten the poor lady with a football crowd. Let's go round the back, too. I always go round the back." He burst into a cloud of little giggles and led them unprotesting to the kitchen door.

Minnie received them on the concrete platform outside the window of Uncle William's deserted room. She was seated on a low stool, shelling peas with Westy and George Meredith to help her. There was a half-hundredweight sack of them on the stone beside her and both she and the boys each had a small basin which they emptied into a huge punchbowl of blue china which stood in the centre of the group. It was warm in the sun, and just below them, at the foot of a flowery bank, the river ran golden water. She glanced sharply at Campion and he noticed with dismay that her face was drawn and set.

"I'm so sorry I can't get up," she said, smiling politely at Luke. "If I do I shall spill all these. Boys, will you be lambs and go down to the village to get the table-silver? You know where it is. Mrs. Claude has been cleaning it for us, bless her. Oh, of course, you took it to her. Well, go and get it, and take it into the studio.''

Fred South beamed. "You put it all out as piece-work, do you, ma'am?" he asked, seating himself in Westy's place. "That's a good idea."

"I bully my friends to do it," she said, laughing. "I'm so grateful to Amanda, Albert. She's slaving on that wretched wherry. Rupert is with the twins in the dining-room. Emma is icing cakes there. I never feel a party's a party without little pink cakes. Lugg is spud-bashing, as he calls it, with Dinah, and old Harry is in the back kitchen cooking hams. He has some secret way of doing it which is terrific. Pinky should be here soon, too. She's going to do the flowers. It's a dreadful set-out, but everybody's being so good."

Mr. Campion motioned Luke to George Meredith's seat and sat down himself on the edge of the platform.

"Tonker, I take it, is still in bed doing the cross-word puzzle?" he suggested.

Minnie's characteristic snort escaped her. "I'm afraid he is, the old cad," she said. "Do you want to see him?"

"In a little while, ma'am. We just want to have a word with you first." The Superintendent was twinkling at her and Luke cleared his throat warningly.

"We want to talk to you about Leonard Terence Dennis Ohman, Mrs. Cassands," he began gravely. "I have to tell you that his dead body has been found not far from here. Did you know him?"

Minnie nodded. "Poor Little Doom," she said unexpectedly. "He's been lying out there for a week and we never knew. I don't know what I shall do without him."

The reaction took Luke out of his stride and there was a moment's silence in which Minnie blew her long nose and then, observing Westy's empty basin, proffered it to South with a handful of pea-pods.

"How did you know he was dead!" Luke demanded.

"My charlady told me this morning. It's all over the village. Oh, you mustn't blame anybody," she said, intercepting the reproachful glance he cast towards the local man, and handing him George Meredith's basin by way, no doubt, of appeasement. "News does get about. They say he was killed, murdered, but I can't believe that."

"Why not?" Absentmindedly, Luke began to shell peas himself.

"Because I don't see why anybody should. He was a bit of a bore, perhaps, but no one could have wished him any harm."

Fred South picked a maggot out of a pea-pod and flicked it into the flowers.

"You knew what his job was, did you, ma'am?"

"Indeed I did. He collected Income Tax."

"Why did you call him Little Doom?"

"I always have. We called him that twenty-five years ago. It was something to do with his signature."

"Twenty-five years. . . ?" All three men were regarding her in astonishment.

Minnie went on shelling peas. "It must be quite that," she said thoughtfully. "When I first knew him he was the rent collector of the studios in Clerkenwell. He collected for the whole estate."

Luke sat back abruptly and felt in his breast pocket for a document.

"That's right," he agreed at last. "He came to this part of the country in 1942 when London was being pasted." He glanced up and smiled at her. "This is a statement made by a Mr. Henry Angel, who is a retired insurance agent. He lives in the road where Ohman lodged and seems to be the only person who knew him well. They played chess together at a club. Angel says here 'Ohman came to this town in the war and secured a temporary post in the Inland Revenue Collector's office, which was shorthanded at the time. He had a very modest job with them until the January of this year, when he became redundant and left.' "

"Really!" Minnne was astounded. "I didn't know he'd lost his job. He didn't tell me. But then perhaps he wouldn't."

Luke hesitated. "He appears to have confided very thoroughly in Angel, Mrs. Cassands," he said at last. "It says here that Ohman was in the habit of writing letters for you. Is that true?"

She met his stare with eyes as sharp as his own. "Suppose I tell it," she suggested. "Then you can see if the stories agree. That's what you want, isn't it?"

He sighed and smiled. "It would help," he said.

"Well then—" Minnie's fingers moved faster and faster among the pea-shucks "—I hadn't seen or heard of Little Doom for quite twenty years, until he turned up here one morning saying that he had come from the Department of Inland Revenue and waving a demand for five thousand pounds odd. The whole thing was a shock to me, because I hadn't very much money and until that instant I had not known that the fifteen thousand pounds which my husband had given me eighteen months before to pay our debts in back-taxes with wasn't real money. I mean, I hadn't known one couldn't pay anything with it."

"You didn't know there was tax due on it?"

"That's right. Well, Little Doom and I recognized one another and we began to talk. Naturally. Anyone would."

"There was something to talk about," murmured South.

"Yes, wasn't there?" Minnie regarded him gravely. "He explained there'd be the same amount to pay again in six months and he guessed about seven thousand in surtax later. Both my husband and I had earned some money as well in the same year, you see. It took me a long time to understand it all, and when I did I'm afraid I was very angry with my husband." Suddenly she laughed. "Poor Little Doom was very nearly as terrified as I was."

Both Luke and South were disposed to be considerably alarmed *now*, Mr. Campion noticed. They sat looking at her in a kind of fascinated horror. Luke was the first to collect himself. He returned to his typewritten statement.

" 'Ohman confided to me,' " he read, " 'that he observed at once the lady had no idea of the machinery of Income Tax, and out of pure kindness and for the sake of old acquaintance he roughed out a few letters about expenses and allowances for her to send to the Inspector's office, which, of course, was quite separate from his own. He knew he was taking a great risk in doing this, but the subject fascinated him and later he read all manner of books on it and quite wore himself out.' "

"Oh dear," said Minnie ruefully, "doesn't it sound frightful? It was, too. He was very conscientious, you see, and liked to make certain for himself that we really were doing what he had arranged. He timed the gardener with a stopwatch and things like that, but he saved a lot of money and took all the drudgery of the thing off my shoulders by doing all the writing."

"Did you pay him for his work, ma'am?" South said curiously.

"Very little. He was very exact and fanatically honest. I painted a portrait of him to make up, but unfortunately I kept thinking of Tonker's beastly present all the time I was doing it and so it came out rather fierce. He liked it, though, and bought an awfully expensive frame for it. It's in the studio now. He lent it to me for the show on Saturday."

Luke shifted uneasily in his chair. He was eyeing the document in his hand with deep misgiving.

"It says here," he began slowly, "that Ohman finally arrived at the conclusion that your husband and yourself should—er—separate for financial reasons."

Minnie flushed scarlet. "It says. . . ? Oh well, I suppose he had to talk to someone. That man is rather the Recording Angel, isn't he? What else does it say?"

"Not a lot." Luke was trying to sound soothing. "But is it true?"

"Yes, it is. You see, Little Doom found out suddenly that my working extra hard only made things worse, so he said we'd have to think of something else. He went into it and suddenly decided that the only thing for it was that I should get divorced. He worked it out very carefully. He said that if my husband and I parted for ever, and were very careful never to stay in the same house again, the Inland Revenue would consider us single people, and that if I went on earning at the high pressure I'd had to lately then I should save seven hundred a year in tax each year. Then I could pay that to the Inland Revenue and in time I should get out of the spiral we'd got ourselves into, by paying arrears of Income Tax with the sum Tonker got from his glübalübalum. It's quite simple when you get the hang of it, but very dull. Like crochet, all circles.'' She paused and her brow cleared. ''Little Doom meant well. The subject had got hold of him.''

''When he put up this idea, didn't you feel very annoyed with him?'' Superintendent South was getting ready to pounce. Mr. Campion glanced at Minnie nervously. She appeared to be considering the question.

''No,'' she said at last, ''I don't think so. I think I realized he was only being dead keen. I was a bit startled by the law. I mean, Income Tax is one thing and if you owe it you must pay it, but I don't think they ought to corner one into abandoning one's marriage. It's so high-handedly inefficient, isn't it? It can't be what they want.''

South retired to wait again, and Luke continued cautiously.

''According to this statement, Ohman told Angel that he had 'had it out with you, and had warned you that he intended to appear at your husband's party on Saturday to make certain of catching him. His idea was to put this proposal before him at a time when he would be compelled to listen.' Is that so?''

Minnie laughed. ''Poor little man, he did have horrible ideas,'' she said. ''I told him I'd kill him if he—hullo, darling?''

The final question was addressed to Annabelle. The little girl had come dancing along the brick path from the kitchen. She shot a sidelong glance at the visitors and went on up to Minnie.

''Uncle Tonker has sent these down to you,'' she announced, handing her a slip of paper. ''He says don't over-exert yourself, but if you happen to spot the answers please let him know, because the problem is holding him up.''

Minnie took the note and the policemen on either side of her craned their necks. Obligingly she leant back so that they could both see.

"One," she read aloud for Mr. Campion's benefit, "flatulent statement, novel aftermath. Four-four-three-four. Two, typewritten exercise, tail tip. Three-two-three-five. Bless the man . . . All right, Annabelle. I'll see to it. You go and collect the vases for Miss Pinky, who should be here at any moment. Off you go, my pet."

As the child trotted away, Minnie returned to Luke.

"They're cross-word puzzle clues," she explained. "They're a fearful waste of time, but if you want to see Tonker we ought to do them, because he won't get up until he's finished *The Times*. Let's see now—"

"No," objected Luke firmly. "Let the gentleman rest. You were telling me, Mrs. Cassands, that you told Ohman you'd kill him if he—"

Minnie stared at him in scandalized amazement. "I *didn't* kill him, if that's what you mean," she protested. "Good heavens, how dreadful! You can see how valuable he was to me. I haven't worried at all since he appeared, except over this divorce business. I was very grateful to him, and quite dependent on him. He worked like a beaver and loved it. Do you know," she went on, shaking a pea-pod at him, "that there's a cupboard in this house ten feet by seven which is absolutely chock-full of carbon copies of letters written by Little Doom? He loved his work as much as I do mine."

"When did you see him last, if you please?" Luke was completing his notes.

Minnie considered. "About a fortnight ago, when he 'had it out,' as he called it. But he was over here last week on the Thursday."

"How do you know?"

"Because he brought his portrait back, or someone did. I borrowed it from him to show on Saturday, and when I saw it just inside the studio I knew that he had been, but I thought he must be still angry because he didn't wait."

"I see. Was your husband in the house that day?"

"Yes, I think so. In fact I know he was. He took two days off down here, working on a scheme they're getting out for some margarine people. They may flavour it and sell it in different colours—honey, clover, paprika, cheddar, and so on."

"Wouldn't he work in the studio?"

"No. Little Doom wouldn't allow that. It was something to do with heat and light and expenses. Tonker had to work in the drawing-room."

"Could he have seen the man without your knowing?"

"I don't think so. He'd have mentioned it. You must ask him."

Luke smiled. "I hope to. First of all, though, I want to see a Mr. Jake Bernadine. We hear from Angel that Ohman didn't like him."

"Well, naturally he wouldn't." Minnie looked embarrassed. "Jake threw him into a beehive and the little man didn't know it was empty."

"When was this?"

"Oh years ago, last summer. Little Doom kept bothering to know if they paid me any rent. He wouldn't believe me when I said they didn't and so he went and tackled Jake, which," she added in sudden apprehension, "is never a very wise thing to do, so be careful. Look out for the donkey, too. He doesn't kick, but—"

"I know," said Luke, getting up, "he bites."

When the two senior policemen had vanished round the side of the house, Mr. Campion remained where he was.

"They'll be back," he ventured at last.

"I know they will." She raised a worried face to him. "My goodness, what a mess, Albert. Can you get us out of it?"

"I don't know," he said honestly, "it rather depends."

She looked out over the river, her eyes sad.

"I'm so sorry. The man was absolutely invaluable, and in a way I'd got to like him. He did take the problem seriously. Still, that can't be helped. Oh Albert, no one could have murdered him. It's fantastic!"

Mr. Campion ran a finger round the inside of his collar.

"Minnie," he said, "when exactly did you spring all this on Tonker?"

She did not answer immediately but sat looking at him, making up her mind.

"I had to tell him," she said at last. "It was getting so near the party. I wasn't sure of Doom. He did some very tactless things. It was on the cards that he really would turn up and try to start something."

The thin man shook his head. "I know why you told him, my dear. I said, when?"

"On the Wednesday night. Tonker was livid, quite furious. One of his Grade-A rages. But we made it up in the end, Albert, we did really. We swore that whatever happens we won't split up, and that is what has cheered me so. I'd been scared to death, wondering what his reaction would be. After all, they can send him to jail when we get old and can't pay, can't they? I mean, I knew he was very fond of me but I felt it was testing it somewhat."

There was a long silence after she had spoken and presently she leant forward to talk earnestly.

"Albert, this is the literal truth. This morning, at six o'clock, Dinah came up to tell me that the dead tramp was Little Doom. I was horrified and I woke Tonker and told him, and he said 'Damn!' And I said 'Good heavens Tonker, you don't know anything about it, do you?' He turned over and said, 'Clear your mind. I'm not round the bend. But what an unholy nuisance just now, just before the party. Otherwise, jolly good show, of course.' So that really is all right. He wasn't lying. I always know when he is."

"How?" inquired Mr. Campion, who had known Tonker for thirty-five years.

"I can't tell exactly, but I do." Minnie spoke with deep conviction. "Probably he smells differently. I was reading somewhere that everything is smell. Anyway, Tonker wasn't lying and he would know if he'd killed somebody, wouldn't he? Besides, he wouldn't do it. Tonker wouldn't really kill anybody. He might give them a tap, but he wouldn't kill them. Don't be silly."

Mr. Campion swallowed. "How angry was he with the man?"

Minnie shrugged her shoulders. Colour had appeared on her cheekbones and her eyes were flickering.

"He was very cross with everybody, including me. He says there's a general feeling against marriage just now, and of course he's quite right. Look at Dinah."

"Miss Diane?" Campion was diverted in spite of himself. "She says she's not married."

"She was once. I remember her in Clerkenwell twenty years ago. She used to clean the offices opposite the studio. She was married to an absolute horror who used to wait outside on a Friday and collect her earnings and knock her about. I don't suppose she ever saw me but I recognized her. Early in the war she turned up here as a single woman who had lost her identity card and ration book. She got new ones at the Food Office and I think she took the opportunity to change her name. I imagine that she saw her chance and just ran away from the old brute. I never asked her or let her know I knew her."

"Where does Old Harry stand in all this?"

"Oh well, she just moved in on him in the modern fashion. Even if her husband is dead, she'll hardly marry him. If they stay single they get just enough to live on when they're old, but once they're married, fifteen bob is knocked off her old-age pension."

A new possibility occurred to Mr. Campion. "The wages of sin, fifteen bob," he remarked absently. "Very modest. But if her husband is still alive and drawing a pension, while she is taking a single woman's pension down here, she's probably committing some sort of offence. Little Doom came from Clerkenwell. Could she have known him in London? Could he have recognized her if he saw her down here?"

Minnie hesitated. "She was remarkably clever if he didn't know her," she admitted grudgingly. "As I keep telling you, he was the rent collector. But don't you go getting any frightful ideas about Dinah having killed him, Albert," she commanded. "That woman is the only professional help I've got, and there are quite eighty-five people coming to dinner tomorrow, if something terrible doesn't happen to stop them. Oh my dear, don't make things worse.''

There was a somewhat helpless silence between them and eventually Minnie took up the sheet of cross-word clues.

''Of course Tonker is naughty,'' she observed placidly. ''This is the sort of thing that can cause an awful lot of trouble. See what that first clue is? Flatulent statement, novel aftermath: that's 'Gone with the wind,' isn't it? And the other, 'typewritten exercise': that's 'Now is the time for all good men to come to the aid of the party,' and the 'tail tip' is 'aid of the party,' so Tonker's message to me is 'Gone with the wind. Aid of the party.' Tonker's gone off. He borrowed a car to come home with last night and left it at the end of the lane. I saw the message at once and I heard the car go off when Annabelle was here.''

Mr. Campion was staring at her in horror. ''D'you mean to say he's cleared out now, at this moment?''

''I'm afraid so.'' She took up yet another handful of peas. ''He didn't come into the drive at all, so he avoided the police cars altogether. He is a cad. He's just thinking of his old party, and he's relying on us to keep these police quiet. He's worried that there may be awkward publicity on this 'Death of an Income Tax Man' angle, and is afraid it may spoil the show. I wonder how he'll get around that one.''

''He won't.'' Mr. Campion, who was deeply shocked, spoke with conviction.

''He'll think of something,'' said Minnie sadly. ''Let's hope it's not one of his clangers. Of course he's only gone to London. How was he to know the police might want to see him? They didn't ask to. And even when I suggested it, they brushed it aside as unimportant. You fix it for me, Albert. Go up and telephone the office, and tell Wally he must make Tonker call us back the moment he gets in. He's trying to save the party, and doesn't see how it may look.''

Mr. Campion rose unhappily. "This is going to be very difficult," he said. "A murder has been committed . . ."

"Oh, I *know.*" She sounded utterly exasperated. "But you're mad to worry about Tonker. If anybody killed Little Doom intentionally it must be that man Smith."

"My dear girl!" Campion was aghast. "How can you make such a wild accusation? Why Smith?"

"Because," said Minnie unreasonably, "he's got the face for it, and nobody else has. Find out what he's been up to, and while you're about it, discover why on earth he wants my house. I had a note from him this morning confirming that I'd invited his friends to the party, and asking me if I'd ever thought of going to live in Eire or the Bahamas! I think everybody has gone quite mad. Call up Wally soon, please dear. I don't want those policemen to misunderstand Tonker."

At that moment a shadow fell over the stone and they turned to see Superintendent South coming back, his little box in his hand.

"I forgot to ask the lady," he said, twinkling at Campion. "Look ma'am, have you ever seen this bead before?"

Minnie peered into the box and her eyes were sharp and interested. Presently she took up the bronze bead and held it in the palm of her hand, while she turned it over with an exploring finger.

"Why yes," she announced with great satisfaction. "Where did you get that? Don't lose it. We must put it back. That's off Tonker's party waistcoat."

CHAPTER X

The Bottom of the Garden

"Yes, well, there the waistcoat is," said Emma Bernadine, holding her sticky hands well away from herself.
"Don't bring it near the table, for goodness' sake, or I
shall get icing all over it. Small Fry, get out of here
darlings. Go and help Minnie shell peas."

The inner kitchen appeared to be a sea of small coloured
cakes, and the three men, determined in their official
capacity but as human beings acutely aware that they were
in the way, stood back against the inner door.

Rupert and the twins, jammy-faced and excited, scram-
bled off the floor and herded into a corner, where they
stood hesitating, hoping to be forgotten.

"Be off!" Emma was harassed. A wisp of dark hair had
escaped her white head-dress and she dared not touch it
but had to keep blowing it out of her eyes.

"Many happy relations," Rupert ventured softly, but
something had gone wrong with his spell, for so far that
day he had had no success with it.

The twins, who were more practical, put the inevitable
retreat to account. Blue Drawers gave one hand to Rupert
and took a cake with the other, while Yellow Drawers took
two cakes. All Rupert had to do was to open the door to
the back kitchen. Emma was still talking.

"That's the only beaded waistcoat in the house, or in
the county for all I know," she was saying, as the children
trooped off shedding crumbs. "It's genuine Victorian bead-
work and you can see for yourselves that its never been

worn. I bought it at a sale of work in the village, and brought it home in my shopping bag just as it was, half done. Miss Knipp turned it out. It was made by her grandmother who died before it was finished. I left it in the cloakroom to get ready for the party. It's to be a surprise for Tonker. And it's hung where you found it for quite six weeks.''

Superintendent South, who had been with Luke into the small square room beyond the wash-basins to find the garment, now carried it over to the light. Both police officers were a little at sea, for beside the usual country house paraphernalia of gardening boots, guns, and golf clubs, the cloakroom at The Beckoning Lady had yielded a large red false beard hanging on a hook, a cavalry sword, a racing crash helmet, and a small black human skull which had proved after some excitement to be part of an articulated skeleton such as can be found in most art schools.

The waistcoat, which had been on a hanger hidden under an oilskin cape, was an impressive affair of tan watered silk, embroidered in a bold masculine pattern of acanthus leaves in bronze, black, and white beads. But the embroideress of long ago had never seen her work in use, for the sheets of notepaper which she had used to protect the pattern as she finished it were still tacked in place, and only the final quarter-inch or so remained to be done. The button-holes were made, but as yet there were no cat's-eyes to correspond with them. Where the pattern remained to be finished the beads were loose.

South turned it over and finally hung it against his chest for a moment, before comparing it with the bead he carried about. There was no possible doubt about the similarity. He glanced at Luke, who shrugged his shoulders, and the Superintendent returned the waistcoat to its hanger.

''I should like to see the gentleman actually wearing that tomorrow,'' he remarked, ''so perhaps we won't borrow it after all. These beads seem to be all over the place. Ohman could have picked one up anywhere.''

"Little Doom probably tried the waistcoat up against himself just as you've done," said Emma. "It's the sort of impudent thing he would do."

"Impudent?" Mr. Campion fastened on the word hastily, lest relations became strained. "That's a new word in connexion with Little Doom."

"Is it? Then the only person you've discussed him with is Minnie, and one doesn't have to be three detectives to tell that." Emma began to beat up a bowl of icing as though she disliked it personally. "I expect she simply told you what a help he was, and how he took a load of worry off her shoulders. No one else found him anything but a menace."

Her powerful forearm rested for an instant and she pointed a dripping spoon at South.

"That man was one long prying nose," she announced. "Hasn't it occurred to you all that we're taking your inquisition remarkably calmly? Don't you think it peculiar that we're all getting on with our work and letting you poke about as if you were nothing out of the ordinary? Well, let me tell you you're not. We're used to this sort of thing. We have it every day. We're not surprised to open our kitchen doors and find that someone has undone the stove to see how much fuel we're burning. We're not astounded to be asked who we've telephoned or why, or where the half-bottle of gin that was on the sideboard last week has gone to, or if the new piece of soap in the cloakroom was really necessary. That's the kind of insane life we've been leading, and the reason for it is that Minnie let the little brute into the house and then daren't get rid of him. If he really is dead, I tell you I'm more than glad. I'm hysterical with joy."

Luke made a sudden movement but a hand like a band of steel closed over his arm and he was forced to keep silent as a little sigh escaped the Superintendent.

"Jake was the only person who treated him with any intelligence," Emma continued, her round face flushed and her eyes bright. "He started on Jake and Jake threw him on the hive, and that was the last we saw of him in our cottage. Tonker hid from the man and Minnie encouraged him. Minnie always feels that if she suffers she'll be lucky, that her work will sell, or get better, or something equally idiotic.''

"Oh I don't know," murmured Mr. Campion. "I think Minnie felt she'd like a visible irritant."

Emma laughed bitterly. "This way we all shared it, certainly," she said. "Do you know, he actually came and timed me working on those rooms upstairs? Oh, he *did* enjoy his little bit of power."

South was beaming. "You ought to stop and have a cigarette," he said, feeling in his pocket and looking hopefully at Campion. "You've been working too hard. It's not worth it. When did you see this difficult gentleman last? Do you remember?"

"I haven't spoken to him for some months. We weren't on speaking terms." Emma waved Mr. Campion's cigarette-case away and continued to beat the icing. "I saw him last week on Thursday afternoon, some time between four-fifteen and four-thirty."

"Did you though?" Luke came back into the inquiry with a rush, and the force of his personality lit up the kitchen and silenced the busy spoon. "How do you know the time so exactly?"

"Because," said Emma, looking at him critically for the first time, and responding suddenly to something she saw in him, "my husband and I were in our cottage listening to Mrs. Dale's Diary on the radio, as we always do at four-fifteen. We *like* it," she added defiantly.

"Do you? So does my mum." Luke was beaming at her, his eyes alive and bright and his dark face friendly. "So does *his* wife, I'll bet," he added, with a ferocious grin at South. "You were listening, were you? That's all right. Your husband didn't tell us that. Come to that, he didn't tell us much."

"Jake doesn't admit he likes it," said Emma.

"I know." Luke was happier. "He just happens to be doing something quiet in the room when it's on. That's natural enough. You saw Little Doom?—this name is going to get me into trouble, I can see that. It'll sound well if I come out with it in court. You saw Little Doom while you were in your cottage listening to Mrs. Dale? Where was he?"

"Haring down the drive, apparently for his life," said Emma calmly.

"Away from the house?"

"Yes."

"Anyone behind him?"

"No, not a soul. I watched to see. He was all right too. I mean there wasn't any—he wasn't hurt."

Luke turned inquiringly to Mr. Campion and the thin man answered his unspoken question.

"He wouldn't have got very far with the injuries I saw. How do you feel about that, Superintendent?"

Fred South shook his head. For once he was not laughing. His comic face wore an expression which was almost thoughtful.

"Was he running away or running to, ma'am?" he said at last. "It's a different kind of run."

Emma did not answer. For the first time her hard brightness had wavered and there was a lot of colour in her face.

"I—I don't know," she said at last.

"Were you surprised to see him?"

"Surprised to see Little Doom? I wouldn't be surprised if I saw him coming down the chimney or up out of the copper! I noticed him particularly that day only because it was unusual for him to be on the drive. As I said, he avoided our cottage after the hive incident, and the donkey didn't like him. But I wasn't surprised. In the normal way he came down the footpath from the village, crossed the lane, and took the path across the meadow by the barn to the front door. I didn't see him arrive, and I was in the cottage all day, so since he left his portrait in the barn, probably he came the way he usually did."

"But left running down the drive?" said South.

Luke was frowning and she took up the palette knife with which she had been spreading the icing and drew a rough plan for him on a slab of sponge cake.

"Look," she said, "this is the map of the place. It's like an arrow in a bow. The lane is straight and the drive is roughly a half-circle on one side of it. It is a very big half-circle, and inside it there is a meadow and the barn and various other outbuildings. Our cottage is down here, about twenty yards from the lower gates. That's the bow. The footpath from the village is the arrow. It meets the lane in the middle of the half-circle and one can go on into the meadow and along by the barn. Got it? From our cottage we can't see anyone approaching the house by the barn, because of the hedge and the bank between us and it."

"Wonderful," said Luke, putting out his hands for the cake, "we'll take it with us."

"I should say so!" Emma was laughing, her temper restored, and the tapping at the door which led into the back kitchen continued for some seconds before anybody noticed it.

The new arrival proved to be the village constable, a large elderly man, very red and profoundly uneasy. He stooped automatically as he passed through the doorway, as he who habitually wears a helmet must, and looked from one to the other of the plain-clothes men anxiously.

"Could I have a word with you gentlemen in private?" he inquired in a slow, deep, wondering voice. "I've come up against something."

Luke and South followed him at once but Mr. Campion, seizing the opportunity, lingered.

"Emma," he said with the unconvincing carelessness of the would-be borrower, "do you know if there's any dormital in the house?"

"Dormital? I should hope not." She ceased her work to look at him. "Never take that, sweetie. If you happen to mix it with alcohol it's death, just like that. Or so they say."

"Really?" he inquired mendaciously. "How do you know?"

"Know? The papers have been full of it, or they were last winter. I don't believe you townees read any more.

It's the same as that stuff that ends in sodium. I thought they'd stopped it being sold. I don't suppose one would kill you if you had a drink some time during the same day, but take a couple or so and an ounce or two of whisky, especially if you're one of these people whose livers are a bit brown round the edges anyway, and you go out like a light. What do you want that sort of filth for? If you ran about a bit in this air you'd sleep all right."

"I see," he said, sounding deflated. "I only thought Uncle William might have had some."

"William? Good heavens, he wouldn't have had any within a mile of him." Emma's glance was concentrated on the pale green glue she was spreading over a cake. "William was petrified of that sort of filth. I used to help Dinah to get him to bed when Minnie had to go to London, and you never heard such a set-out as he used to make over the pluminol which the doctor left him. I told him he'd have to take the best part of a box before it hurt him, but he didn't believe me. Poor old boy, he did so want to live. Wasn't it a shame?"

"A beastly shame," said Mr. Campion with more feeling than he had intended. "And so is this other business," he added hastily.

"Little Doom?" She shrugged her shoulders. "It will be, if it rots up the party. Albert, for heaven's sake don't let them spoil my party. I just couldn't bear it. I mean it. It's an Orphan's Outing for me. I shall die if anything stops it. They seem all right, those men. One of them is a bit sensational, isn't he? Glowing with it. Who's the lucky girl?"

Mr. Campion sighed. "Prune," he said.

"Prune?" She was appalled. "Oh no, *not* hopeless love."

" 'Fraid so. Forget it."

"I shall try to. Jake calls her the Snow Queen. I call her the Marble No-Bust. She's no earthly good to that chap. He's alive."

"So far," said Mr. Campion sadly, and went off to find the others.

He came out into the yard just in time to see Amanda standing on the drive talking to a curious gnarled figure whose earth-coloured garments had such a quality of stiffness that the whole man seemed to be made of old wood. They did not appear to be saying very much, but the way they stood suggested the wordless communication peculiar to the countryside. As Campion stepped out of the house the old person moved off in the direction of the barn meadow, and Amanda turned her head towards her husband, who had paused in astonishment. For after he had touched his forehead, one of Old Harry's thumbs had turned upward in a gesture both modern and explicit.

Mr. Campion advanced upon his wife and took her gently by the back of the neck.

"Helping?" he inquired.

"Justice must be served." Amanda's cool voice was dangerously offhand. "I should cut along after Old Harry if I were you. I think you'll find they've got the weapon. What's all this about Tonker?"

"You heard it on the bell-bine, I suppose?" Mr. Campion murmured impolitely. "He's gone to London."

"How do the police feel about that?"

He shrugged his shoulders but his eyes were worried. "It's not as ugly as it might be, or as it will be if the idiot doesn't telephone by three o'clock. They know they're at fault by not asking to see him at once. Anyhow, Wally has promised to stand over him and see he calls the police the moment he appears. But he may easily drift off to lunch before going to the office. You never know with Tonker."

To his surprise she grinned. "I like old Tonker. He's got such a valuable sense of proportion. Oh by the way, you can take it that it was Old Harry who removed all the reading matter from the body. He didn't do it until he found out who the man was, then he thought Miss Diane might be involved so he removed the evidence of identification in case—that's who that was."

"Was it, by George? How's he going to justify that."

"He isn't. Old Harry hears nothing, sees nothing, says nothing. He's the proverbial cartload of monkeys. Those papers will never be heard of again. They weren't valuable and didn't mean much, and if you try to question Harry you'll not only never find out anything at all, but all your rabbits will die."

"I see. Is it permitted to inquire how you know?"

"Oh," said Amanda. "I was born here. I really should go along now, if I were you."

"Why?"

A smile, singular both for its sweetness and its guile, flickered over the heart-shaped face.

"Because if you don't you may miss something rather good. I say, I hope you won't mind if Lugg and Rupert and I stay here and get on with our work. Honesty Bull will give you and Luke some lunch at The Gauntlett. It ought to be giblet pie."

"Why ought to be?" he said.

"Because it's Midsummer's Eve, of course." Amanda turned on her heel. "I tell you, to get on here you have to know the place."

Mr. Campion crossed the drive, let himself through the white gate, and walked round the barn which smelled sweetly of tar in the morning sun. When he reached the lane he paused. A knot of men was standing on the dusty flint surface, looking at something on the bank under the hedge. Luke, South, and the constable were waiting for the sergeant-photographer who had gone back in the police car for his gear. Of Old Harry there was no sign at all.

Luke beckoned Campion over. "Look at this," he said. "The original not-so-blunt instrument. Same as Cain found out the original trick with. They tell me they leave these about all over the place." His bright eyes in their triangular sockets opened wide. "No wonder we cockneys think the country dangerous."

He pointed to a nest in the rank grass, where lay a ploughshare of the ancient pattern, very long in the shaft or cray, and broad in the wing. Using his handkerchief, although there could be no hope of prints on the gnarled and rusty surface, South picked it up and turned it over.

"See that?" He pointed to a faintly darker stain on the

broad bevel of the straight side of the iron. "This is it, all right. My chaps scoured the meadow as soon as it was light, but they didn't think of coming right out here in the lane." He giggled. "Getting very close to the pretty house, isn't it?"

"Put there this mornin'." A small elderly voice, rising from somewhere in the region of their knees, startled everybody. Old Harry had materialized among them and was bending close to the grassy nest. "Put there this mornin' while the dag was wet." He straightened himself on the words, but remained a good head and a half shorter than Luke and South, who were both big men. He made the peculiarity greater by keeping very close to them, so that they had to look vertically down upon him while he lifted his shy, rosy face to them like a child.

"Crikey," said Luke under his breath.

But South, who like all countrymen was not so unwise as to disregard the native, began to grin and sparkle again.

"That's what you think, is it, Dad?" he asked civilly enough and shot an inquiring glance at the constable, who had become as wooden as a soldier on parade.

"Harry Buller, sir. Old-age pensioner. Has worked round about 'ere all his life. Bird-catcher, sir."

"Ain't much I don't know. I'm a very knowledgeable old man," said Old Harry, very fairly as Mr. Campion thought.

The boast, however, delighted South, who was pleased with himself and in kindly mood.

"How d'you know it was put there this morning, chum?"

Luke brought a city intelligence to bear. "Did you put it there?"

"No no. I see you a-lookin' so I looked, and I see dags under it."

"Dags—doo," said South. "Doo of the morning. Like rain, but it ain't," he explained. "I see what you mean, Dad. You don't think it's been there long?"

"No no, grass'd be yellow." Old Harry appeared to become very excited and he made a curious high-pitched trumpeting sound, scarcely recognizable as words. "Yeller-

anwhoitanoddmedods, yelleranwhoitanoddmedods, yelleranwhoitanoddmedods.''

Since everyone else was defeated, the constable, who
was sulky and the least bit nervous, was forced to translate.

'' 'E says that the grass would be yeller and white
beneath the iron, and that there would be slugs, snails, and
other small vermin under it if it had lain there for any
length of time, sir,'' he said to Luke, adding mendaciously, ''I was wondering along of that myself.''

Old Harry stretched up a hand which looked like part of
a pollarded willow to South.

''Give I a holt of that, mate,'' he commanded, and took
the ploughshare, holding it carefully with a handkerchief.
''I seen they do this here on the tellyvision,'' he remarked
with awful cunning. ''But that little old tellyvision ain't
never seen what I be a-goin' to do.'' And very solemnly
he smelled the iron all over like a dog.

It occurred to Mr. Campion, who was enjoying himself
despite his anxiety, that townspeople betray a superstitious
attitude towards the sense of smell. It was as though, he
reflected, they realized they had lost a valuable asset and
felt nervous about it. Certainly South was watching the old
man with tremendous interest, while Luke was as dumb-
founded as if confronted in fact by a talking hound.

''Har,'' said Old Harry at last, a secret joy lighting up
his apple face. ''Har. Don't you notice nothin', sir?''

The Superintendent hesitated, but it was clear what was
required of him and he took the share by the cray and
sniffed at it deeply and noisily.

''I can't say I do,'' he said at last, offering it to Luke,
who declined it with a gesture. ''What are you getting at,
Dad?''

Old Harry took the weapon once more and repeated his
truly remarkable performance.

''I'll take you where that's bin the last few days,'' he
volunteered. ''That's lain in wormwood, that's been near
rust, that's known Johnwort. And that's smelled the fire,''
he added with sudden enthusiasm. ''You gentlemen follow
me.''

"You'll open your mouth too wide and you'll slip in of it." The constable spoke involuntarily and the venom behind the statement showed far more clearly than he had intended. Both South and Luke turned slowly round and regarded him with cold appraisal. Fred South returned to Harry.

"Where is this place where all these things grow, old 'un?" he demanded.

"You gennelmen come with me."

"Not yet. Where is it? Where do you think the plough-share has been?"

"Battus Dump. That's the place. 'At's where the worm-wood grow. Don't grow no other place, lest in the churchus, and there ain't no fire there. Battus Dump, Battus Dump, Battus Dump." Old Harry was dancing a little in his excitement. It was a masterly little cameo, innocent pride, anxiousness to help, simple rusticity, were all knit together with the enthusiasm of a child with a chance to show off.

The wretched constable, unmasked by witchcraft, made a feeble effort to defend himself.

" 'E's nothin' but a silly old man, sir," he began. " 'E—"

"I know all about that. But you told me that you'd just found this ploughshare lying here, and it's got dag—I mean doo, under it."

The constable took a deep unhappy breath.

"Could I speak to you private, sir?" This time he had indeed come up against something.

South led him a yard or so down the lane and a soft but considerably animated conversation took place between them, while the London man smiled tactfully at the toe of his boot and chatted to Mr. Campion about the weather, and the greenery, and how to him the whole place smelled of honey. Old Harry retired to the footpath's edge and looked earnestly at tracks which not even he could see. When South returned he was angry but triumphant, and the constable, lingering in the background, had a silly smile on his face and dumb misery in his eyes.

"I'm sorry for that, gentlemen." South was laughing to

himself, as usual, but not quite with his customary enthusiasm. "I think I've got the truth now. This silly juggins fell over something on the footpath in this next meadow on Tuesday night this week. He picked it up and carried it to the rubbish dump just outside the village. Yesterday he remembered it, and last night he went back and found it. Then, because the meadow had been searched yesterday, he had the bright idea of planting it here. As for you," he went on, swinging round on the unsuspecting Harry, "you didn't smell anything. You saw the constable hunting for the share last night, and put two and two together."

"That ain't right." Old Harry spoke quietly and even calmly, but an expression of such scarifying malignity darted out of his innocent blue eyes that everybody was made slightly uncomfortable. "Oi don't think much to talk like that, mister," the old man continued, using the fearful formula which is the east country's strongest protest. "Last night I was too drunk to see nothin', and just now I smelled that as powerfully as I smell you—Richardson's Violet Bear-cream, that's what you've got on your 'ead. 'Owever, seeing as 'ow you don't want no help, I'll bid you good-day."

He plodded off through the gate, back to the meadow round the barn. There he glanced back.

"Sence you feel so 'appy alone, I 'ont show you where that old share has laid these fifteen or twenty years, as I've seen with my own eyes."

They got him to come back with some difficulty. Superintendent South, who had become self-conscious about his favourite and indeed only cosmetic, kept pulling his hat down closer over his head without realizing what he was doing, and Luke, supremely tickled, but keeping well to leeward of the witness, set out behind him along the footpath to the stile and the bridge where Little Doom had come so quietly to rest.

Old Harry walked across the plank bridge, climbed the stile, and dropped down on his knees just beside the post.

"Now," he said, "bring that here."

South carried the ploughshare carefully over the stile

and Luke and Campion leant over the rail behind him.
Beside the right-hand post, and half hidden by the long
grass, there was a clear triangular shape cut in the moss
and the lichen. Root threads were still white in it, and that
small grass which had persisted was brown and burned by
the suffocating weight of the iron.

Very delicately, and still using a protecting handkerchief, Old Harry slid the ploughshare into the natural
sheath. It fitted exactly, even to the worn edge at one
corner.

"Fifteen year, mayhap twenty. Mayhap that were there
when I were a little ole boy. Seen it there a score o'
times. They don't forge that shape no more. Cray's shorter
now."

"Well I'll be damned," said South with tremendous
satisfaction. "How long since it was taken out of there,
Mr. Buller?"

The use of the name and prefix put Old Harry exactly
where he wanted to be, on top. He gave no sign that he
had heard, but he swelled a little and became intent on
doing his best. He touched the worn place, laid his cheek
against it, examined the corpse of a woodlouse he found
among the matted roots, and finally ate a piece of the
young grass from beside it.

"Mite more'n a week," he said finally, which was, as
he knew by more ordinary methods, not far out.

South grunted. "Where did it go after that, I wonder."

Old Harry rose up and looked about him. He was far too
much of an artist to give himself away, but he was most
anxious to continue to shine. After a decent interval he
clambered over the stile and went round under the oak
tree, where he knelt down and held his head sideways, so
that the contours in the dust stood up high in his vision.
Suddenly he saw quite plainly what he was looking for and
his grunt was astounded quite as much as it was gratified.

"Come you here, come you here," he shouted and
Luke, who was already on the right side of the stile, leapt
down to join him. On being shown how to look he was
amazed to see the imprint of the ploughshare not once but
several times on the soft crumbling earth. He was fascinated.

"How did that happen?" he demanded.

"Once when that fell," said Old Harry, adding "I doubt not" lest he should be misunderstood. "When that was throwed from the Battus' side."

"Battus?"

"That little old mound or wall, like. That's the Battus."

"I see, chum. And then what? How came the other imprints?"

Harry shook his head. He was on dangerous ground. "Mayhap that were kicked," he suggested. "That was lying in the footpath, the policeman said."

"It might have been kicked. But it's been here all right. Take a dekko at this, Mr. Campion. It's amazing."

"Wait, if you don't mind, Chief." South was grinning down at them. "I've got the inquest at two o'clock. I wonder if you agree with me how this was done? The murderer must have stood here, on the far side of the stile, probably on the step."

Luke went over at once and together they worked out the crime with a painstaking thoroughness which surprised even Harry. The old man enjoyed himself. As a reward for his assistance, and since like Little Doom he was small, they permitted him to be the victim in their reconstruction. Mr. Campion sat in the grass and watched the pantomime, while the constable skulked in the background.

"That's it, then," South announced as he helped Old Harry up out of the ditch for the eleventh time. "The victim followed the murderer on to the bridge, advancing from the meadow. The murderer climbed first and then, looking about for a weapon, caught sight of the ploughshare ready to hand. He snatched it up and, stepping back on to the stile, struck the victim one tremendous blow which sent him reeling against that low rail, so that he fell over down into the greenery below. The murderer next threw the weapon away and it fell under that tree, which is just where it would fall. If the ploughshare fits the wound, we've got it. How's that?"

Charlie Luke, who was hot and dusty, leant back against the stile and felt for a cigarette.

"And what did the bloke do next? Continue down to the village for a quick one, taking his steam hammer with him?" He frowned and went on talking, the physical power of the man apparent in the very tones of his voice, which set the leaves vibrating. "I've not examined this wound, as you know, but I've not lived a sheltered life. I've seen a few head injuries. What does this relic of the iron age weigh? Three to four pounds at most. One blow from it to kill a normal man stone dead? I don't believe it. I don't believe one man in a million could deliver such a blow, even from above with the wind behind him. Come to that, I don't believe I could do it myself." Seizing an imaginary Little Doom by the throat, he whirled his arm over his head and brought it down upon his closed left fist. "Solid reinforced rubber, human skulls," he said.

Superintendent Fred South did not speak for a moment. His colour had heightened and a gleam, which was apprehensive rather than mocking, had appeared in his twinkling eyes. At length he made a soft, tooth-sucking sound of decision.

"Constable, you can go and collect my chaps and tell them to bring both cars round to the village end of this path," he commanded. "Are you going with him, Mr. Buller?"

"No, I ain't going walkin' with he for a while." Old Harry made a long and ruminative noise of the pronouncement. "And I'm a-goin' up to The Gauntlett to get myself a pint, and I'm a gointoputatdowntoyou."

The final words were so run together that since there was no constable to translate they were unintelligible. He touched his cap and stumped off, smiling, his lashes lying modestly on his rosy cheeks.

Luke dug in his trousers pockets but Campion shook his head.

"I think you'll find all that has been mysteriously laid on," he murmured. "My crystal tells me that Old Harry has joined your service. You'll be seeing him again. What is it, Superintendent? Something worrying you?"

"It ought to." The man in the tight tweeds sat down on

the rail of the bridge and took out a pipe. "It's been enough trouble to me all my life." He cast a sly upward glance at Luke. "The long and the short of it is that I can't bring myself to trust a man until I've worked with him for a bit. It's what you might call a kink in my nature. It affects my memory at times." He paused, hopefully, but there was an ominous silence, broken only by the rustle of the grasses and the murmur of the bees in the clover. "Of course," he went on, scratching his ear and grimacing, "a trait like that can be remarkably bad for me. For instance, when a smart young man who, as I can see now, will go far, is sent down by the Central Office—"

"Oh all right, I'll buy it." Luke spoke with sufficient suppressed ferocity to preclude any promise of weakness. "What have you been holding out on me? The P.M. report?"

"Not the report, son. I'm not barmy if I'm butter-fingered." South was laughing again, but warily. "It hadn't come in when we left, but it'll be waiting for us now. But I did happen to have a word with the County Pathologist on the telephone. You'll see it all in black and white in a minute. But as far as I could understand from what he told me, our corpse wasn't very normal, not in the skull."

"Oh Lord." Luke spoke, but both listeners had stiffened abruptly at the intelligence. "Not one of these darned thin-skulled cases?"

South began to nod like a mandarin, winking and flashing and conveying unspoken secrets through every pore.

"The thinnest he has ever seen. Equal to the thinnest ever recorded. One forty-seventh of an inch. He said it was only one blow, struck by an iron bar approximately three-quarters of an inch wide, which is about right for the bevel edge of the cray of the ploughshare, and it had about the same effect as a kid hitting an egg with the back of a knife." He started his teetering giggle again, but smothered it. "So you see," he said, "any blessed soul could have done it. Ladies as well, if they were cross enough."

CHAPTER XI

Lunch in Arcady

Charlie Luke had had little sleep, and now that noon was past, three o'clock came nearer and nearer, so that his private worries obtruded into his thoughts, suffocating him with sick apprehension. The case looked as sticky as any he had ever known, and his chances of finding himself Local Enemy No. 1 seemed more than high.

Mr. Campion was on edge, which was unlike him, and the lush fairyland in which Luke found himself like a cockney on an outing was strange and even alarming in its little surprises. For instance, he had just discovered that the excellent pie which he had enjoyed was made largely of peacocks. The comfortable elderly party who said she was the daughter of the old landlord had just told him so when she came in to apologize for having to serve them in the little back room, since the large front one was crowded. She brought them each a tail feather tip to put in their coats for luck.

"Wear them, and the pie won't repeat," she said cheerfully, placing a plate of processed cheese, five dry biscuits, and some margarine before them. "Or would you like a junket?"

"This," said Luke firmly, seizing the cheese, which he detested but at least had eaten before. "Do you—er—eat a lot of peacocks round here?"

"Oh no." She seemed scandalized. "They're a very rare bird. Old Admiral Bear from Bandy Hall at Girdle has his roast peacock club dinner here every twentieth of June.

He's done it for years and years, and his father before him. He breeds the birds and we cook them. Then on Midsummer Eve we make the pies out of the giblets and the left-overs, and that way every customer gets a taste. That's why the house is so full today. Oh, there's a lot goes on at Pontisbright. I made sure young Amanda had told you."

"My wife's at The Beckoning Lady," volunteered Mr. Campion.

"Ah yes, with poor Miss Minnie." She lowered her eyes, as at the mention of a family embarrassment. "Horrid little person," she said. "Fancy going down there to get done in. Cheek, eh?"

A shout from the other room sent her hurrying to answer it and they were left alone.

"I didn't notice anything peculiar about the pie, did you?" Mr. Campion was not really thinking what he was saying. "I didn't notice it. Like Lady Macbeth, it should have died hereafter."

He was hunting beside him as he spoke and Luke produced a wilted bundle from the floor at his feet.

"Here are your flowers, if that's what you want," he suggested.

"Oh thank you." Campion, who had called in at the Mill for them on his way to The Gauntlett, took the herbs with relief and spread them out on the table. "Snapdragon, that's all right. But this thing ought to be Wild Liquorice, which is beyond me."

"That's Mint," said Luke, dragging his mind from his own troubles.

"I know." Campion took a piece of stamp-paper from his wallet, affixed it neatly to the woody stem, and wrote "Liquorice (Wild)" on it in small printing. "Then there's Meadow Saffron," he said, "which is out of season, so the tiresome chap must have the bulb, and good luck to him. And a sprig of elder, which has to be tied to it. Finally there's this handsome bloom, the best of the lot."

"Petunia?"

"Exactly. I wonder if I could bother you, my dear chap, to take these into the next room for me. Somewhere there you will see a man who looks like Little Doom."

"What?"

"I have it on my son's authority. He's probably quite different, but will certainly be a clerkly type, wearing a raincoat—or perhaps not at his meal. Anyway, I think you'll spot him as well as I should, and if you'd just go over to him and say 'The Mole Insurance Company?,' and then, when he admits it, 'The roots for Mr. Whippet,' you will be doing me an eternal service."

"Yes, I'll go." Luke got up, his dark shiny eyes very curious. "Snap-dragon means 'No.' "

"That's perfectly correct." Mr. Campion was temporarily jaunty. "You and I have no secrets, Charles, I hope? Snap-dragon, 'No.' Wild liquorice, 'I declare against you.' Meadow Saffron, 'beware of excess' coupled with Elder, 'zeal.' And Petunia, 'keep your promise.' I ought to have added a red red rose."

"Which means 'love'?"

"How true. It's a very laborious method of correspondence but it has its uses."

" 'No. I declare against you. Beware of excess zeal. Keep your promise. Love,' " said Luke. "That's a funny message to an insurance company."

"Well, *is* it?" asked Mr. Campion. He was drinking very bad coffee when the Chief Inspector returned looking slightly dazed.

"I found him," he announced with frank bewilderment. "Wizened little chap. He took them without batting an eyelid. Said 'Ow, thank you very much.' I say, there are about forty people in that room, Campion, all eating peacock pie because it's Midsummer's Eve. I could do with some coffee."

"So could I," said Mr. Campion with feeling, "but don't despair. She's coming back with some of the Admiral's other left-overs. She says it's Napoleon and you never know."

The comfortable landlady brought two thimble-glasses,

frighteningly overfilled, and withdrew. Whatever it was, it was wonderful.

"Napoleon?" said Luke after the first sip. "Alexander! That's better. My feet are touching the ground again. Campion, I don't want to interfere but should I offend you if I asked you in confidence what the Mole has promised or to whom?"

Mr. Campion sat looking at his little glass.

"You wouldn't offend me, my dear chap," he said, "but you'd embarrass me. I haven't the faintest idea. Moreover," he continued earnestly, "I just don't see at all how there can be a claim on them—that is, of course, if they and myself are talking about the same corpse. However, that's their look-out."

Luke was uneasy. Mr. Campion's strange world of nods and hints and mysterious understandings among people who trusted each other because they were or were not related, or had been to school or served in a ship or a regiment together, both bothered and fascinated him. His own plate was embarrassingly full, but he was still inquisitive.

"The corpse you have in mind is the old gentleman's, isn't it? Mr. William Faraday, your old chum?"

"Yes."

"Anything funny about that death?"

"The reverse." Mr. Campion sounded bitter. "He was one of the best old boys in the world. He was dying, and he wanted to live until Bonfire Night. And he wasn't allowed to make it."

"Not allowed? What do you mean?"

The thin man put his hand in his pocket and took out a telegraph form. It had awaited him at the Mill and he had picked it up when he collected the flowers. Now he re-read it and threw it across to Luke.

"Supposition confirmed. Pritchard."

Luke blinked. "The analyst?"

"Yes. I sent him a couple of the pellets which were on Uncle William's mantelshelf. I said I thought they might be dormital, and if they were would he let me know."

"Dormital?" Luke was frowning. "We've had a crop of suicides with that lately. Take it with al—I say, Campion! Your old friend believed in alcohol, didn't he?"

"He was never without it." Mr. Campion spoke with misleading lightness. "He said it would be the death of him and it was. He thought he was taking pluminol. They look very alike, and the dormital was planted in his normal box. He washed it down with what Minnie considered a decent nightcap for a drinking man—the equivalent to four stiff ones, I should think."

"But Campion—" Luke was sitting bolt upright, "—that's murder."

Mr. Campion remained lounging indolently in his chair, one arm over its back, the other elbow on the table.

"Prove it," he suggested.

Luke was frowning, all his shepherd dog instincts aroused. "I'll have a damned good try."

"No." Mr. Campion did not smile. "Impossible. Consider it. Suppose you have him up, what will you find? A liver like a breadboard, possibly a trace of the stuff left—it deteriorates very quickly—a body which was worn out anyway and was only kept going by will-power and affectionate nursing. No, you'd be wasting your time. The stuff isn't even a poison. A lot of people take it habitually—people who don't drink, of course."

"Who benefits?"

The first question asked in any case of unnatural death by any good policeman escaped Luke involuntarily.

"No one whom I can find. Minnie loses money. William gave her the bulk of his possessions four and a half years ago, and she let Little Doom know. Little Doom filed the information and with his natural bossiness insisted on a formal Deed of Gift, although it was nothing to do with him. Since the old boy did not live the statutory five years from the date of signing, this estate is still considered his for the purpose of Death Duties. She'll have to pay. I should think it would be an embarrassment to her. There simply isn't anybody else. He was very much loved, he was looked after like a baby, everyone was sorry when he died.''

Luke ran his fingers through his shorn curls until he looked like a black lamb.

"Wait a minute," he said. "Why did you send that 'All Clear' message just now? The original inquiry, if I remember, talked of an enemy. How did it go?—'Mourning, Danger, A Deadly Foe is Here, Do not Refuse Me, Make Haste.' Wasn't that it?"

"It was." Mr. Campion had the grace to look embarrassed. "That's the Mole's point of view. To understand any letter, you have first to consider your correspondent. Alas, I know Whippet and his Mole. Once I decided the message came from him, I knew it meant 'There is a case of mourning at hand which interests the Mole. There is danger—to the Mole. A deadly enemy—of the Mole—is at hand. Do not refuse—the Mole. Make haste to save— the Mole.' I've had a bucket or two, as you yourself, Charles, might say, of the Mole before. Old Whippet always was a lazy beggar. He made me do all his Mole tending most ingeniously, once, while he pinched the young woman on whom my eye had lighted at the time. I was at school with him, and so was Tonker. That's why he knows he must tread very warily or look a clot.''

"So you told him it's all clear?" inquired Luke, suspecting a serious flaw in this interesting form of cricket by which he had recently become so fascinated. "How do you square that one?"

"Not at all." Mr. Campion was hurt. "I've told him it wasn't suicide. That's the only query which he could possibly be raising. If you are murdered your insurance company can't back out. If you commit suicide, it can."

"I see." Luke sat back. "There's a lot in it," he said at last.

At length the silence became uncomfortable. The friends knew each other well, and the shadow of the Superintendent's revelation of the morning had hung over them ever since he had made it. Finally Luke took the plunge.

"You're right," he began. "The old gentleman is your

business. But the other bird is mine.'' His eyes met Campion's own. ''That's the sort of crime I understand. I'm used to it. I deal with it every day. There are strong motives there, you know.''

''I suppose so.'' Mr. Campion sounded unhappy.

''Oh yes.'' Luke stubbed out his cigarette. ''That's marriage. We hear a lot about marriage in the Barrow Road. No two are quite alike. People fix up the most extraordinary arrangements between themselves.'' He smiled wryly. ''You know what we say about marriage. We say it's like the kitchen clock. If it goes better lying on its side or even standing on its head, leave it alone. As long as it ticks and tells the time, keep your hands out of the works. In this case it's pretty clear to me that this silly little Big-'ead put his paws in the machinery and where is he now?''

Mr. Campion swallowed. ''What do you think happened?'' he ventured.

''I don't know yet. I want to see the man.''

''Tonker? You'll like him.''

''I expect to. That's just my luck. I'm all on his side. If I found any stranger in my place talking to me about getting my missis to divorce me to save money I might hit him.''

''Tonker's not like that. He's an artist.''

''Artist!'' Luke spoke with withering contempt. ''People talk about artists as if they went about in flying saucers. The only artists I've ever met were just like me only more so. Well, guv'nor, I hope for all our sakes that there's some other explanation—but who else is there? I don't think an acorn fell on Little Doom, do you?''

''What about Jake Bernadine?'' Mr. Campion spoke reluctantly.

''Him?'' The Chief Inspector smiled. ''We didn't get very near him. He was grooming his moke, for one thing. He's a chap who reminds you of opening one of those cellar lids outside a backstreet London shop. You look down into a great dark empty place. There's something alive down there, but it might be just an old woman or pussy. No, I think he's in the clear, and I'll tell you why. That chap is a thrower and not a hitter. They're utterly different.''

"He hit a man once," said Mr. Campion, still reluctantly, "and knocked him out."

"Did he? I bet you'll find he picked him up and threw him down so that he hit his own head, or fainted. Besides, I believed that girl with the cakes when she said he was listening to the wireless. I believe her altogether. Her story's the only hope we've got.''

Mr. Campion eyed him curiously. "Doom was running away?''

"No! He was running to something. That's what the old Super noticed, and he's no one's fool, tricky old monkey. The same thing showed up at the reconstruction. The murderer was *over* the barrier, on the far side of it. Little Doom was advancing on him. Why? The whole crime is just a little bit back to front." He sighed wearily. "I've been thinking about that extraordinary little dog-man this morning. He's absolutely new on me. He *was* incapably drunk last night, by the way. I checked it with the bartender just now when I took your flowers. Oh, and he's put us down on the slate for three pints, if you please. One each. His mind works. He doesn't do it all through his nose. Who *is* he? Is he a type? Do you get a lot of them?''

"He reoccurs." Mr. Campion restrained an impulse to glance sharply behind him. "You meet him from time to time. Long ago it was thought expedient to give chaps like that a nice sort of nickname, just to be on the safe side.''

"How do you mean?" Luke was intrigued. Anything which was right out of his experience held an unholy fascination for him. "Pal, or something?''

"Or even more crudely, Good-Fellow," said Mr. Campion and broke off abruptly.

The lady of the inn had returned in a fluster.

"There's London papers keep ringing up, Mr. Campion," she said. "Gentlemen want to come and stay here. Dad says would you advise him?''

Mr. Campion grimaced at Luke. "Its caught the evening

editions then," he murmured. "Well Dolly, they're coming down. Nothing on God's earth will stop them. I should telephone your brewer, stock right up with spirits, and air the beds. You'll find them very nice generous gentlemen, but they'll keep late hours. Tell them anything you know, but nothing you don't. Your father need not worry. They're all right. They'll pay their bills."

Luke's dark face was mischievous. "Good-Fellows all," he said. "How much of the Admiral's brandy is left in the bottle?"

"Barely three little glasses, sir."

"Bring 'em." Luke spoke recklessly. "It's the one safe hiding-place."

Miss Dolly said she'd rather have a small port, so they split the third glass and went out into the village street feeling fortified if not sanguine. As they paused for a moment on the edge of the heath, blinking in the dazzling light, the Postmistress put her head out of the door of the shop and beckoned. She had a telegram for Campion handed in at a West Central London office at ten minutes past two. He read it and passed it to Luke.

GETTING LIFT PRESS CAR STOP SEE YOU AND POLICE
TEATIME STOP HOPE AM RIGHT IN PRESENT BELIEF
THAT OBTRUSIVE ITEM WAS FOUND ON LAND OWNED
PONTISBRIGHT PARK ESTATE STOP PLEASE CONFIRM
AND PUBLICIZE SAME WITH VIGOUR STOP TONKER

"Obtrusive item is good." The Chief Inspector was grimly amused. "Is he right? Where is the Pontisbright Park Estate?"

Mr. Campion explained in detail. "It may be that the stile is on their property," he added at last. "Leo said it wasn't on Minnie's, and I hear they've been buying up land round here lately. Trust Tonker to think of that conjuror's misdirection. He's trying to save his party from the Press."

"Which is not like a bloke who's done a killing unless he's lakes." Luke used the ancient slang which decrees that Lakes of Killarney shall rhyme with barmy. "Well, good luck to him. He may get away with it. South is bent on keeping Angel dark, and I doubt if they'd touch him at this juncture anyway. That tale of his is sheer dynamite. What about this Pontisbright Park Estate? If the owner isn't in residence, who is there?"

"A shocker called Smith, who is preparing it for sale, I think. He was there yesterday. And his car must be still in the village. I know that for a fact."

"We'll look him up." Luke sounded as if he were grasping at straws. "Come on, we're justified . . . just. Let's have a bash."

CHAPTER XII

The House without a Back

"Christmas!" said Luke as he brought his small car to a standstill in a newly laid out drive as big as a bus park. "Is this a house?"

Mr. Campion made no attempt to move but sat looking wide-eyed at the "improvements" which Miss Pinkerton had warned him had overtaken Potter's Hall, Fanny Genappe's little farm where the larks once had nested. It was a melancholy prospect. After his first wave of dismay, it became obvious to him what had occurred. A rambling Tudor farmhouse, not unlike The Beckoning Lady, had been embellished at some time during the past century with a pretentious Georgian front one room deep, while a fine range of hunting stables, complete with clock tower, had been added at the northern end. Possibly the result had not been unpleasing, but that there was now no way of telling. Now the whole of the older buildings, gardens, trees and duck-ponds, had been smoothed away so that all that remained was something which looked like an architect's elevation, or the façade in a child's box of bricks. The house had no depth and remarkably little character. Everywhere was very tidy, very newly painted, very bare.

The same disconcerting clearance had been made to the surrounding land. Not a hedge, not a tree, not a ditch remained, only a bare open plain sloping gently to the river some quarter-mile distant where a fringe of greenery still flourished, and away in the southern valley a large unwieldy knot of trees, roofs, and pocket-handkerchief fields which was the ten-acre Beckoning Lady estate taking a deep bite out of the area.

Luke was so silent that Mr. Campion turned sharply to look at him and discovered him staring ahead with strained concentration, his narrow eyes soot-dark and even tragic. It took Campion some seconds to discover that he was looking at the stable clock.

"Five past three," Campion suggested helpfully.

The D.D.C.I. shook himself free from some secret enchantment. He had coloured slightly.

"Yes," he agreed. "I've sent someone down to see my mum at her little house in Linden Lea. They should be together now." There was a pause and he added abruptly, "It isn't a bit like this."

Mr. Campion regarded his friend with respectful surprise. He never knew which he admired most about Luke, his common sense or his courage. His present preoccupation appeared to have demanded a considerable quantity of both. He opened the door of the car and returned to the Pontisbright Park Estate.

"That's a matter for profound congratulation," he murmured. "This does not appeal to me as a place for anybody's mum. It's like one of those terrible Irish fairies who have no backs. When you look over your shoulder at them you see they're hollow as jelly-moulds."

Luke collected himself with a start. The fairies, haunts, and spells of Pontisbright were getting under his skin.

"Get away," he said. "What a horrible idea."

"Isn't it?" Mr. Campion seemed happy. "Like Tonker's skin-deep masks, yet not unsuitable on Midsummer's Eve. Let us ring the bell of this blank-eyed shell and see what comes out. The vertical half of an empty bottle, perhaps."

Ten minutes later it was evident to them both that nothing at all was going to come out of the narrow house. The place was deserted. Mr. Campion tried the door. It was unlocked and he eyed Luke.

"Suppose you tried to find a gardener," he suggested. "There must be somebody about, if it's only to sweep the drive."

Luke did not argue. As a private person Mr. Campion had certain advantages. He strolled off at once and the man in the horn-rimmed spectacles melted quietly into the house.

It was in use but deserted, and all about there were evidences of Miss Pinkerton's bright impersonal efficiency. Every flower vase had four neat blooms in it, every cushion was set in a diamond shape, every newspaper was folded with its title showing.

The kitchen alone betrayed traces of a more human personality, but this too was deserted. The stove was banked up and closed, and the back door was locked.

On the table the thin man discovered the key to a simple situation. A well-spaced typewritten note was propped against the brown sugar crock, and as he read it the picture became clear.

Mrs. Beeton. Mr. Genappe has telephoned to say that he is back in London, so have had to hurry off. Do not know how long I shall be, but you have menus and should be able to manage. If lobster was unobtainable, tins are in back of cupboard. Make up all beds as some guests may stay. Have left note for Mr. Smith in my office. Should Beeton bring him back late tonight instead of tomorrow morning, do not bother to get up. It will be soon enough if he has it first thing and you must keep fresh. Since car has gone shall take bicycle. Clean towels in all rooms, please. E. Pinkerton.

With the S.S.S. man, the chauffeur, and Miss Pinkerton away, and the cook shopping further afield than the village, since no one in their senses would even hope to buy lobster in Pontisbright, it seemed to Mr. Campion that he had little to worry about. So he continued his wandering. The house was planned in the only possible way, which is to say like a corridor railway coach, with a staircase at each end of the corridor. Upstairs he found little to interest him. The bedroom used by the S.S.S. man yielded a fine assortment of pomades, eye-drops, and blood-pills, but no dormital.

Miss Pinkerton appeared to take no medicine at all, and the Beetons, man and wife, to take everything Mr. Campion had ever heard of except opiates. In a bathroom he found some aspirin, but nothing more.

He went down again and inspected the liquor cupboard in the dining-room, where there were most things except, rather surprisingly, gin. And finally he discovered the small room at the opposite end of the corridor to the kitchen which was Miss Pinkerton's office. He knew this because, somewhat unnecessarily one would have thought, it had her name on the door on a small typed card.

The office had all the orderly charm of a dentist's surgery. The window looked on to the stable wall, and green filing cabinets lined every available space. The desk supporting the covered typewriter was in the centre of the rug, and the rug was in the centre of the floor. The note addressed to S. S. Smith Esquire was in the centre of the mantelpiece, and there was another addressed to an R. Robinson Esquire beneath it. But these were the only items which could conceivably have been called personal. In the entire room there was nothing intimate, not a cigarette-box, not a flower vase, not a tea-cup.

Mr. Campion looked at the filing cabinets. Each drawer was labelled and he let his eye run over them casually. Architect. Contractor. Builder. Demolition Merchant. Miss Pinkerton had been busy.

He was turning away when a label marked *Findahome* caught his eye and he pulled open the drawer behind it. The size of the file surprised him. It was three inches thick. But he was even more astonished by the fact that it was tied up with tape like a parcel and was marked "Correspondence: proposed purchase Beckoning Lady." Underneath in much fresher ink was the single unequivocal word

"Finished," followed by a date, "15 June," which was becoming memorable to him as the one on which Little Doom must have died.

He was considering just how unethical it would be to open the parcel forthwith when the problem was settled for him promptly by the sound of voices in the front of the house. He closed the drawer softly, raised the window sash, and slid quietly out into the narrow way. When he emerged round the side of the house, the first person he saw was Tonker Cassands, looking solid and doggy in tweeds only a little darker than his sandy hair. There were three men on the drive, Luke, Tonker, and a hatless young giant who was looking at the house with the same blankness with which Mr. Campion himself had greeted it. Beside them was a small and dusty car marked *Press* on the windscreen.

Reflecting that the modern fashion for labels ought to make life elementary, Mr. Campion advanced upon the party and reached it just in time to catch Tonker's closing remark.

"I'll leave you here then, George," he was saying. "You're certainly the first." He turned to Luke as to a friend. "If, as you say, the gardener thinks the old cook is coming home on the Sweethearting bus, she'll be here in fifteen minutes. Do you want to see her, or can I get a lift back to the village from you? If not, I can cut across the fields."

"No, I'll take you." Luke was grinning slightly.

"Splendid fellow." Tonker sounded unconcernedly pleased. "Well George, as soon as you're through, look us up. Minnie will be delighted. Anyone will tell you the way." He returned to Luke. "Since you say you can't tell this chap much now, where will he find you? At the Mill? Good. Well, well, that's settled. Hullo, Campion."

When the introductions had been accomplished, the young man went off to find the gardener and Tonker led the way to Luke's car. He was jaunty, as usual, very cheerful and intent on his own serious affairs.

"So sorry I had to clear off this morning," he said frankly to Luke as he took the seat next to the driver. "Are you all right at the back there, Campion? I couldn't help going. These dear eager chaps could ruin the party by sheer inadvertence. We've just got to keep clear of the morning editions, that's all. Once people are on their way it doesn't matter what anybody prints, as far as I'm concerned. But we don't want all this dreary rigmarole about Minnie's crazy finances popping out *before* the fun starts. Very off-putting, homely finances. Take the joy out of anything." He looked about him. "I say, Campion, have you noticed all this? What do you think of it? What a clot the man Smith is, eh?"

Mr. Campion saw Luke's neck muscles stiffen. He had started the engine but did not let in the clutch, and they sat looking at the open plain, golden in the afternoon sun.

"It's a rum place," said Luke suddenly, his voice sounding deep after Tonker's lighter tone. "I couldn't get any explanation of it out of the gardener, who only seems to work here the odd day or so. It's got a familiar look. It's like the beginning of a racecourse."

Suddenly there was a deep silence in the car. Presently Tonker began to laugh, his solid shoulders shaking.

"Minnie's in the way over there, isn't she?" he observed contentedly, waving to the distant oasis. "Spread out like an Ascot hat just about half-way down the second mile. I don't know what the good Sheikh Hassan Ben-Sabah would say to that, the blackhearted old buzzard."

"Sheikh Ben-Sabah of Murdek, forty-three?" Luke turned in his seat to Tonker. "Were you there?"

"*I Corps, Deception.* Were you?"

Mr. Campion caught a glimpse of popping sugar-bag eyes as Tonker fielded this gift from God.

"Was I not! *S.I.B.*" Luke spoke from the heart. "What a rat that chap Ben-Sabah was."

"Oh, an excrescence!" Tonker was blowing gently. "A veritable shower of unwanted grease."

Luke grunted. "A darned dangerous finger," he announced, adding as he recollected himself somewhat, "and a very wicked man. He got at blokes I'd have gone bail for, and they weren't the only ones."

"By no means." Tonker was wagging his head like an elder prefect. "Far too many chaps who ought to have known better fell for it. One body-snatcher in particular. Ben-Sabah had the necessary ackers, dear boy, the much publicized alchemy of the East. He made the thing too easy. Do you recall exactly how it was done?"

From his seat so close behind them Mr. Campion became aware that he himself was receiving instruction, and he wondered for the hundredth time during his long acquaintance with Tonker just exactly how the old villain always managed to divine what exactly one was up to. He had a gift for it, just as remarkable in its way as Old Harry's. Luke, who had been taken out of himself for a moment, was falling in with Tonker's present requirements in the most obliging way, completely ignorant of the part he was playing.

"Yes, I do," he said at once, "only too well. I was up against the brute, trying to pin him down. We never did it. He licked us. It was watertight."

"Of course it was." Tonker was encouraging. "First of all, he nobbled the bloke he wanted to bribe. And then he sold him a horse, cheap."

"That was it." Luke was leaning on the wheel, his thoughts far away in a dusty fly-blown land. "First the chap had to buy the horse. The sale was put on record. Then Soapy Sabah kept it and raced it for him, and told him when to back it. Sometimes it won and sometimes it lost, and it all went down in the books. And then one day, soon after the motor-tyres or back axles or whatever Sabah was trying to get hold of had mysteriously disappeared, the horse won again, and that time the owner happened to have put a packet on it, and the odds were very right. What could you do? You could grill him until you were tired, you could examine his bank balance, you could search his kit, you could shake up his friends, you could instruct the people at home to frighten his family, you could court-martial him, but you couldn't beat the record. There it was, all straight, all in order: win two quid, lose two quid, lose again, lose again, win again, and then, just at the right moment, a ruddy great win at ruddy great odds. It was the one safe way of bribing a man who was being watched. Oh well, it couldn't happen here."

"Why not?" Tonker was dangerously quiet.

"Because," said Luke innocently, "you need a crooked little racecourse to work it."

"Of course," Tonker purred like a cat at a cream jug. "I overlooked that, eh, Campion? You can't start a racecourse in England without sanction from the Jockey Club, and they'd look very closely at the man who wanted to lash out in such a sensational way just now. A lad like Genappe, who is absolutely Caesar's wife, might manage it, but no one else. He's an old man and he might sell it of course, after a year or so, not realizing what was happening, but even then I expect it would all be looked into. Wouldn't it, Campion? They'd make terrific inquiries, get someone whose opinion they valued to vet the whole thing, wouldn't they? I mean, say someone wanted to start a racecourse here, for instance, and the Jockey Club sent for you—"

Mr. Campion began to laugh. "I don't think there's anything to worry about, Tonker," he said. "Let's get going, Charles, unless you've set your heart on waiting for the cook."

Luke let in the clutch. "Some other time," he said. "She left the house about nine this morning and hasn't been home all day. There's a secretary, though. The gardener hasn't seen her since yesterday, but he says she's usually in the village."

"That's Miss Pinkerton." Tonker was helpful. "She'll be at Minnie's. She haunts the place like the Fairy Nogood. A little bit of tidying here and a little bit of tidying there. She flitters through life hiding things. That's where she is and that's where I ought to be. If I mistake not, there's some intensive organization to be done down there before tomorrow. Last time I saw it, they'd secreted the whole of the liquor supply on the wrong side of the river, which they propose to make impassable. That is the sort of grave error into which the poor muggins fall without me. Do you propose to keep me long, Chief Inspector."

Luke suppressed a smile. "I sincerely hope not, sir," he said and trod on the accelerator.

Superintendent Fred South, his green hat square on his scented head, was sitting by the porch of the mill-house when they pulled up beside the race, and as they got out of the car he rose and came grinning towards them. Tonker took one look at him and stepped back a pace.

"Oh dear, it's got a bend in it," he murmured to Campion and chuckled at his bewildered expression. "Haven't you heard that yet? You must have been out of Town a week. You'll be sick of it tomorrow. It's the Augusts' latest catchphrase. Very telling. You'd be surprised. Now then, what do these chaps want? Do you know? Thumbs down the seam of the trouser leg, Tonker, and speak up."

He was still truculent when they all trooped into Aunt Hatt's formal dining-room and sat down round a gate-legged table which had been thought a pleasant possession when it was new and the men who sat round it wore lace at their knees.

Charlie Luke was dog-tired and his private affairs were giving him a physical pain in his chest. Left to himself, he would have been content with a brief questioning, turned the man loose, then watched him for twenty-four hours. But as it was, with Fred South sitting about like a Chinese with a joke, there was nothing for it but to do the job properly.

The inquisition began formally. "Now, Mr. Cassands, as you know, we're inquiring into the death of Leonard Terence Dennis Ohman. Do you recall when it was that you last saw the deceased?"

"About March the twenty-fourth," said Tonker promptly.

"I spoke to my wife on the telephone as soon as I reached London this morning, and she told me you'd been to see her. Naturally I guessed you would ask about the fellow and so I worked it out. March the twenty-fourth. I know I'd just won a tenner on the Lincoln and I was on the stairs of The Beckoning Lady, when I saw this shadow flitting by in the passage below, and I thought to myself then, 'Thank God I've won the doings and not Minnie, or that depressing sight would get his grabbers on it.' So it must have been about the date the race was run. I wouldn't be thinking of it weeks after, would I?" He looked at South. "Or before it happened," he said distinctly. "I haven't spoken to the man for over twenty years."

Luke's tired eyes flickered upwards. "Not at all?"

"Not once." Tonker produced it as a minor record. "I was not drawn to him many years ago when he was the rent collector, and when I heard he had reappeared in an even more sinister guise I'm afraid I left him to my poor wife, as indeed I often did then."

"Very well, Mr. Cassands. Can you recall what you did all day on the Thursday of last week?"

"Yes." Tonker spoke readily again. "As I think my wife told you, she and I quarrelled about an outrageous suggestion the fellow had made. It was about us divorcing to put his books right, or something equally fantastic."

Luke nodded.

"That was on the Wednesday evening," the sandy man continued. "On Thursday we were late up because we did the cross-word puzzle together in bed, and we had a scratch lunch about twelve. Then my wife went along to the boat house with Dinah and I shaved. Then I went in to poor old Will and had a chat, but he was very tired and very deaf, and so finally there was no help for it and I had to settle down in the drawing-room and do the work I'd brought with me. That was very interesting. Do you want to hear about that?"

"No." Luke spoke hurriedly. "When did you settle down?"

"About three. I was still in pyjamas and a dressing-gown."

"How long did you stay there?"

"Oh, until supper. About eight, I suppose."

"Didn't you see anybody at all, all that time?"

"I don't think so. Dinah brought me a cup of tea. I remember I got up and unlocked the door for her."

"You'd locked yourself in?"

"Yes, I did. I thought I heard somebody in the house, and I thought it might be some visitor. I wasn't dressed, and I didn't want to be disturbed, so I locked the door. Safest way."

"Didn't you know who it was?"

"Nor did I care," said Tonker cheerfully. "I work very hard, you know."

Luke sighed. "Mr. Cassands, how did you know that I should be interested in what you were doing on that particular day? Why did you think that Ohman died on the Thursday?"

The sandy man was pulled up short. He appeared astounded.

"That's clever," he announced, conferring as it were a minor accolade upon the Chief Inspector. "How did I know? Wait a minute. Yes. The portrait reappeared. We found it on the Friday, when Will seemed a bit queer. Minnie said Little Doom must have brought it back, and I was annoyed with her for giving it to him. Then at dawn this morning my wife woke me and said that Little Doom had been dead in a ditch for a week, and I suppose I assumed that she meant that he'd died when he returned the picture. What else?"

"What about this?" Fred South had risen from his chair with his now familiar little box in his hand. He appeared to have a story-book detective's fixation about idiotic exhibits, Luke reflected gloomily.

Tonker screwed up his eyes. "What is it?" he inquired ungraciously of South. "A beetle?" Finally he recognized it. "That's off some dreary fancywork hanging in the

cloakroom at Minnie's. A Victorian waistcoat, old-hat as
the dodo. I think they hope to make me wear that
tomorrow.''

"Aren't you going to?" South sounded almost disappointed.

"Not if I can help it. I've got something better."

The Superintendent put his bead away. "I think you
smoke Blue Zephyrs, Mr. Cassands?"

"So I do, and I've run out and had to get some of these.
But they sell 'em in the village. Why? Am I the only
person who smokes 'em down here?"

"Er—no." It was evident that South had inquired. "No,
they are sometimes sold to other people."

"Too bad," said Tonker, misunderstanding the entire
situation. "You'll have to light one of these and be
thankful."

South refused the cigarette and went out of the room, to
return almost at once with a ploughshare, which he placed
on the table. It was not the murder weapon but one very
like it, and it lay on the black oak, rusty and ancient and
decorative. Tonker regarded it with great interest.

"What a nice thing," he remarked, taking it up by the
cray so that it was like an axe in his hand, the point of the
triangular wing downward. "It's a ploughshare, isn't it?
Make a good tomahawk." His eyes widened as the significance occurred to him. "Good Lord, is this what it was
done with? What a horrible pecker!" He put it down at
once, dusting his hands. "You ought to test that for finger-
prints," he said seriously. "They've got a wonderful new
process."

"We've seen to all that, sir." Luke spoke quietly. He
was looking at South steadily and gradually the twinkling
eyes gave way under the stare.

When the gathering was once more under control, he
returned to the hieroglyphics on the crumpled pad of envelopes in his hand. He looked very tall and tired, and his
fine head drooped a little.

"Very well," he began. "I think I've got all I want

from you at the moment, sir. I'll just confirm this one point. You assure me that you have never, within the last twenty years, had a conversation with this ex-employee of the Inland Revenue, and that during the whole of the time he was employed by your wife you. . . ?"

"What!" Tonker's snarl of rage was a triumph even for him. To those unprepared for his lightning temper it had all the electrifying effect of a sudden manifestation of mania. "Say those unutterably idiotic words again." He had bounded to his feet. His hand had closed over the cray of the ploughshare and his eyes seemed to be bursting from his head. Both policemen stared at him in amazement. "Do you mean to tell me," demanded Tonker, shaking the ploughshare as if it were indeed a tomahawk, "that Mrs. Cassands *paid* that man to make her life a little hell? Answer me, did she do that?"

"I understood she paid him something to write the letters, sir." Luke had no desire to become involved in a domestic squabble, and indeed had done his best to avoid it all along. "I think she . . ."

"Then I give up." Tonker slammed down the ploughshare and every hair on his head, face, and tweeds appeared to bristle. "I'm surrounded by lunatics. There's only one thing for it. If the law of this land is going to persist in its delusion that my wife and I are the same person, and that person is me, it must be logical about it. My wife must lose her vote, or pass it to me. They must rescind the Married Woman's Property Act. And every time the lady signs her name to anything or employs anybody, the contract must be endorsed by me. Otherwise the position is untenable, as anyone can see, I should have thought." He paused and stood steaming. "And I didn't murder the man," he continued with a sudden return of fury. "I may have felt like it, but I didn't see him. What I did do when my wife told me of this latest and most monstrous demand was to lose my temper, black her eye, and break a window. That I was ashamed of. But this final piece of insanity of which you have just told me makes me want to do it again. Good afternoon."

On the last word he strode out of the room and nobody attempted to stop him. Tonker's confession had been made.

The silence was broken by Superintendent Fred South.

"He held the share the wrong way," he said, "and he wasn't acting. I don't see that we've got anything on him, Chief. Nothing that will stick, at all." He paused and went on dreamily, almost, his dangerous twinkle returning. "He's got a temper though, hasn't he? Just right. Sudden, and clean off the handle for a couple of minutes. It wouldn't take any more."

Luke turned helplessly to Campion.

"That woman Dinah," he remarked. "She's the next to go through the hoop. I wonder if she left Mrs. Cassands for long that afternoon?"

CHAPTER XIII

Three in a Row

With a high top wind sending the cloud, as ragged as the countries on a map, coasting across the moon, the bright studio light streaming across the meadows and the soft house ones glowing in the dusk, Midsummer's Eve flickered over The Beckoning Lady with traditional excitement. There was a streak of red in the west, so the weather was safe. Preparations had nearly reached the blessed stage of "leave it alone or you'll spoil it." The big back larder, which was a white elephant on any other day of the year, was full to overflowing. The cream was on the ice and the hams were setting nicely.

There was considerable noise in the front of the house, where Tonker had set up a Press Bar in the drawing-room, and the river was rising well. But the barn was busiest of all.

Mr. Campion was helping Emma, or rather he was standing about ready to help her as she did something mysterious with hundreds of knives, forks, and spoons at a temporary sideboard some twelve feet long just inside the big doors, which were open to the sky. She was as fresh as if her youth had returned, as no doubt it had, and her cheeks were glowing like a Dutch doll's.

"I don't mind telling you," she was saying, "for half an hour I thought the party was off. I *like* Tonker. I'm not one of the people who can't see that it's not old buck with him. It's just singleness of purpose. But there are moments when he's the edge, and if that dates me I couldn't care less. Fancy coming home like the wrath of God and starting a fight now of all times in the year. And what about, I ask, and what about? Whether a man who's been dead a week was paid or not. Really, Tonker wants his head decarbonizing. And Minnie's as bad. One day she'll have a stroke, and she'll see if she's as strong as she thinks she is. Red Indian blood! Red Indian motorbicycle blood.''

"But everything is all right now, I trust?'' Mr. Campion looked as foolish as he had ever done.

She threw up her head like a horse shaking its mane. "Till next time,'' she said. "Let's hope they wait until the people have gone home, that's all. Oh!'' It was a cry from the heart. "Do you realize that in forty-eight hours it will be over? *Over!* How dreadful! I can't bear to think of it. Count these forks. There should be fifty.''

Mr. Campion counted twenty-five and decided to judge by weighing the two bundles.

"Emma,'' he said, "last Thursday week, before you settled down to listen to the radio and saw Little Doom in the drive, did you come up to the house for any reason? Tonker thought he heard someone.''

"And didn't investigate, I suppose?'' she demanded. "How like him. If Tonker's working, a coach and four could drive up to the front door and remove every stick of furniture, and he wouldn't bother to come out to inquire. No, I didn't come up. But if he heard someone, someone was there. Now the spoons. Don't thumb them, they're polished.''

"Who would walk into the house unannounced?''

"Any one of about forty people. This is the country. Everyone walks round until they find somebody.''

"Do you want these knives counted?''

"No. Now I've got to rush off to see to the flowers. Pinkie let us down. Apparently Genappe has returned, so we shan't get any help from her. Anyway, I've picked the flowers and I've got Annabelle at work on them in the wash-house. I'll just go and see what she's made of them. The boys can finish the cups.''

She jerked her head to the far end of the barn where Westy and George Meredith were unpacking piles of blue and white china, dusting the teacups, and setting them out in rows.

"Tea is hell." Emma spoke with feeling. "It's more difficult to serve than anything else. I can't think why people want it at a party. Do go and look at Jake's picture. Minnie came and got it from him and there was a row, but he likes it now."

She swept off, her white head-dress flapping, while Mr. Campion went on down the room obediently and found himself looking at a charming, gentle design in various tones of grey. The snail was still the main motif but was now not three-dimensional. The picture was lazily attractive, restful, and comforting. He felt he could live with it.

He was standing looking at it when he became aware of a young voice on the other side of the table behind him. Westy was talking to his sombre friend, who was doing little with the cups but much in grim moral support.

"I certainly realize that I am in no position to judge." The soft New England voice was very earnest. "And it may well be, George, that you are at an advantage, being virtually a stranger here. But it does occur to me that they make life unnecessarily complicated. I may be wrong, and of course Minnie is peculiarly close to me because we share the same blood, but as I see it she doesn't need anything but her Art and never has."

George Meredith contributed a strange inarticulate sound.

"That is very true," said Westy miraculously, "but I admit it does seem to me to be so elementary. Why clutter yourself with Tonker, who is a good fellow enough in his way—that I will not deny—but he can only be an interruption. In fact, a definitely disruptive influence in a life which should be entirely and solely devoted to the production of very beautiful things. From this angle, you know, my dear chap, I cannot help but think that life is extraordinarily simple if it is approached with deliberation. Why fall in love at all? Is it so necessary in a civilized person?"

There was a minor upheaval behind the table and Mr.

Campion, who felt a fool as well as a cad for listening to
something which made him feel so antiquated, nerved
himself for an experience. The child was about to speak.

"I say, hold on, old fellow," said George Meredith in a
very high-pitched British middle-class voice indeed. "Think
of the Race."

So they were all right, and so was humanity, and Mr.
Campion turned down the room again to where, under the
platform made by the floor of the inner studio, Amanda
and Lugg and Rupert were finishing the resuscitation of
the glübalübali.

"How nice you look," said Amanda for no apparent
reason. "Cool and respectable and mildly entertained. Aren't
we having a glorious, glorious time?"

"Speak for yer perishin' self." Mr. Lugg disentangled
himself from the embrace of one of the monstrosities and
gave it a cursory rub with a duster he was carrying. "I
don't like these 'ere. I don't think they're the article.
They're common, like elephants' insides."

"More common to you than to me," said Mr. Campion
impolitely. "How has it gone?"

"Jolly well." Amanda as usual was very interested in
the practical problem. "We've got two to play, one to
grunt, and two for show. Tonker must have an amazing
mind. The principle of the mechanics of this instrument—"

"Is low." Mr. Lugg spoke savagely. "Principally low.
And you can talk as informed as you like, but it won't
alter it. Mr. Tonker may be a remarkable organizator,
but 'is mind belongs to the Spirit Dead-Egg."

"My hat yes." Amanda rose dexterously from the floor
where she had been sitting cross-legged. "Do you know,
Albert, Tonker came into the house, got all the champagne
moved to four separate highly sensible strategic points, had
the wherry brought down the stream and fixed in position
as a bridge—we're not to wait for the Augusts to make a
triumphal entry, because no one knows how, when, or if
they'll arrive—set up a Press Bar of hard liquor which
he'd bought at the pub—he came down from the village in
The Gauntlett's van—got hold of Minnie and had the

fiercest row I have ever heard in all my life with her, and got himself changed, all in one hour and three-quarters flat. Oh, and he also had an omelette. He really is remarkable."

"Reorientations. He got my reorientations right, too." said Rupert, attempting a running tackle at his father. "Uncle Tonker is a conker, silly bonker, I am like Uncle Tonker."

"God forbid," said Mr. Campion. "Bed for you."

"Not yet." It was Amanda. "Not yet. We're all going to sleep late tomorrow, and then we're going to dress up and come to the party looking very clean and elegant in our best clothes, and be suitably impressed by all our clever handiwork which we shall not brag about except in private, or . . ."

"Casual-ly," said Rupert, who had evidently heard the plan before. "Where is Charlie?"

"Luke? He's talking to Miss Diane. They're upstairs on the landing. It seemed the quietest place. Superintendent South had to rush back to his office to see the Chief Constable."

"Good." Amanda was studiously polite. "I fear he may have his hands full. I've not been exactly eavesdropping or anything indelicate like that, but I did happen to overhear one of the reporters say that the local office of the Inland Revenue is simply livid with the way Little Doom has been described as an Income Tax man. They say he was declared redundant months ago, and that he was incompetent anyway, and they only took him on as a 'temporary' in the war, and that he wasn't their class and they never did like him. It's jolly hard on them because apparently they're rather good. If they stick to their guns, the whole thing may fizzle quietly away as a story, the reporter said."

"Except that the silly fellow happens to be dead," murmured Mr. Campion. "That's inescapable."

Amanda raised her eyebrows inquiringly and he shook his head.

"This wretched marriage business is a nuisance," he said softly.

"After I have married you," said Rupert to his mother, to make certain that she should not feel overlooked, "I shall marry the fattest twin."

"Which one is that?" Mr. Campion was interested. "I thought them both well covered."

"The fattest *then,* of course." Rupert seemed to find him stupid. "And I shall shout at her and put her across a bed and smack her until she cries, and then I shall kiss her until she laughs, and we shall go downstairs and pour out drinks for a lot of visitors." He took a short run round the group, looking under his lids at them, to see if his somewhat oblique method of reporting gossip had gone home. Satisfied by their startled exchange of glances that it had, he returned to Lugg, having nothing more of interest to impart to them at the moment.

"You quit pertending to be young." The fat man's murmur was a growl. "You think you're so clever, you'll run parst yerself. Shut up, and let persons 'ave a bit o' private life in their own 'ouses. I'm ashamed of you be'aving as if you was an ole woman come to tea."

Rupert flushed but his eyes were dangerous.

"Dinah's got a bicycle bell," he said.

"What if she 'as?" Lugg was truculent. "What if she 'as?"

"Well, she wanted one," said Rupert. "She said so. She's wanted one for a very long time."

"And so Old 'Arry come along and give 'er a brand-noo second'and one for 'er birthday, which it ain't. Orl right, orl right, we've 'eard it. Now come orf it and shut up."

"But she was de-lighted," Rupert insisted wickedly. "De-lighted. She kept saying so until he told her to holdergab."

"Now then, now then," Lugg's voice rose in warning cadence, "that's enough. That will do. Bed you. I'll see to it meself."

He swung the child under one mighty arm and turned to the parents.

"I'm seein' to this," he said firmly. "A lot of namby-pamby just another hower will make a little spiv of 'im.

You shut up, my lad. I don't orfen put my foot down, but when I do . . ."

"You ring a bicycle bell," muttered Rupert, half suffocated, and he hung scarlet-faced but silent as he was carried off.

"It's a good thing," said Amanda, regretful but philosophic. "Lugg is tired too. I fear he's had words with his lady friend. Old Harry won her back with gifts. Old Harry is quite rich, they say," she added as an afterthought. "He keeps his gold in a tin biscuit box, bound up with barbed wire."

"*Barbed* wire?" Mr. Campion echoed in astonishment.

"So they say." Amanda seemed to find the fact interesting but not extraordinary. "He's very much of a country person. I don't know quite where the gold comes from, but he picks things up and sells them, and I should think he makes quite a bit on the side. Odds and ends, you know. He's just given Dinah a bicycle bell which he must have got from somewhere. They were oiling it because it was very wet, but it was quite a good one."

They wandered into the house together and joined Minnie and Tonker, who were sitting placidly in the drawing-room amid a welter of dirty glasses, talking amicably about the probable reaction of Lady Glebe and The Revver to Prune's affair with Luke.

"The woman may say anything," declared Tonker. "She's insane. She was a Gallantry. The Revver won't notice it happened for about ten years, and then he'll hope it wasn't true. That dreary man . . ."

"Put up with you jolly well," finished Minnie. "He wasn't angry for long and even laughed a little in the end."

Tonker's expression of concentrated villainy was lightened by a gleam as he poured his old friends a nightcap.

"Did you hear about my appearance in the parish magazine?" he inquired.

"I heard in the village that you'd been 'advertising of yourself,' " said Amanda. "You had a row with The Revver actually in church, didn't you?"

"Wasn't it frightful!" Minnie was appalled. "There was no service at the time, of course."

"There was no real row," protested Tonker, passing the glasses. "It was simply this. Judge for yourselves. I don't get along to the old boy's dreary services, as you know, because I'm not always here. But I walked up to the church one day, because I wanted to look at some wizzo lettering on the Pontisbright Tomb. I was mucking about very peacefully, admiring things, when I suddenly thought I wasn't being very respectful. I thought 'God Tonker, you are a stinker, only coming up here when you want something,' so I got down very decently and said something—not aloud, of course, but something simple—like 'O God, make me a good Tonker and let Mr. Guggenheim pass that scheme.' Something perfectly normal and ordinary." He cocked a wicked eye at them. "And then I noticed the old Revver. He'd been watching me from behind the vestry curtains, the old so-and-so, and presently he came creeping down to me and paused just in front of me where I was kneeling and said, if you please, 'Are you all right?' I didn't get up but I stared at him and I said—in a whisper, you understand, the whole conversation was conducted in whispers—'What do you mean? Of course I'm all right.' And he said very nastily, 'Oh I thought you couldn't be. You never come to worship.' And I said, 'Well, what on earth do you think I'm doing now, you fathead?' And he said, 'Don't be blasphemous, Tonker.' He did, he really did! Well, after I left him, which was pretty smartly, he went round the village telling people I'd gone off my head and got religious mania. I heard it at The Gauntlett half a dozen times, and I resolved to teach the man a lesson."

Minnie was trying not to laugh but the tears were creeping out of her eyes and rolling down her long nose.

"It was very naughty," she protested.

"It was not. It was very dignified. I knew he'd never apologize, the rat. You know what a parish magazine is like, Campion?" Tonker turned to his friend. "It's a solid wodge of family matter which is the same for every parish—

syndicated stuff—but the outside double page just under
the cover is printed separately for every community. It
opens with a letter from the local parson to his flock, and
the whole of the rest of the space is taken up with two-inch
ads inserted and paid for by local tradespeople. You know:
'My bread is good bread. B. Bunn, Baker,' 'Have a
good coffin while you're about it. H. Hearse, Undertaker,' and so on. Well, I went to my old friend the
wheelwright, who has the centre of the back inner page,
and came to a deal with him, and the next month in his
space there was my announcement. 'Apology accepted. T.
Cassands.' That caught The Revver in a cleft stick. He
didn't notice a thing until he'd delivered the whole lot by
hand on his bicycle, which he does as an act of humility. I
knew he wouldn't.''

"And then he laughed," said Minnie, "so it's all right.
He's forgiven you.''

"He hasn't you know," said Tonker. "He doesn't like
me, and he thinks I'm veering to Rome, secretly. I can see
it in his eye. Anyway, I expect he has a bucketful with the
old lady. She believes in all the religions, Polytheism,
Sufism, Fire Worship, the Water Cure, Buddhism, and
Rosicrucianism—the lot. Come to think of it, that girl
must have quite a time between the two of 'em. No
wonder she looks a bit blah.''

"I think she's in love now," ventured Amanda.

"Love!" Tonker spoke with withering contempt and he
glared balefully out of the window behind her at the
moonlit garden. "Pah! What's love? How much can it
stand?''

"That," said Minnie with some asperity, "is a thing I
sometimes wonder.''

Meanwhile, on the landing upstairs Luke was finishing
his interrogation of a frightened but very shrewd-eyed
Miss Diane. The Sergeant, whom he had borrowed from
South to fulfil regulation requirements, was a dark shadow
in the background. But at the end of the hall there was a
grandfather clock and on this the Chief Inspector kept his
eye. The last train from London was due in at Kepesake
station in something under half an hour.

"For the last time, Ma," he said, dropping into the vernacular of his beloved London manor, "forget it. We do not care two penn'orth of gin if you're married to the King of Siam. Forget the subject of pensions. The only pensions the Sergeant and I are worrying about at the moment are our own, and we shan't live to collect those if you don't get on with it. I only want to know if you and Mrs. Cassands spent the whole of that Thursday afternoon together. We don't care about the morning. We know by the bus when the deceased arrived at Pontisbright. And we don't really care about the late evening. We just want to know about the afternoon."

"I was with 'er from two o'clock until we got Mr. William settled for the night about eleven, and that's God's truth."

"All the time?"

"Well, I come in and made the tea, but she was scrubbing the shelves in the boat house then, and she must have stuck to it or she couldn't have done so much. She's a good worker, I'll say that."

"I see. Very well." Luke let snap the elastic band which kept his packet of envelopes together. "Go on. I'll see you tomorrow, I expect. But don't worry."

"Are yer satisfied?" A damp hand clutched at his sleeve in the gesture now so familiar to him from his years of work amongst the women who were so like her. "You're not keeping nothink back from me, dear?"

"No." He patted her shoulder, which was as solid as a side of bacon. "No. Run along. I'm not laying information. And when I get back I'll look up your husband for you. He's dead, you know. Blimey, he'd be about a hundred and ten by all accounts, even if he got away from the bombing, which is unlikely."

" 'E'd be seventy-three," she said softly, "and oh, he was a one, 'e was a one. I'm 'appy 'ere. I ain't ever been 'appy before."

"Well then, shut up." Luke was firm. "Come on. Sergeant. You've got your own transport, have you?"

"Ho, I'll see to '*im*," said Miss Diane.

Luke flung himself out of the house and into his little car. But half an hour later he had driven it into the garage at the Mill, and had walked out on to the silent moon-drenched heath alone.

The stubby train, which was but four coaches long, had waited less than a minute at the single platform before panting off again on its potter through the night. The yellow lamps had flickered palely in the moonlight. The few passengers had bustled away to their waiting cars. Prune had not returned.

Now, on the springing turf of the heath where the wild thyme and the coltsfoot made the air aromatic, Luke felt younger and more alone than at any time since his baby-hood. The world he knew so well, and in which he was counted a sophisticated member, was suddenly set apart from himself so that he could look at it from the outside. It was a new and frightful experience and he had a glimpse for the first time of a state in which colours and comforts and warmths and familiar delights had lost their virtue.

He was no Shakespearian, nor was he a countryman, so that he was not concerned with being absent in the spring. Bird song and the deep vermilion of the rose meant little to him at any time. But he was now faced with a vista of grey pavements, little bars bright behind raindrops, traffic, ex-citement, telephone calls, the chances of taking risks, good-tempered dirty faces, friendly words from doorsteps, the smell of new bread rising from a grating, a radio lovesong trilling in the night adding to a city's enchant-ments, all of them spoiled, dulled, devitalized for ever.

He was aware of the whole experience in one terrible revelation, swift and awful, like the discovery that the unforeseen accident has broken one's back, a peep into emptiness. He threw himself down among the little flowers and the scented herbs, and thrust his forehead into them in an agony of dismay. He was not thinking at all. The little house, the familiar blue overall his mother wore, the tidy curtains, and the spotless yard, their inadequacies were too exquisitely painful to bear contemplation at this juncture. Even Prune herself was a vanished dream. There was only one absorbing picture in his mind, himself, shadowy and alone, in a drab flavourless city for ever.

The night wind blew over him and the earth was kind and he was so tired. He slept like a log. The voices on the road and at the Mill, the cars rustling by, the laughter in the village, they passed without him hearing them at all. He lay there exhausted and out, like a dead man.

When he awoke it was an hour past dawn on Midsummer's Day, the day of Tonker's party. The sky was like a pearl, clear and flawless, the air was thin and cool and breathtaking. His first surprise, even before the black sorrow of the night returned to whisper to him that Prune had found upon inspection that it would never do, was to discover that he was quite warm. He was covered with sacks, and there was a large wild rhubarb leaf over his head. It took him some seconds to grasp the significance of these phenomena, and by that time he had realized that he was not alone.

Old Harry was lying propped up on one elbow some three yards away. His own bed was of pulled thyme and he rested there contentedly, a long grass stalk between his fine new Government teeth. The Chief Inspector sat up slowly, aware again now of his private sorrow but still himself and still game. The rhubarb leaf slid on to the ground in front of him and he took it up.

"What's this for?"

"To shade yer. Let the full moon soak into yer this time o' year and you won't never be the same man again. Not a half of him."

Luke stretched his broad shoulders and his dark face was sad.

"Too late, chum," he said. "You should have told me before."

He fingered the sacks, which were wet with dew.

"Thank you for these. I was all in."

Old Harry accepted the gratitude with an approving nod.

"They say you're the *Head* policeman," he remarked, slowing his normal high-pitched gabble to a reasonably intelligible pace. "The Head of 'em all, come from Lunnon."

"So I am." Another great packet of worry shouldered its lumbering way back into Luke's unwilling mind. "How's your nose? Smelled out anything else since I saw you last?"

A secret smile, which he was unable to suppress, passed over Harry's rosy face and he lowered his eyelids coyly as Amanda had noticed before.

"I dunno," he said idly, and added as soon as he judged his disinterestedness was sufficiently established, "I reckon you'll hear of another death today."

"Eh?"

The old man rose with agility and stood for a moment to stare into the white glare of the eastern sky before going off like a cracked alarm clock.

"Three in a row, three in a row," he chattered, turning round. "There's allus three in a row."

"Oh." Luke settled back. If it was a case of superstition only he was not interested. "I don't know so much about that."

"Aha! But I do." Old Harry was laughing with ancient glee, and all about him stretched the lush green countryside in which there were to every acre a thousand hiding-places, deep and wide and quiet enough to hold so small and worthless a thing as a single unit of mortal clay. "I *do*. Tha's the humour of it, I *do*! I'll see you later, sir, at the Feast. Good-day."

CHAPTER XIV

Fine Goings-on

I

In the normal way Tonker slept late. Even in these, his late middle years, he was able to lie unmolested in an amiable torpor from midnight till noon. But on the morning of his party he awoke like a bird at a quarter to six and went down in his dressing-gown to open every outside door in the house. Then he put a record on the gramophone and went out to run up the Union Jack on the flagpole at the north end of the barn.

Five minutes later, Minnie, aroused by a gale which sent the curtains of the painted bed flapping about her, the *Soldier's Chorus*, and a sense of fury, rose also, and with her Mother-Hubbard over her nightgown strode down to rescue the record, to shut the doors, and to run up the Stars and Stripes at the southern end of the same building.

An hour later, when the boys had come in, Annabelle had appeared already dressed for the party, and breakfast was on the table, there was still no sign of Tonker and a deep general suspicion arose that he had gone back to bed.

Presently, however, he appeared, a little wet round the legs from the dew but beaming and bearing with him all the papers. Having thoughtfully arranged with the village shop and Miss Diane that she should bring them with her first thing, he had gone down to meet her at the stile.

He took his seat at the head of the table, adjusted his reading glasses, and turned up his thumbs.

"It's all right," he announced with tremendous satisfaction. "Saved! The *Bibful* says more than anybody else, of course, but even they are cautious. Would you like to read it, Minnie, or shall I?"

His wife pushed her hair out of her eyes, gave George Meredith a second egg, passed the butter to Annabelle, took the frying-pan off the stove, rescued the teapot, and sat down herself. Her mouth, which had been the least bit tight, relaxed into the ghost of a smile.

"You read it, Tonker."

"TAX MAN'S DEATH
MYSTERY BODY LIES
SEVEN DAYS ON
MILLIONAIRE'S FARM
from
George Apgeorge
Pontisbright, Friday

A lonely man, keeper of many secrets, kept his own dark mystery unsolved in this remote East Anglian village today. Leonard Terence Ohman (54), ex-temporary civil servant, was a man of few friends. His battered body lay for a week in a deep ditch by a stile on a millionaire's farming estate at Pontisbright, yet no alarm was raised at his absence. At the inquest this afternoon in the romantically named township of Kepesake, adjourned after formal evidence, only one clue to the mystery was offered. Ohman was until recently a tax collector. His visits to the area which he served never brought good news to those upon whose doors he knocked. He was a man apart, at whose approach neighbours turned their backs. Tonight all is quiet in this old world Tudor village, where the white-faced inhabitants look at each other with an unspoken question in their eyes. Few can have earned sufficient to have merited Ohman's attention, and it is too soon to tell what tale of fancied right or wrong may be uncovered. Superintendent Fred South, smiling stalwart of . . ."

"Oh no!" Minnie put down the teapot with a clatter. "Oh, no, Tonker, they're not going to take that line? How frightful! Poor Little Doom was only trying to help."

"Do you want to hear any more?" Tonker lowered the paper and eyed her balefully over the top of his glasses. Now that he had come to read the story carefully after merely glancing through it for unwelcome names, he was not quite so cheerful. "It goes on like this for quite a bit, and then there's a paragraph to say that the estate belongs to Fanny. Are you going to listen?"

"No." Minnie spoke with unexpected savagery. "It terrifies me. What are they going to say tomorrow?"

"Tomorrow?" Tonker shrugged his shoulders. "Tomorrow the party will be over. We'll meet tomorrow when it comes. The important thing is, you silly girl, that everything is quite all right for today. This stuff won't stop anybody coming. Probably bring 'em." He looked her firmly in the eye and indicated the children, who not unnaturally appeared mildly alarmed. "Don't spoil everything when it's going all right," he protested virtuously. "Accept the gifts of heaven as they arrive. It's a wonderful morning. If I have time at the end of my life I shall make a point of getting up at this time of year. It's quite an experience in the meadows. I wouldn't have believed it. I think it could be capitalized. Er—well, we've all got a great deal to do. Boys, have you shut the sluices?"

Westy turned to him at once, glad of the reassurance. "You don't have to worry about that one little bit," he announced cheerfully. "That was done at four a.m. just as the water touched the mark we fixed. We've got it trickling through at a rate which George calculates will keep it pretty well exactly at the same level all day. Isn't that so, George?"

By turning a dull puce, threatening to choke, and overturning his cup, George Meredith indicated that indeed this was so, and Tonker grunted his satisfaction.

"That's all right, then. You'll get over that shyness one day, Meredith my boy. It'll drop from you like a cloak. Now we have to check the essentials. Sanitary arrangements, liquor caches, glasses, car park, food, lighting, first-aid equipment, rugs, cushions, garden chairs, and so on for people to sit on, in that order.''

"Tea and washing up,'' murmured Westy.

Tonker scowled. "Women's work,'' he said airily. "What are you wearing?''

"My Suit.'' Westy spoke with reverence.

Tonker chuckled happily. "I'm not,'' he announced, as he glanced up at the clock on the bracket. "Wally can't get here before eleven, I suppose. Minnie, I did tell you that Wally and Tommasina would be here for lunch?''

"Who?'' Minnie slammed down the paper she had been reading and her eyes, from being merely dark with worry, became pits of horror. "Who's coming to lunch? Tonker, if you've invited—''

"Wally and Tommasina, my dear. Our oldest friends.''

"Oh. Oh well, that's all right then.'' She threw the paper on the floor in disgust and picked it up again at once because of the need to keep tidy. "Wally and Tommy are all right. They'll eat in here and like it, bless them. I don't mind them.''

"I trust, my dear—'' Tonker spoke with crushing dignity and acid forbearance, "—I trust that you're not going to 'mind,' as you put it so charmingly, anybody whomsoever on this tremendous day, because, my sweet and gentle Minniehaha, we have only absolutely everybody we have ever met or heard of coming down all this way to ENJOY themselves, dear. ENJOY is the operative word, Smile,'' he added ferociously as he glanced round the table. "Happy carefree smiles. Cut that out, and you might as well call the whole thing off. Understand? There is only one must at a party. Everything must be fun. Nothing unpleasant must occur. No frown, no ugly reminder must intrude to spoil the happiness of all.''

Minnie sniffed ominously and George Meredith hacked Westy on the shin with sudden violence.

Breakfast being over, the boys rose, collected Annabelle in passing as if she were an overcoat, and burst out into the yard in a minor explosion.

"Nerves." A hoarse high-pitched British voice, which nobody in the house had heard before, spoke from out the whirlwind.

At the sound of it Minnie looked about her with absent-minded superstition, and Tonker growled.

"Pup," he said, and rising, went round the table to kiss his wife. "Don't cry, Minnie. If you cry you'll get a headache, and if you get a headache you'll be sick. What's the matter? Don't worry. *I'm* here."

Minnie's smile broke through. "I know you are, God help me, but what about this dreadful business, Tonker? It looks quite terrifying to me. They can't leave it here. They must go on. Poor little Bossy's dead. Somebody killed him."

Her voice died away and Tonker took up the nearest newspaper again. Despite the flowing folds of his spotted gown, he looked remarkably masculine, and his freckled forearm was sandy-haired and tough.

"I see what you mean," he conceded. "It's got an ugly side, I grant you that. But don't let it get you down. We're over the first fence. We'll take the next when we come to it. Keep your heart up, old gal. All our life has been like this, hasn't it? Hasn't it, Minnie? Keep on going. We always have. Courage, old lady."

Minnie was dabbing her long nose in a minute mirror and her snorting laugh escaped her.

"Stop talking to me as if I really was a horse."

"That's better." Tonker patted her. "That's my Minnie. That's the spirit. Now we'll pull up our socks and make it the best day anybody's ever had. And you'll see something will transpire. Something will turn up at the party. Something will come sailing in. I can feel it in my bones. Keep your eyes skinned."

"The postman's brought nothing." Miss Diane's cheerful roar reached them from the outer kitchen. "The postman's brought nothing, I say. Only a handful of them buff envelopes and a circular from Mr. William's bookie."

"Put them all straight in the boiler!" shouted Tonker in a rage.

"No you don't." Minnie's voice was equally powerful. "Slip them in the kitchen drawer, Dinah. Oh my God, now I've got to see to that lot alone. Damn you Tonker, help me clear away."

II

Miss Pinkerton was quite dead when her body entered the water. The river was deep at that particular point and the stream was a limpid green, sparkling now in the full sun. The body slid in gently, feet first, and the blue cotton dress with the starched petticoats beneath it spread out on the dazzling surface and bore it up, so that like Ophelia she floated for a time, looking strangely comfortable in the glittering bed, her dark head lolling deep in green cushions.

Since it was now some hours since Westy and George Meredith had almost closed the sluice gates far down in the fen meadows beyond The Beckoning Lady, the flow was very gentle and the body drifted slowly for some fifty yards or so into a tunnel made by a double line of overhanging willows. Here it was cool and secret and the stream grew shallow. Midway along this watery corridor there was a temporary dam caused by a mass of dead rushes which had broken away from a dense bank of them which grew by the Sweethearting Road, and had become entangled in the knotted roots of the old trees.

It was not much of a dam. Later in the day it would lose its hold, inevitably, and would float on down towards the oasis of flowers where the boat house shone so gaily in its new paint. Yet now it was firmly lodged and was just strong enough to hold up the new piece of flotsam.

There for a long time the body rested, waiting.

III

Old Harry and Miss Diane lived in what Pontisbright was pleased to call a hole. This was no term of opprobrium, but a literal description of a cottage whose thatched eaves were level with the outside world. Behind this dwelling there was an even lower piece of ground, enclosed now with enormous hollyhocks and burgeoning with sufficient greenery to feed a cow. In the midst of this again there was a very small shed, covered with an old and sunken thatch, and inside, safe as a field mouse in its nest, was Old Harry.

He had just finished taking the bicycle completely to pieces. The tyres and inner tubes had been removed and were now hanging up in someone else's shed, The Revver's in point of fact. They were quite safe there. The old gentleman would not attempt to climb those dusty stairs until the next apple-picking. The chain, newly greased, was hanging in the well-head at The Gauntlett, another abode of a family of fixed habits. The handle-grips, which were unusual, had been destroyed. The wheels were here, under the bench, as dusty as if they had lain there for years. The lamps were in a rabbit burrow in the garden. The saddle-bag was in a hollow tree. The mudguards were on the Battus Dump, and the bell, which had no marks on it save the maker's name, which was famous, was on Miss Diane's own machine.

The frame, which was a good one, had been regretfully consigned to the river, but was in a pool which could be investigated again later if all went well. Old Harry had been sorry about that. Yet it seemed only fair that the stream which had brought him this glittering prize should have some small return. It had done its work so gracefully. He had scarcely believed his eyes when he had first seen the present from the gods borne to him, shining and intact, on a tangle of logs, straws, and moorhens' nests. It had not been in the water more than three or four hours then, he suspected, and since it was afternoon, and there were police about as he very well knew, having spent the best part of the late forenoon with them, he had merely rescued the gift and covered it with pulled grass.

At dusk he had returned to it and before beginning his dismantling had detached the bell and had won back Miss Diane's wayward heart with it from the foreigner.

Much later in the night, when most of his trove was

garnered and safe in its hiding-places all over the village,
he had made a special journey up the stream to find out if
there was any good reason for the bicycle's presence in the
water at all.

Under a tree some few yards from the field path which
led up to the house without a back he had found one.

Old Harry's ethics were peculiar in the sense that they
were special to himself, but such as they were they existed
and accounted for his most thoughtful treatment of Luke,
both at night when he had assuredly saved his reason from
being spirited away by the dangerous rays of the moon,
and in the morning when he had as good as reported the
body to him if the man had any understanding at all.

So now, at noon on the day of Mr. Tonker's Feast, or
party as people were calling it nowadays—names changed
with the years in Old Harry's experience, but Feasts mercifully did not: Man and his Belly they stuck together,
modernize them how you liked—here he was, richer, happier, and in Midsummer mood.

He fortified himself with a draught of the wicket wheat
wine of his own making, which he had broached for the
late evening's celebration when he had a mind to show the
Londoner a few wonders, and went round to the back of
the shed where, under some cabbage leaves by a little
spring, he had some of his posies waiting for the ladies.

These were tight bunches of flowers, very formal and
conical in shape and doubtless of some ancient significance, but they were beautifully made out of the choicest
blooms which the gardens of Pontisbright could produce,
as Old Harry well knew, having made a tour to collect
them just after he left Luke. There was one for Minnie,
tipped with one of her own red roses, another for Emma,
one all-gold for Amanda, for she was of the nobility, and a
small white one for Annabelle. But the best and biggest of
all was a glowing crimson pyramid smothered in buds and
cradled in maidenhair, which was "special for a lover."

Old Harry took down a dusty waisted basket, relic of
some Edwardian wedding, and placed the posy inside.
Then he went down to see his new friend, the Head police-

man, to whom he had taken a fancy because he was such a splendid, well-furnished young man, a pleasure to the eye.

IV

"I take my hat off to you, Minnie. It's a species of miracle. I wouldn't do it for mink and millions. The work, woman, the work!"

Tommasina, wife of Wally, Tonker's friend and boss, sat on Minnie's bed and made up her mouth with a lipstick as red as a raspberry. Like Minnie, she had never had the disadvantage of having been born beautiful, but unlike Minnie, in something over forty years, she achieved something very near it. She was as rounded as a girl, and genuinely elegant, and her white and navy dress made the very flowers look countrified. Minnie grinned. She was very pleased to see her, and was secretly delighted to find that the old elixir which the prospect of a party had always poured into her own veins had not failed her once again. She could feel it now, a recklessness and a gaiety which killed worry and anxiety as an alkali kills acid.

"It's going to be all right," she said and crossed her fingers in the pocket of her new print dress. "It wouldn't be fun if one didn't do it oneself for people one likes. These business do's could be awfully dreary, and then they'd defeat their own object."

"You're telling me." Tommy spoke bitterly. "I see enough of that. Who's coming? Everybody, I suppose. Wally's been as nervous as a cat. What's old Tonker got on?"

"On?" Minnie started violently. "I don't know of anything special."

"Oh well, then, forget it. I only wondered. I don't know a thing. I only know that he's fixed up something with the Augusts."

"The Augusts?" Minnie groaned.

"It's nothing destructive." Tommy was holding her arm. "I only know it's some sort of patter, and if you mention it they'll neither of them ever forgive me. Seri-

ously, angel, I only know that, whatever it is, Tonker
came down here to fix it over the telephone because he
wanted to give them long, quiet instructions and wouldn't
do it from the office at all."

"What?"

"That's all I know and all Wally knows. That's terribly
important." She laughed. "Yet it may be all crackingly
silly. You know what they are."

"Oh well," Minnie dusted her nose with a mighty
powder puff, "it can't be worse than we've known."

"That's true." The other wife of Perception and Company
Limited echoed exactly the tone of mingled pride and
resignation. "Are all the old gang coming as well? Jenny
and Robert and Eve and Cocky and Poppy and the
Whippets—"

"And the kids." Minnie spoke with a certain pride. "I
do a deal," she said mysteriously. "We do all the work
and I trade friends in for extra help."

Tommy laughed. "You're mad as a coot. Wally says
you take the inquisitors too seriously. What do they do?
Demand to see a visitors' book with each name's probable
value accurately assessed?"

"Not now." Minnie was giving her nails, which she
wore in the old-fashioned way, a final burnish. "But oh
dear, my little snooper chum is dead. I keep remembering
him."

"He's not the one in the papers, I hope?" Tommy's
voice had a dangerous inflection.

"Well, yes he is. Was, I mean."

"Minnie!" Her visitor's mascara'd eyes had widened.
"Wally was muttering about this all the way down. I say
Minnie, if there was a scandal now, it really would be
unadulterated hell, darling. You do realize that, don't you?
The new client is coming down and is bringing old Lord
Tudwick himself. Wally and Tonker have been simply
slaving on some business for them for months and months.
Oh dearest, it would be too cruel if something frightful
broke."

"Oh I know." Minnie was shaking her head. "You're
telling me. Fang wrote me yesterday. He's bringing . . ."

"Listen, Minnie." Tommasina's eyes were unnaturally bright. "Let's face it. Tonker hasn't the temper of an angel. You don't think that . . . I mean you are sure . . . ?"

"Tonker says he didn't," said Minnie flatly, "so don't be ridiculous. It's going to be the best party we've ever had and there's nothing whatever to worry about. It's going to be the Lions and Lovelies Party. Tonker wouldn't call it that if he'd—well, if he'd thought the police were interested in him. We'll be all right. Put a bit more colour on. What a glorious dress that is."

Tommy was reassured because she wanted to be and momentarily sidetracked.

"It's good, isn't it? The Paris house of the Old Firm, there's no one like them. They charge the earth but you do get heaven. I bought it over there when I was doing a little publicity job for Lemesurier's. Alarmingly hard work. I had to spend the whole of a long dreary Thursday afternoon at Auteuil with S. S. Smith and some appalling pals of his. I didn't escape them until nine in the evening. He'll be here today, they say."

"Yes." Minnie was thinking. Her eyes had narrowed and she seemed half afraid to ask the question in her mind. "Which Thursday was this?"

"Last week. Does it matter?" Tommy had captured the mirror again. "Not the day before yesterday. The Thursday before that. Anything of great importance in that?"

"No."

"Darling, what on earth is the matter? Do you care where the S.S.S. man was last Thursday week?"

"Yes, I do, rather." Minnie spoke absently, and then, catching the other woman's expression, bridled like a girl. "Oh, don't be silly," she protested. "Don't be so disgusting. Whatever next?"

"That wouldn't please the V.I.P.," Tommy was beginning, when a handful of stones splattered over the window. There was silence outside, followed by a school-boyish guffaw. Minnie looked out and Tommasina joined her. Two stocky figures stood side by side on the path outside the window, with their backs to the house. Wally was very decently clad in formal grey, but Tonker had put on his party garment which his friends had brought down for him. It was a very early M.C.C. blazer, just a little large for its present wearer and cut with all the pyjama-jacket respectability of the Victorian sporting mode, in quarter-inch thick flannel. The stripes of scarlet and yellow were but little faded, and the effect was both gay and grand.

"Ripping!" said Minnie, fishing out the right word. "Absolutely whacky. Bang on."

The two figures, still making smothered noises, turned slowly and there was a squeal from the window. Both Wally's magnificent black beard and Tonker's sandy grin were hidden by "beautiful girl" masks, ill-fitting but still horribly lifelike. Tonker's blazer, buttoning almost to his chin, added to the revolting incongruity. Wally screwed up his face and thrust his chin forward, and the supple rubber of the mask moved also. Tonker covered his eyes.

"It's got a bend in it!" he shouted and they both roared with laughter.

Tommasina turned to Minnie. "I'd believe anything of them after that," she said.

V

After lunch, instead of getting dressed, Amanda and Rupert were romping. The enforced rest in the morning seemed to have produced an unnatural energy in both. They were also excited. Old friends had telephoned, Old Harry's posy had been a success, and the weather was much better than anyone could have hoped.

After being merely silly, Rupert suddenly got very naughty and refused to put on his new long white trousers. Amanda, who was half-dressed herself, was so ill-advised as to chase him, and they tore all over the top of the house like lunatics, finishing up in Aunt Hatt's bedroom. Rupert took a flying leap at the bed; Amanda, seizing the opportunity, caught him by the leg; and with a shriek he snatched up the tortoiseshell hairbrush from the high chest beside the bed, hit her over the head with it, and flung it away from him into a corner where it broke.

Mr. Campion, coming up to see if the goats had got in, arrived in time for the lamentations. Rupert was weeping in an agony of remorse, Amanda was rubbing her head, and they were both rather appalled about the hairbrush, which was a "good one." Mr. Campion had to have the entire business explained to him in detail, a difficult matter since no one had been thinking very clearly at the time.

"I didn't mean to do it." The ancient wail went up in the old house, which must have heard it a hundred times before in its long history. "She was trying to catch me. I didn't think. I didn't mean to do it. Honestly I didn't mean to do it."

The silence which followed, and which was only broken by Rupert's sobs, went on so long that after a time both warriors glanced cautiously at Mr. Campion, who appeared to have forgotten them. To their intense indignation, they discovered that he had. He had wandered over to the window and now stood looking out into the garden with unseeing eyes.

"Of course," he said at last in a surprisingly matter of fact tone. "Of course. What a silly chap I am." Turning, he appeared to notice the two insulted faces for the first time. "Yes, indeed," he said, "you two must hurry up, mustn't you?" And, swinging round, he strode out of the room and ran lightly downstairs, leaving them sobered and flat but partners in adversity.

As he reached the hall, the telephone began to ring and he was advancing upon it when Luke, a little flushed and misleadingly businesslike, hurled himself out of the dining-room to answer it. Mr. Campion stepped back obligingly and was sickened to see the nervous possessiveness with which Luke's long hand closed round the receiver, and immediately afterwater, was the crimson posy Old Harry had made. It gleamed gruffly, "Lugg. For you."

At the other end of the wire the thick and familiar tones were heavily mysterious.

"That you, Cock? No luck yet, but I've got a bit of a lead. I'm pressin' on."

"Good. Where are you?"

"In a perishin' general shop, with a pack of bullocks' eyes glued to me . . . That's shifted 'em." The background noises were various, including the strange soughing of a distant sea which he gathered with astonishment was his caller breathing.

"In Kepesake?"

"No, I've gorn on to Ring and now I'm makin' for 'Adleigh. I've met a pill-basher 'oo's sendin' me to 'is 'ead office, got that?"

"Yes. Keep at it."

"Orl right. Thump a willin' 'orse, you know what 'appens."

"What?"

"The noble animal gets ruddy fed up. You take 'Er Ladyship and the Gawd-ferbid to the party, and expec' me when you see me. Tell 'em I'm coming. I've got a lot to do down there, and if you're right on this lark there'll be a bit more."

"So there will." Mr. Campion sounded non-committal. "It's important, though, because I've got an idea."

"Chalk it up." The flat voice was derisive. " 'Old on to it. Don't let it escape yer. That's what the bloke said 'oo 'ired me my transport."

"Good heavens, what is it? Equine?"

"No. One of them little motor-scooters you can drop by parachute. A Sealy'am."

"Corgi. My hat Lugg, are you all right? Be careful."

"That's what they all say." Lugg was heavily amused. "I got a percession o' motors be'ind me all follerin' to see me blow up. A very ignorant type of person in'abits these parts. Under-entertained. Every now and again I show 'em—look, no'ands! Wot yer."

Mr. Campion hung up and went into the dining-room. Luke was sitting at the table before a portable typewriter and the inevitable sheaves of tidy papers all round him. The C.I.D. sergeant, a slender quiet-eyed young man, who had been sent down to help him, was sitting at the small desk in the corner tabulating notes. On the table, in a tumbler of water, was the crimson posy Old Harry had made. It gleamed like a wound on the dark surface of an ancient wood. Mr. Campion looked at it sharply in passing and glanced at Luke, who was in shirtsleeves, his face hard and preoccupied.

"I think I shall drive down there now. It's after three and we promised to be early. You'll follow, will you?"

"I don't know." Luke was trying not to appear surly. "There's a lot to do. The Chief Constable is in a flap. He can't very well go down there, socially of course, and the Press are nagging him. We got some more names and addresses out of the Inland Revenue office with a great deal of difficulty. They're hopping mad, of course. It's very bad luck on them. He was off their strength. However, we shall have to make a thorough check. We did a few this morning. It's a miserable job."

Mr. Campion hesitated. "I had a sort of idea," he ventured at last. "It's a very long shot."

"Long shots are getting me down." Luke spoke with uncharacteristic bitterness. "I'm sorry, guv'nor, but if I could only get a single blessed fact which would stand up for ten minutes I could sew the thing up and get out of here."

The cry was too vehement altogether. He flushed angrily and returned to his typewriter.

"I may be along to give it the once-over if I can get through this lot," he said briefly. "South will be there."

Mr. Campion turned away. He was not offended but his idea was still too insubstantial to impart. So much depended on anything Lugg could dig up from the chemists' shops of the district.

Once again as he passed the posy caught his eye.

"I know where I've seen that extraordinary arrangement before," he observed, surprised into inaction. "On a piece of antique French tapestry. It's in the Victoria and Albert, I think, on top of a little coffer. In the fifteenth century they used to make them as wedding—" He broke off abruptly. He was not usually so gauche.

"I hate the damned thing," said Luke.

After a while Mr. Campion drove his wife and son away. They were exquisitely tidy and slightly overawed by their own elegance. Amanda's shantung suit and small straw hat were spit-new, and Rupert had never worn such elegant white flannels before, so they bowed to people they knew as they passed them in the road, and addressed each other formally as they commented on the weather and admired the well-known view.

Meanwhile, in the dining-room at the Mill, laborious work went on for a long time. Luke let the telephone ring for a minute as he finished a sentence, but he signed to the sergeant that he would take the call himself, and presently rose and wandered out to it.

"Hullo. Is that you?" Prune's ridiculous voice was unnaturally subdued.

"It is." What with controlling his breath, fighting back fury, and preserving what shreds of dignity remained to him, Luke succeeded in sounding stagy. "Can I help you?"

"Aren't you coming to fetch me? It's terribly late." Luke had never been murderously angry with a woman in all his life before. Blind unreasoning rage consumed and almost choked him.

"Why didn't you telephone before?"

"Ought I to have. Your mother said that the one thing one must never do is to . . ."

"Oh, you saw her, did you?" Luke was hunching himself over the telephone as if he was preparing to squeeze into it. His normal vitality was coming back. The little brass ornaments on the mantelshelf over the fireplace began to vibrate at the sound of his voice.

"Yes. My dress wasn't done, so I stayed there the night."

"At Linden Lea?" Luke, who had the most vivid recollections of the upheaval which had preceded the week-end visit of an aunt way back in 1936, was astounded.

"Yes. I was asked so I jumped at it. I was going to get in at Brown's, but your mother said . . ."

"Where are you now?"

THE BECKONING LADY 205

"At the Rectory, waiting. The Revver and Mama have gone on, ages ago. I'm all ready. I've locked up, I've—"

"Wait." Luke glanced first at his shoes and then at his nails. "Wait. You're there alone, are you? Stay exactly where you are."

"Of course I shall. I've been waiting . . . I say Charles, I've got the necklace."

"What necklace?"

"*The* necklace. The jade. The one your uncle brought from Shanghai. Your mother gave . . ."

"She gave?" Luke nearly hung up, he was so relieved. "Listen," he roared into the telephone, "listen . . ."

"I *am* listening."

"All right then. Don't move."

"Very well. But Charles, there's one thing I must know. What is our attitude towards this murder business?"

"Our attitude?"

"Yes, dear, ours," Prune said patiently. "Ours. Ours. The official attitude of the police."

"Hold on. That is, ring off," said Luke, hanging up. "Stay where you are," he said to the telephone and went back into the room for his jacket. "You'll carry on then, will you?" He addressed the sergeant absently. "None of this stuff matters a damn, you know. The whole centre of the thing is down there at The Beckoning Lady. I don't quite see the set-up yet, and it may be a most unfortunate mess, but it can't be helped. The only thing to do is to plunge straight in and—er, sew it up. Stay here, I'll get you relieved later."

The younger man was looking at him curiously. He was something to see, standing there preening himself like a great black tomcat, his bright eyes gleaming and an obstinate curl at the corners of his mouth. He set his tie straight in the mirror, settled his cuffs, and grinned.

"Leave it to me," he announced and went out, only to return immediately for the posy, which he took out of the glass and wrapped in his handkerchief. He looked the sergeant firmly in the eye. "I shall need this," he said.

VI

In the cool silence under the willows, where there was no
breeze, the water had slowly penetrated into the billowing
skirts which had supported the body and it had begun to
sink by the feet. At the same time, a further mass of rushes
and sodden blossoms from the trees had swept downstream
to join the rest, and because the body was tilted had slid
half under it, making a pillow for the dark head. Meanwhile the original dam, never very strong, was straining
under the new weight and its hold on the roots was gradually giving way. About five in the afternoon the final
tendril holding the tangle broke under the gentle pressure,
and very gently the whole terrible burden began to move
slowly towards the opening where the leaves ended and the
sun shone on a bank of yellow irises further down . . .

CHAPTER XV

Tonker's Guests

Edging his way adroitly through the crowds on the lawn, Tonker came up behind Minnie at last and slid an arm round her.

"It's all right. Poppy's arrived," he said hoarsely. "Leo locked her in, but she climbed out of the window and changed in the car, the gallant old trout. She's safe behind the bar, pouring it all over old Tudwick, who is just her cup of tea. Wally has stopped biting his nails and is taking nourishment, so that hurdle's past."

"Oh how good of her." Minnie was still using her social vocabulary, but as ever her gratitude was sincere. "Dear Poppy, how like her and how very sensible."

Tonker grinned wickedly. "Locked her in, eh? That's a bit much, isn't it?" Above his high-buttoned blazer his freckled face and deep blue eyes were gay. "It shows you what some marriages are like. He's standing on his dignity as Chief Constable. Fantastic old buzzard."

Minnie regarded him blankly as the significance of the move dawned upon her.

"Oh Tonker, how frightful! Oh dear, I'd forgotten."

"Then go on forgetting," he said doughtily. "Everybody else is. It's going with a bang. Fang is looking for you, by the way. Don't forget your own pictures. I saw some very distinguished-looking birds in the barn. I don't know 'em, so I suppose you must. Now then, don't flap. No hurry. Gosh, have you seen Prune?"

"Prune?"

He laughed. "I see you haven't. You must. I wouldn't have believed it." He paused abruptly as he caught sight of the posy in her hands. "You've got one of those things. A lot of the girls have. Where did you get them?"

Minnie turned the flowers over. "Old Harry. They're rather formal and nice, don't you think?"

Tonker looked at the bouquet dubiously. "I suppose so," he said. "Yes, well, why not? I say Minnie, I suppose that bridge is perfectly safe?"

"The wherry? Oh yes dear, does it look all right?"

"Very good. But there's a lot of grass and leaves and stuff collecting against one side. I suppose that can't be helped."

"No." She was apologetic. "No, I don't suppose it can. There are always odds and ends floating by in the river. People expect that. Is it bad?"

"No. Nothing to worry about. Everything's wonderful. The champers is excellent and I'm glad to see some intelligent child, Annabelle as a matter of fact, has had the sense to set herself up in a soft drink bar. The ice cream was a brainwave too. Who thought of that?"

Minnie looked startled. "Do you know, I don't know. I've been noticing it. Everyone seems to be eating it. There must be gallons of it." She was looking round her with swift preoccupied eyes, watching for the lost young woman or the odd man out. "Things just happen at a party like this. It's very nice. Tonker, there are two people I don't know, looking at you, just over there by Agnes Glebe."

Tonker turned his head. "Ah yes indeed. Be seeing you." He sailed away, hand outstretched, smile delighted, and Minnie was claimed at once by a very elegant young man who had carried his elders' most recent fashion for aping the modes and manners of their grandfathers to the alarming point of growing exactly like one of them. He had been designed by Charles Dana Gibson as a foil for a young woman who had vanished, and he looked therefore a little lonely in his loose-jacketed masculinity.

"Mrs. Cassands, I've been sent to fetch you," he said taking her firmly by the hand. "There is a very distinguished gathering in your studio. That is over in the barn there."

Very cold blue eyes were looking into hers and she controlled a rising panic. It was thirty-five years since she had been confronted by this sort of dominant male, and then he had been elderly.

"They want you to explain your remarkable picture." He eyed her again. "They like it very much, so you have nothing to worry about."

"What picture?" Minnie demanded, her mind's eye making a lightning review of the canvases on show, and pausing guiltily at the portrait of Little Doom.

The young man lowered his voice. "The modern one."

"The *modern*?" In a flash of intuitive divination Minnie remembered Tonker's unexplained absence before breakfast. She had not glanced at the pictures since. The young man continued to hold her hand in a compelling grip.

"I think you must come along," he said.

"My word yes." Minnie spoke grimly. "I think I'd better."

As they ploughed through the crowd, the young man gripping her elbow so that she should not escape, he made an inquiry in a tone whose studied casualness belonged to other eras beside the turn of the nineteenth century.

"There's a girl here. I think her name is Prune."

Minnie raised her head. "Was she alone?"

"Er—no," he said sadly, "no, she wasn't."

Meanwhile, on the other side of the lawn Mr. Campion was standing talking with a knot of old friends.

"Why do these ridiculous parties of old Tonker's *go*?" said the woman who was Mrs. Gilbert Whippet and had once been Janet Pursuivant, Sir Leo's only daughter, with genuine bewilderment in her voice. "Daddy's heartbroken he can't be here. It's some sort of business, I don't know what. But Tonker really is extraordinary about these do's.

You never know when he's going to have one. He doesn't actually invite anybody. There are no servants at all. And yet everybody turns up including, really, the most amazing people. Look at that man over there, for instance. And it's *always* a fine day.''

"It always seems fine," said Mr. Campion, smiling fondly at her because he was so grateful that she had not married him. "And that man is your father's Superintendent."

"Oh well then—" She was a little pettish because she knew quite well what he was thinking, and although she was very fond of her husband, who was an even vaguer edition of the same type, she held it ungallant of him to be happy too. "Oh well then, consider *those* people. Who on earth are they?"

"Look at the light on those trees," said Mr. Campion hastily, turning her attention in the opposite direction and lowering his voice discreetly. "Those are two of the wealthiest men of the year, Mr. Burt and Mr. Hare and their ladies. And the man with the crushed face is a very influential person called Smith. I shouldn't worry about them. They're virtually gate-crashers."

Janet could not forbear a well-bred peep. "He doesn't look happy, anyway," she said contentedly. "In fact he doesn't even look bored. He looks sick. Perhaps they're being difficult. They look as if they're thinking of buying the place."

"Some people are always thinking of buying whatever they're looking at," murmured Mr. Campion. "Is Gilbert here?"

"Yes. Gilbert Whippet, Chairman of the M.O.L.E." A wraith in pale smoke colour emerged from some point just behind Campion's left shoulder and proffered a limp hand. "I'm here. I've been here all the time. Wouldn't miss it for worlds. I say Campion, have you seen Prune?"

"Not today. Why?"

"I don't know. I only wondered." Whippet was blethering, as usual, and Mr. Campion restrained an impulse which dated from his first meeting with him at Totham School, to tread firmly on his foot to keep him from wandering away. "I only wondered," he repeated. "She used to be such a dull girl."

"She's still a dull girl." Mr. Campion spoke with unwonted bitterness.

"Oh no, my dear fellow." Whippet conveyed what was for him passionate excitement. "Oh no, I don't agree with you. You're wrong there."

Mr. Campion seized his elbow with much the same force as Minnie's young man had taken hers, and led him a little apart.

"How's the Botany class?" he inquired. "Thank you for your communication. I trust you got mine."

Whippet blinked. "Nice of you," he said vaguely. "I just needed to set our mind at rest, you know. Minnie happy?"

"I don't know. Should she be?"

A faintly puzzled expression, if the term is not too specific, passed a leisurely way over Mr. Whippet's indeterminate features.

"Oh yes," he murmured. "I really think she should be. Do I see Solly L. over there?"

Campion looked round. Far away, among the confetti-coloured crowd, he caught a fleeting glimpse of a grey bowler hat. When he turned back again Whippet had gone. Mr. Campion set off through the chattering company, but before he could catch up with the grey bowler he was waylaid by no less an obstacle than old Lady Glebe, Prune's mother, who had ditched The Revver somewhere and was wandering about loose. She was one of those large pleasant old women whose very soft flesh has black patches on its surface, and is attached to the main structure by a series of tight ribbons, one round the neck, one lower down. She stepped nimbly in front of Campion and looked deeply into his eyes with very nice if misguided grey ones.

"Hallo, young man," she said flatteringly. "How's your father?"

"As well as can be expected," said Mr. Campion, who had been orphaned for twenty years.

"I'm so glad. I thought he was dead. I want to see you."

She tucked her arm through his possessively. "This young man of Prune's . . . ?"

"Yes?" Mr. Campion was defensive.

"I don't know him."

He hesitated. "He's a very distinguished man in his own line."

"Oh, I know he is." She spoke with a warmth which surprised him. "And entertaining. He spent an evening with us, when was it?—the night before last." She paused to make a deep grunting sound which he assumed to be laughter. "Kept us in stitches," she said, using the term as if she had just invented it.

Mr. Campion swallowed. "You liked him?"

"Oh, very much." She lowered her voice, with elderly wisdom. "So kind. She's wearing his jewels, you know."

"Really?" said Mr. Campion.

"Quite the finest jade I've ever seen."

Mr. Campion took a firm hold of himself. She was a Gallantry, he remembered. One must hold on to that.

"So knowledgeable, that's what I liked," the gentle voice continued. "He listened to me as no other young man has ever listened, and I told him all about the societies I belong to, the ones I have my long correspondences with. I told him all about Professor Tarot, and the High Priestess, and Madame Delaware, and that man who runs the Guild of Light—what's his name, you know him."

"I don't," said Mr. Campion with some dignity.

"Ah, perhaps not. But Charles *does*," said Lady Glebe with sudden distinctness. "That's the amazing thing. He knows each one of them personally. Some of them live in his manor—that's his district, you know, a technical term. He knows them well, and he was able to tell me about them first hand. A most useful man. Prune seems delighted and he's doing her good. She looks quite pretty today. The Revver pointed it out."

When Mr. Campion left her at last he felt giddy, but he was a determined man and he pressed on to where he had last seen the grey bowler. He located it at last just outside the house. The man under it was seated on a low parapet which enclosed a small terrace outside the glass doors of the drawing-room. He was drinking champagne and talking to Amanda. Solly L. was a Jew and a bookmaker of great reputation, and since he was also a sensitive person he had settled his private problems in his own way and always made a point of dressing the part. In figure he was not unlike Mr. Lugg, and it was said of him that he always took a copy of the latest joke drawing from the sporting papers when he visited his tailor. At the moment he made a colourful and splendid figure.

"No, I don't like rings," he was saying to Amanda as Campion came up. "Never wear 'em. Get in the way if they're big enough to see. Hullo Mr. C. Enjoying yourself? What a day, eh, what a day."

Mr. Campion sat down beside him and Amanda gave him her glass.

"It keeps getting filled," she said. "I don't quite know how."

Solly laughed, the essential sadness of his boldly moulded face brightening with amusement.

"I do," he remarked. "Look at 'im. Good Old Tonker. He's conducting this party as if it was a piece of music for massed bands. I've been sitting here looking at him while I've been chatting to Her Ladyship. It's beautiful to watch. He does it all by ear." He nodded to where Tonker was standing in his beautiful blazer, stomach in, rump out, pads springy, and invisible whiskers quivering. He was talking to a group who were laughing at him, and was sipping his wine, but his eyes wandered from time to time and every now and again someone, usually a child—and there seemed to be millions of them—came up to him and received some casual instruction.

"Do you know what he's saying?" Solly flicked the ash off a property-sized cigar. "I do. I listened to him once. He says 'It's too quiet over in that corner. Go and see why and come and tell me.' Then it's 'Go and get a bottle from Auntie Poppie. She's only a famous actress and the Chief Constable's wife. And three or four glasses. And take them up very carefully to the back landing where

you'll find three old gentlemen, one of them's only Genappe, sitting about smoking. Just hand it to the one who's
awake and come back.' Then, to a legal eagle who looks
as if he's still on the bench, 'My dear feller, how
charming to see you. And you, and you. You need a
drink. I wonder if you'd mind? You see this french window here? Go through it and on the left you'll see a
bureau. Open it and you'll find all the necessary. Start a
little bar. Do you know the Lord-knows-who, and General
Whatnot? I'll bring them over.' '' He ducked his head and
laughed. "It's a poem," he said. "It's a gift. What a
maître he'd make if ever he capitalized it. But he wouldn't,
you know. It's an art with him, the same as her painting is
with his good lady. He'd do anything for his parties,
Tonker would. Commit murder. Anything."

The husband and wife both looked at him sharply, but
he had spoken innocently and was holding up his glass to a
willowy nymph who, with George Meredith in earnest
attention, was pouring nectar from a golden vase.

"I like to see the youngsters waiting on the old 'uns,"
said Solly. "Gives 'em something to do. The old 'uns
have got their uses too," he added, permitting his liquid
eyes to rest on Campion for a moment. "Poor old William, eh? What a punter! What a friend!" He raised his
glass and they followed him, Mr. Campion having acquired one from a strange small boy who had placed it
carefully beside him as he passed by, intent on some other
errand.

"Uncle William." Amanda's honey-coloured eyes were
soft. "He was a pet. I know he was old and tired but I'm
sorry he's gone."

"So am I. Ought to be." Solly's sidelong glance was
full of hints. "No. But I mean it," he said. "I do indeed.
I liked the old boy. He was straight and he was sporting
and I wish there were more like him."

Mr. Campion who had pricked up his ears, was forming
a delicate question, when Amanda sprang to her feet.

"It is!" she cried. "Look, Albert, right over there.
Mary and Guffy and the children."

Mr. Campion followed her gaze to where, in the far distance, he saw a friend of his youth and Amanda's elder sister so surrounded by golden striplings that the whole bunch looked like a sheaf of daffodils with buds. Amanda sped away but Campion lingered. He was curious and for the first time he thought the Mole's flowery way was beginning to show a gleam of reason. He made a guess.

"One thing about Uncle William was very characteristic," he began cautiously. "He always wore both belt and braces."

Solly began to chuckle. He laughed until he coughed, and slapped his checkered thigh.

"That's one way of putting it," he agreed. "Covered himself every time."

Mr. Campion was pretty sure of his ground now, but there is a rigid etiquette in such matters and he did not wish to transgress. He guessed again.

"Does Minnie know?"

Solly ceased to smoke and leant forward, heavily confidential.

"D'you know, I was beginning to wonder that," he said. "I made certain she'd get my letter this morning. He opened the account for her and made the bet in her name, you see, without telling her. I never pay out until the end of the week, of course, and I was a bit late because I didn't hear of his death until Monday, and then I had to take it up with the people I'd laid the bet off with, didn't I?"

"The Mole?"

"You know a lot, my lad." Solly was suspicious. "William told you, I suppose?"

"He said something last time I saw him," said Mr. Campion not entirely untruthfully. "It must have been a most unusual bet. Why did you accept it?"

Solly shrugged his shoulders. "Why bring that up? He was an old client. He begged and prayed of me. It was the only way he could beat the death duties, and it didn't seem much of a risk, really, because we had all the posh specialists, you know. Oh yes, we did the thing fair. I had the reports on my desk a week after they'd examined him. They said he was good for a couple of years, as far as they knew. Anyway, I was satisfied and that was that.''

"The Mole didn't kick?"

"Why should it?" Solly was truculent. "I wasn't kicking. They take their time, you know, but I got the okay yesterday. The bet covered the last six months of the five-year gift period. If he hopped it in the last six months I agreed to pay, and I have. Minnie's got the money, or she ought to have it if the letter's not lost, and my money's real money, you know. It's the only stuff of its kind that is. There's no tax on it. She can pay her debts or go to Paris on it. Or both," he added after a pause. "There's plenty there. Seven-to-two in thousands. Good old William. I don't grudge it him."

He broke off to raise his hat to a passing vision.

"See who that was?" he inquired. "Lili Ricki. Lovely voice, lovely woman. Everybody's here today, ain't they? Lots of Press too. I didn't know Tonker went in for that. But I've seen Kidd and Green, and I thought they were crime. The Augusts are due, they tell me. They're cards." He hesitated. "You don't think she knows, then. You don't think Minnie's got the letter."

"I should be very surprised," said Mr. Campion. "She's not reticent."

"Oh, well, I feel better for that. A pleasure to come." The bookmaker drained his glass and, putting it carefully in a flower-bed, rose to his feet. He was laughing at himself again. "I felt a bit flat," he confessed. "I'd got it in my head I'd be received with open arms, see? And as you know, I love children. And I'd prepared a bit of a surprise. I've got an old-fashioned hokey-pokey box in my car, and I got five and a half gallons of ice cream at Chelmsford as we came through, and I drove up and . . .''

Mr. Campion could hardly bear to hear it. The vision of Solly playing the elephantine uncle at this most sophisticated of gatherings was bad enough, but the actuality was far more exquisitely painful.

"Oh dear," he said.

"But of course she didn't know!"

The Fairy Ginsberg, that indefatigable sprite from the East who is always turning up in the most English of Athenian woods, was joyously reborn in the melting eyes of Solly L. "That accounts for everything. She just came up and said 'Hallo Solly dear. Nice to see you. Here's Tonker,' and when I turned round my chauffeur had taken the stuff out and it had been seized on and carted away by a crowd of rotten little kids and a woman dressed in wallpaper." He laughed and lit a new cigar. "Still, they enjoyed it," he said, "and if she doesn't *know* I must tell her. What a nice little place, eh? I like a river. I'm a bit of a poet myself, you know. I can see anything floating down that stream on a day like this—swans, roses, anything. There's some smashing girls here. Look at that one. What an eyeful, eh?"

Mr. Campion turned his head and remained staring. The crowd had parted for an instant and Prune and her escort were before him.

Prune only knew of two dressmakers, Miss Spice in Pontisbright and Edmund Norman in London and Paris. Because it was to be the greatest day in her life she had gone, not unnaturally, to Norman. She had told him everything about herself and left it to him. She had the height and figure of a model, and at the only school she had ever attended they had taught her how to walk, if little else. The rest of the miracle had been performed by Charlie Luke, who walked now a little behind her looking as if he knew it. Her dress was made of tailored cream, which flattered her skin and her hair, and her shoes and long gloves and little handbag were all fashioned from the palest milk chocolate, or something very like it in tint and texture. Round her throat she wore the jade necklace, which deepened rather than echoed the colour of her eyes, and in her hand was the flagrant posy for a lover which Old Harry had wound according to the ancient way.

She was so ecstatically happy that she glowed with it as if she wore a glory, and every man who set eyes on her that day remembered her for the rest of his life.

When she passed Mr. Campion she smiled at him so warmly that in spite of himself his face smiled back.

"A knock-out," said Solly, sniffing sentimentally. "I like the look of the bloke too. I've seen him about somewhere. Happy as a lord, isn't he? You could warm your hands at him. Well, I must go and find Minnie. I'm enjoying myself, I don't mind telling you. I can't think of anything that could spoil a day like this, can you?"

Mr. Campion did not answer. His attention had been caught by the little knot of people who were standing on the river's brim near the wherry bridge. The S.S.S. man did indeed look strained, and his two solid companions, with their broad secret faces, were glancing about them with the cold predatory interest peculiar to the body-snatching kind. Their womenfolk were with them, but they were in the background and were openly unimportant. Burt and Hare, male and watchful, were the dominating factor.

Campion was interested because he saw that they had taken up some sort of grandstand position and were clearly waiting for something. The crowd broke over the little rock they made and flowed on either side of them. As Campion stood watching, he became aware of a commotion on the drive behind him. A small blue van labelled "Bacon Bros. Wet Fish. Billingsgate," and driven rather recklessly, had turned off the gravel and with much hooting and screeching had bounded on to the lawn and bounced its way to within a few yards of the body-snatchers and S. S. Smith. Instantly, and without any other visible cause for the transition, the gay garden-party quality of the gathering turned into something wilder. The setting sun shone brighter, the wind got up. Rupert and the twins, with Choc bustling behind them like a nursemaid, all petticoats and agitation, dashed through the legs of the company shouting, "Many happy regurgitations!" Tonker appeared on the balcony of the boat house. Emma, sensational in a long gown which would have appeared normal in the thirties, stood poised at the drawing-room door, flushed and joyous. Minnie, with a bearded dignitary on either side of her, came sailing round from triumph in the barn.

As soon as the van stopped the door was opened and five small and wiry fishmongers in striped aprons and straw hats emerged in a state of great excitement, and began handing out more and more unlikely seafood, including two large blonde live mermaids complete with rubber tails, shell brassières, and Tonker's masks. One fishmonger rushed up to old Lord Tudwick, who was balancing on the wherry, blinking in the unaccustomed light and fresh air, and planted a plaice in his hand.

"It's got a bend in it," he explained in the squeaky voice so well known throughout the land.

"Oh well," said Minnie, putting her hand on Mr. Campion's shoulder, "the Augusts have arrived. Now, of course, we're for it."

CHAPTER XVI

All Right on the Night

The body floated on its back among the irises just above the flower garden at The Beckoning Lady. It had been there for nearly two hours, ever since it had drifted into the bank at the turn. As the stream was scarcely flowing, it remained there, borne up by the air in the lungs and in the clothing.

The night had turned warm. The breeze had dropped and the moon, which was at the full, was just beginning to colour the shadows so that the drawn white face was very vivid against the dark water. For some time now the reeds had held the dark bundle almost stationary, and while there was no swifter current there was just a chance that it might remain where it was. But these rushes were the last of the obstacles, and once there was any real disturbance, or the stream began to move at any pace, nothing could stop it floating down to join the other debris collecting against the wherry bridge in front of the boat house.

At the moment the lawn was deserted except for Scat, who was flitting round in his white shoes turning on lights. The main company was at supper in the barn, and the dark building buzzed excitingly like a giant hive. It was a lull, the half-way mark.

The little people had gone to bed. Rupert, who was staying with the twins, was sleeping on the floor in their bedroom, his head full of clowns and Choc at his feet.

The kitchen, crammed with the visitors who arrive on country occasions to assist, was pausing between the serving rush and the washing-up gossip. Old Harry was singing his song, which had a hundred and thirty-two verses, and Miss Diane was pressing the cook from Potter's Hall to try a little American ham.

Mr. Lugg, despairing of any other method of attracting his employer's attention, edged his way through the cigar and brandy fumes in the barn, and touched him on the shoulder.

Mr. Campion rose at once, leaving the civilized warmth, and came out into the meadow.

"What happened?" he demanded.

"Fell orf." The fat man sounded reticent. "Ferget it. I'm 'ere and safe—at last. Nearly missed everythink. You'll 'ave a tidy bill to foot, but we can't 'elp that. I found it, Cock."

Mr. Campion's heart stirred. "Where?"

"The chemists in 'Adleigh. It was a regular perscription. 'E knoo it at once."

"Who?"

Lugg looked about him. There were shadows in the dusk.

" 'Oo we thought," he murmured cautiously.

A long sigh escaped Mr. Campion. "The man?"

"No."

"I see."

"Campion." Tonker's hand fell heavily on his shoulder. "Just a moment, old boy. I want you to stay right by my side, if you will. I am going to show you something." He slid his arm through the other man's own and his muscles were like iron. "I don't want you to miss what's going to happen now. I want you to experience with me one of the more enjoyable spectacles of a civilized lifetime. I want you to see an August talking to a spiv, with the perfect audience sitting round the ring."

Mr. Lugg hesitated. "If you want me I'll be round the back," he announced. "It's to be a bit of a night tonight. Ever 'eard of wheat wine?"

"Oo-er." Tonker bristled and the whites of his eyes

appeared in the moonlight. "My dear innocent fellow, take a tip from a sadder and wiser man. In your present perilous position there is only one road to salvation, and there is no absolute guarantee about that. Creep into the front kitchen and ferret round in the cupboard until you find an old-fashioned cruet. In it there will be a small and sticky bottle, half full of a dreary yellow oleaginous mess. Hold your nose and swallow it, now. And then go forth. You may see wonders as the oafs promise, but the Pit itself will be spared you. Good luck. God bless you. I suppose the dear fellow is of value to you?" he said affably as he led Campion away. "Wheat wine is, as one may say, the hydrogen bomb among beverages. Whole human islands have been known to sink without trace. Now come along, Campion, my dear chap, this should be Tonker's triumph."

All the same it was nearly an hour before the second half of Tonker's Midsummer's Night worked up to concert pitch, and by that time the moon was high and a very potent sort of magic was abroad. The man who suffered most during the first part of it was Westy. When the meal was over and the barn almost empty save for a few couples dotted about still talking, he stood, a lonely figure, shadowy in the blue haze above the guttering candles and gave his portrait a sidelong glance of positive distaste. After five hours of unremitting selfless toil and quiet self-effacing application, Westy was very nearly tired of Art.

The Suit, too, was becoming a menace. The sleeves really were half an inch too short already, in eighteen months only, and there was an ominous tightness under the arms. He even envied Tonker in his abominable blazer.

The great men, the critics and the painters, had been kind enough about the Portrait in the early hours before tea, although he could have done without one black-haired blue-chinned aesthete with his mumbo-jumbo about the "adolescent contours" and "youth's translucent flesh." But there was no doubt about it, the meaningless portrait of Annabelle, which Tonker had sneaked out and hung in place of one of the flower paintings, had stolen all the limelight. Westy was depressed. Not only the pictures, but his heroine had let him down. Minnie had spent the whole dinner sitting between one man who had decided to come in fancy dress as a bookmaker, and another whom she called "Fanny," who looked as if he'd come out of a potting shed. They talked, as far as he could hear it, about nothing more uplifting than money. True, she had looked a little dazed and there was a relieved expression in her sharp eyes which he had never seen before, but to his certain knowledge—for he had kept strict tabs on them—not one uplifting sentiment had passed their lips the whole meal. Only once had she spoken to him and that was merely to ask him to go and look for a bookmaker's letter still in its envelope in the kitchen drawer. The only people who were talking about Art at the moment were Jake, his stomach obtruding again despite the button Westy had sewn on himself, and a dreary wet called Whippet.

They were still at it, hunched over Jake's postcard-sized canvases, which the wet seemed to like. Last time Westy had overheard anything he had appeared to be haggling for a couple of them. It was sickening. The stupidity and obtuseness of the minds of people on the wrong side of twenty seemed to him to be more alarming than any other menace of the era into which he had been born. It was like seeing oneself sailing inevitably into a fog.

Even George Meredith had revealed unexpected flaws. True, he had had all the luck. When the Augusts had discovered the moke and let it loose on the lawn, where it had snapped at The Revver and eaten half of Lady Amanda's new hat, it was George who had retrieved the other half and had been rewarded ceremonially by Tonker with a beaker of champagne.

Ever since that incident George had been an entirely different person, talking as though he had only just realized the years he had to make up, and the willowy blonde he had collected, who was quite four years older and half a foot taller than he, had not stopped laughing.

Now nearly everybody had gone out on the lawn, including the Press men who had given up worrying about boring inquiries and seemed to be quite content to sit or wander about as if the night was going on for ever.

Westy looked at the middle-sized girl who came shyly down the room towards him, and experienced active dislike. He knew who she was. Her name was Mary and she was the daughter of Amanda's sister. She was nothing much to look at, with her freckles and her straight hair, and he eyed her coldly because he guessed she had come on yet another errand from Tonker, who seemed to have had nothing to do all day except to send out trivial orders. Possibly deterred by his expression, Mary's step became slower and slower as she came up to him, and her open nervousness awoke the chivalry which was never very dormant in Westy's New English breast. She stopped dead at the Portrait and stared at it with gratified awe.

"That's you, isn't it?" she said, revealing quite pleasant eyes and the most charming soft red mouth. "Isn't it wonderful?"

"Not bad," said Westy, shooting his cuffs.

She eyed his tight jacket admiringly and was so open about not caring to venture a comment that it was better than any compliment she could have paid him.

"I am so sorry to have to trouble you, but Uncle Tonker asked me to find his masks and see they don't get lost, and although I know where they are I don't quite see how to get hold of them. I wondered if I could trouble. . . ?"

"No trouble at all," said Westy. "Let's go."

She coloured and glanced back at the picture. "It's awfully warm out," she muttered at last, fighting with embarrassment. "And the masks are by the river. A man's got them. I think he might be difficult. I say, I do hope you won't be offended, but I should take it off."

"My jacket?" The beautiful simplicity of the move came as a revelation to him and he unbuttoned it instantly.

Mary took it from him reverently and hung it over the back of a chair. It was a strange and beautiful experience, intuitive understanding at its fairest and best. Westy glowed under it.

"It'll be safe there," she said.

"I don't care if it isn't," said Westy, free and young and uninhibited again in his clean white shirt. "Where is this guy who's got the masks? Come on."

On the lawn the scene was like a Shakespearian finale. Prune, her gleaming dress a focal point, her posy on her knee, was sitting on a high chair in the middle of the lawn, with Luke making a dark shadow behind her, and all about them the little groups of chattering folk in their gay party clothes were sitting about in the light of the moon, the glare from the boat house, and the soft yellow beams from the oil-lit house. Minnie and Tonker, with Fanny Genappe and Solly L., were holding court outside the drawing-room, and Mr. Campion and Amanda were chattering with old friends at the other end of the lawn. The river shone in the lights and the little balcony and the wherry bridge were brilliant against a glowing sky. Private jokes were going on everywhere. Two of the Augusts were playing a posthorn galop on the two best glübalübali, and Superintendent Fred South, who had never encountered anything so truly laughable in all his life before, was being supported by a somewhat scandalized Mr. Lugg.

Mary led Westy down the side of the house to a point of vantage on the top of the low wall skirting the room which had been Uncle William's.

"Look," she murmured. "There."

Westy craned his neck and perceived the difficulty. The S.S.S. man and his alarming-looking friends had chosen with unerring instinct the best place. In the curious way peculiar to them, they had made themselves both comfortable and aloof in the very midst and forefront of an otherwise entirely communal scene. They had taken possession of the little platform which Minnie had built with her own hands for Uncle William's summer bed, and had transformed it into a box at a music hall. They all had chairs and on the coffee table brought out from the drawing-room there were glasses, even an ice bucket, and the pile of masks. The group did not seem to be talking very much, except that two of the women were whispering, and the glow of the cigars alone showed where the men sat in the shadows. They were silent, waiting to be entertained.

In front of them the garden sloped sharply to the open stream. The young people were perched some little way behind them, and were far too experienced to intrude. Uncle Tonker's rules were firm and like life's own: if you made a mess of it once you were sunk.

The man with the squashed face had only to refuse point-blank to part with the trophies and there was nothing to be done about it. The only intelligent plan of campaign was to bide one's time and to acquire them unobtrusively when he was otherwise engaged. At the moment this looked difficult.

Westy sat down on the wall to wait and helped Mary to get down beside him. She revealed the quality which George had lost so sensationally earlier in the day. There was no need to explain to her. Westy accepted the miracle and worried no more about it.

Meanwhile there was growing activity in the boat house. The Augusts, who had been dipping the obliging mermaids in the river, and had been frustrated from following the same course with an angry girl who did not know them, had begun to fool about with some coloured rockets. Mary watched them earnestly.

"When a red one goes up, George is to open the sluices," she remarked, offering Westy half a bar of nut chocolate which she had taken out of her pocket.

He accepted the gift gratefully. "Who's George?" he inquired with a twinge of jealousy.

"You know, the one who can't stop talking. The silly one. He goes to school with you, doesn't he?"

"He's in no fit condition to open a sluice." Westy was contemptuous. "Who fixed it?"

"One of these fishmongers. I happened to hear them talking. George went down to the fen with that big girl who giggles. They're waiting down there near the Indian camp for the red rocket."

Westy shrugged his shoulders. He had the masks to think of now. If George wanted to take over the sluices alone, there would be nothing to stop him.

By this time the Augusts were on the balcony. At least,

two of them were, and the other three were attempting to climb up without using the stairs.

"You buy a horse." The shrill north country tones of the true cross-talk comedian echoed over the moonlit garden and there was a faint movement from Uncle William's platform and one of the cigars went out.

"Me buy a horse?"

"Yes, you buy a horse."

"Why should I buy a horse?"

"Because you want to race a horse."

"I don't want to race a horse."

"Yes, you do."

"No, I don't."

"Yes, you do."

"Why should I want to race a horse?"

"Because the horse will win."

"How do I know the horse will win?"

"Because I say it will."

"Oh, *you* say the horse will win?"

"Yes, *I* say the horse will win."

There was an unnatural stillness on the platform ahead of Westy. He became aware of it despite the compelling quality of the repetitive nonsense on the balcony, which had a magic of its own, inexplicable and ancient.

"Why should I want the horse to win?"

"Because you'll get a lot of money?"

"Oh, *I'll* get a lot of money?"

"Yes, you'll get a lot of money, because you paid for the horse."

"How have I paid for the horse?"

"That's a secret."

"Oh, I've paid for the horse with a secret, have I?"

The shrill, asinine voices echoed over the garden, and one of the crime reporters, who was lying on the grass, turned over to speak to a confrère beside him.

"My God, do you hear this? They're all here. Burt, Hare, Smith, and Genappe of all people, arrived home unexpectedly. This has put the lid on that little deal. This is pure murder. They're giving the whole twist away. Who put them up to it?"

At the same time, on the other side of the lawn, Gilbert Whippet bent over Tonker, who was sitting happily in the darkness.

"You're taking an undue risk, old boy," he murmured. "They'll get you for this."

"Worth it," said Tonker and chuckled into his glass.

Meanwhile, old Fanny Genappe, who was standing next to Minnie, put his hand on her arm.

"Have you ever heard of a man called Ben-Sabah, my dear?"

"Ben who? No, Fanny, I haven't. Is he here? Shall I ask Tonker?"

"No, no, it was just an idle thought. I don't think we'll bother him. Very amusing, these fellows, aren't they? They look so absurd. And their patter's informative."

The cross-talk act went on inexorably, high, nasal, and moronic.

"What's the horse's name?"

"The horse's name is Pontisbright."

Someone pushed back a chair on the concrete platform near Westy and uttered a word which that young man hoped had passed over Mary's head. The Augusts were working up to a climax, shouting and pretending to fall off the balcony. A red rocket went up behind them and Mary jumped.

"See that?"

Westy nodded in the darkness. "I'm watching."

"The horse's name is Pontisbright and I've paid for it with a secret!" bellowed an August.

"Yes, you've paid for it with a secret and the horse will run on my racecourse."

"Oh, the horse will run on *your* racecourse?"

"Yes, the horse will run on *my* racecourse."

"Why should the horse run on *your* racecourse?"

"Because," shouted all the Augusts together, just as a ripple ran through the river and the wherry bridge which they had unfastened began to move, "because it's got a *bend* in it!"

In the next five minutes all sorts of things happened.

Down in the fen meadows a liberated George Meredith, from whom all shyness had dropped like a cloak, had opened the sluices as far as they would go. As the pent-up water began to race, a dark bundle escaped from the irises higher up the stream and began to move swiftly through the garden.

At the same time the wherry bridge moved rapidly, and the two Augusts upon it flung their glübalübali aside and leapt nimbly ashore at the last possible moment, so that nearly everybody on the lawn was drawn to his feet, and most people stepped instinctively towards the river's brim.

Meanwhile, on Uncle William's platform near Westy and Mary, some sort of crisis appeared to be taking place. Angry murmurs were mingled with violent movement and the S.S.S. man snatched up the limp pile of masks just before the table went over. He had leapt down into the garden before the body went by, and was looking towards the river when it appeared.

The wax-white face staring up sightlessly at the stars, sailed down the whole length of the lawn, passed the boat house, and passed the crowd. Somebody screamed, and a sibilant ripple trickled all the way down the line.

The S.S.S. man acted rapidly. Even Westy, who was standing on the wall trying to make out what on earth was happening, did not see what occurred. Smith threw the masks one after the other into the stream. Some fell one way and some another, but they all floated on the tide, so that within a matter of seconds another sightless white face bobbed down the dark pathway beside the lawn, to be followed by another and another, then two together, then one more.

"Masks!" "Only the masks!" "Masks!"

The cries went up all over the garden and laughter, much of it shocked but all of it relieved, broke out everywhere as the crowd receded and there was gaiety again.

Only Amanda, who was standing by her husband in the whispering garden, caught her breath.

"Albert, seven went by. There *are* only six. Get Luke quickly. Down to the fen."

CHAPTER XVII

Mr. Campion Exerts Himself

Mr. Campion closed the drawer of Miss Pinkerton's desk very softly although he knew he was alone in the house, and pushing back the chair on which he had been sitting, stepped across the room and switched out the light. Then he drew back the heavy curtains and left the way he had come, which was, as on the day before, through the window.

The house without a back rose stark and silent behind him and he set off across the long slope down to the river with swinging strides. Away to his left the patch of brilliance which was The Beckoning Lady glowed like a fairground in the night. There were still several hours before dawn, and, judging from the faint roar blown towards him by the light wind, the proceedings had reawakened after the period of comparative quiet.

A little group awaited Mr. Campion under a tree by the river. Luke was there, South, and Amanda, and Old Harry who had guided them. He was sitting apart on a log, very solemn in his Sunday-and-Funeral suit, but sly-eyed and watchful in the moonlight.

"I doubt you had no luck, sir." The Superintendent's tone was difficult to place, but Mr. Campion felt that for once he was not actually grinning.

"It was hopeless," said Luke. "It's been destroyed."

"Wait." Mr. Campion spoke briskly as he came up beside them. "I hope this was not the actual tree where

230

she was found, Superintendent? I don't want to destroy any traces.''

"That's all right, sir. That's the tree over there where Buller says he saw her and thought she was sleeping. Some people ought to have their heads X-rayed, but we can't go into that now. There's an empty gin bottle there but we can't see the bicycle. I have no doubt she hid it because she didn't want to be spotted and in my opinion she probably wheeled it in the river. In that case it may have travelled. The whole stream is choked with rubbish this time of year. You never know, she may have pushed it on to something that looked as if it would keep it afloat and not spoil it. People do crazy things like that when they're thinking of suicide. Well, we shall see. You've come back empty handed, sir, have you? I was afraid you might.''

"I don't know." Mr. Campion leant against the tree which was not the one under which Old Harry had seen Miss Pinkerton's body in the dawn, and felt in his pocket. "I didn't find the actual note, which, as I told you, I noticed yesterday on the mantelshelf under the one addressed to Mr. Smith. That note was for an R. Robinson Esquire, and I give you my solemn word that at that time I had no idea who the man was, and that the whole matter had slipped my mind as unimportant until we all stood up in the Indian camp half an hour ago and looked down at the body we had just taken from the stream. Then, as you know, I did remember it, and I asked you, Superintendent, if you'd ever heard of him.''

"And my reply gave us all the shock of our naturals,'' interrupted South. He was brightening. "How were you to know that our local Coroner wasn't a doctor? Don't tell me you've found the letter, sir?''

"No.'' Mr. Campion still sounded promising. "The note has gone, and I don't think any of us can be very astounded by that. But I have found something. I don't know what you're all going to make of it and I don't know if it will be considered acceptable as evidence, but here it is. I took this sheet from the drawer of her typing desk.''

He took a flimsy paper from his breast pocket and handed it up to them.

"Perhaps I ought to tell you first," he said, "that just after the meal this evening Lugg came in to tell me that he had at last traced the chemist in Hadleigh who supplied Miss Pinkerton with dormital regularly on a London doctor's prescription. She did not drink alcohol in the normal way, so presumably she felt it was quite safe."

Luke produced a torch and both men bent over the letter, their faces hidden in the shadows.

"My God," said Luke, "what do you know? A carbon!" He began to read aloud in his official voice, expressionless and ill punctuated.

*"To R. Robinson, Esquire, the Coroner,
Kepesake, June 23rd.*

DEAR SIR,
I am writing to inform you that I have decided to take my life. I do it of my own free will and am of sound judgement at this time. Yesterday afternoon I had a very terrible experience and the shock of it has unhinged my mind, I think. Without meaning to in the least, I have taken the life of a fellow-man and I see that I shall be found out, and even hanged if they still do that to a woman, and that nothing I shall be able to say will be of the least use in saving me, so I prefer to go in my own way. The man I must have killed was the person called Little Doom by Mrs. Cassands at The Beckoning Lady. I recognized him as soon as I saw his body but lost my head and pretended I thought he was a tramp. The accident happened on Thursday week last. I had gone down to The Beckoning Lady in the afternoon and, finding no one about, I went into the wretched sick room of the old man who was lingering there. He was quite incapable of talking to me and might as well have been dead. I spent some time tidying his room, during which time I accidentally upset some of his sleeping pills. Not wishing to leave him without any, I put some

of my own which I always carry in my bag into his box, and at that moment looked up to see the person called Little Doom peering at me through the window. Not wishing to speak to the man I hurried out of the room, through the cloakroom, and out of the house. But when I reached the stile in the meadows I discovered he had caught up with me and was speaking to me in a very unpleasant way. I hurried over the stile but the hindrance allowed him to catch up with me and he actually laid a hand upon me. I snatched up something from the ground and struck him with it in self-defence. Then I rushed on and was glad to find he had not followed. But a week afterwards on happening to cross the meadows again I was forced to look at the most disgusting sight. I have not slept since. I do not think I shall ever sleep again. I do not know what my employer will say when he hears this. So please be reticent."

His voice ceased abruptly and there was a long silence on the bank of the stream. Luke kept the torch beam on the paper and when Amanda stepped closer he held the sheet down for her to see.

"No signature, of course," he said at last.

"How could there be?" An entirely new quality in Superintendent South's voice impressed everybody. He was serious. The alarming quality of jocund innuendo had vanished from his personality. "You can't have it *all* given to you," he said virtuously. "Sometimes we've got to use our heads and sometimes we've got to be thankful. Well, I can't say I'm surprised. It was in my mind all day yesterday once we'd got the crime figured out. 'It could have been quite unintentional,' I said to myself before I went to sleep last night. 'Quite unintentional'—a man with a skull as thin as that."

The placid effrontery of the statement struck a mundane and recognizable note in the half-lit magic of the summer night. Luke opened his mouth to speak but changed his mind, and Mr. Campion rose from his seat under the tree.

"Of course, a carbon copy does presuppose a fair one,"

he said diffidently, "but I don't know if the Coroner will accept . . ."

"Look sir." The old Superintendent made no bones about interrupting him. "You're a reputable witness. We've got your evidence that you saw a note addressed to Mr. Robinson in the deceased's office yesterday afternoon. At that time you did not know that Mr. Robinson was the local Coroner. That's one point. Then we have your evidence that subsequent to the discovery of the poor lady's body, and after explaining what you were about to us, you went back to the office and failed to find the said note. But you did find this here copy. The lady was a secretary and was used, as we are in the police, to taking a carbon copy of every letter she ever wrote. It was automatic with her, so that it's not extraordinary that in a moment of stress habit asserted itself. That's our case and it's a very, very strong one."

Mr. Campion stood, a tall and secret figure in the half darkness.

"But should the Coroner—" he began.

"The Coroner will accept the truth, sir, and so will the jury." South spoke with the sublime assurance of one who has known each personality concerned for a very long time. "That's what they're there for. Their job is to settle the matter once the facts are before them, not to make trouble. I'm not saying that all the work is done—it isn't. There are two or three questions to be answered, and we shall have to search for the fair copy of the letter and question everybody who might have had access to it, but the truth is out. Now we know where we are. Half an hour ago we had two unexplained corpses on our hands and very embarrassing they were too, to a lot of persons who shouldn't never have been embarrassed, including the Chief Constable. Now we've got a perfectly reasonable explanation. It's a sad business, but we all know that when a woman is startled she sometimes hits out. Ohman had a phenomenally thin skull. As for the lady's reaction when she saw the body and realized she'd killed the little blighter, well I saw that myself and so did my sergeant and so did

the doctor, and so there's no question about that at all.''
He sniffed. "I don't really ought to say that it's satisfactory," he said, "but there's no getting away from it, that's
the right word for it. When she found out what she'd done
she killed herself, leaving a note in a perfectly proper
way."

Luke made a sound which from any lesser man in any
less responsible position might have been mistaken for a
giggle.

"What was she doing in Mr. William's room in the first
place, Super?" he inquired.

"Interfering," said South calmly. "That sticks out a
mile. And if I may offer an opinion—I'm an older man
than you, Chief, even if I am an old country copper—I
don't think that's a subject for us to go into. After all, the
old gentleman is dead and decently buried, and not really
before his time. So no good will be served by discussing
him. Now if you're agreeable I shall go up to this house
here and borrow the telephone. It's an emergency, and I
don't think anyone is going to haul me over the coals for
that. I shall instruct my people to come out to the Indian
camp direct, approaching it from the main Sweethearting
Road so they won't need to go to The Beckoning Lady at
all. That house isn't involved at the moment. I take it
you'll be waiting for me by the body, Buller? You'll be
needed tomorrow, and so will you, Mr. Campion. Is that
how you see it, Chief Inspector?"

Luke hesitated. "It's your manor, Superintendent," he
said at last. "What about the gin bottle?"

"I shall take care of all exhibits myself. You can rely
upon that. I doubt if that one is very material, because the
poor lady probably took enough dormital to put her out
without it. But I know my duty. That paper is the important item."

He held out his hand and the London man handed over
the carbon. They all stood watching South as he folded it
carefully and placed it in a wallet which he buttoned into
the inside of his waistcoat over his heart.

"There," he said with satisfaction. "Now, the only

awkward question which may arise is who put the body
into the water. The answer is perfectly obvious but we
shan't prove it.''

"When Mr. Campion saw the note to the Coroner yesterday afternoon it was under one addressed to Mr. S. S.
Smith,'' said Luke, watching him.

"That's right,'' South agreed placidly. "And it never
got delivered. We can speculate about that, Chief, from
now until Christmas but it won't get us anywhere. Privately we can think that if a gentleman was preparing to
wheel a crowd of likely purchasers round an estate he
wouldn't hardly want the body of a suicide sitting about
spoiling the view. We might think to ourselves that, in his
fright after reading her note to himself, he'd tear up both
that and the one to the Coroner and tip the body out of
sight into the river. But we don't know and we never shall,
not for sure. As it happens it doesn't matter. Luckily
we've got the truth. Down here in the country there's one
thing we never lose sight of. The guilty has got to be
punished but the remainder of us has got to live together
for the rest of our lives. I'll just slip along to the telephone. Buller.'' He peered into the shadows. "Bless the
bloke, he's disappeared. Don't worry, he won't go far.''

When his plump form was no more than a distant dot in
the moonlight, Luke turned to his friends.

"What d'you know about that?'' he demanded.

"Truth is such a naked lady,'' Mr. Campion spoke
softly. "Apparently in well-regulated country families no
one is so indelicate as to stare at all of her at once.''

"That's all very well,'' Luke objected as they moved
away along the bank towards the lights of the distant boat
house. "I see South's point of view but I can't leave it like
that. What I must know is why Miss Pinkerton poisoned
the old gentleman. She must have known the peculiarities
of dormital. She took alcohol with it herself when she
meant to die.''

"Oh yes, she knew what she was doing.'' Mr. Campion's light voice was grave. I don't know if she appreciated
the full enormity of the act.''

"Either she meant him to die or she didn't," Luke persisted.

"She did but she didn't count it," put in Amanda startling them both. "Not as murder."

Mr. Campion was silent for a moment. He was remembering a conversation he had had in the churchyard, and could see again the brisk, efficient woman snipping dead roses from a wreath.

"It's the classic case," he remarked. "When Miss Pinkerton set out that afternoon she had no intention of killing anybody. By all the rules she ought to have got away with it."

Luke grunted. "You think she suddenly noticed that Mr. William's own sleeping pills resembled the dormital in her bag and switched them on the spur of the moment? I'll believe that when I know why."

Mr. Campion hesitated. "I fancy it's been obvious for some time," he ventured at last. "But I didn't spot it. You see, Smith encouraged Miss Pinkerton to help Minnie with her secretarial work, didn't he? That was because he wanted to find out why Minnie wouldn't sell her house. The Beckoning Lady was vital to his plan to turn the Pontisbright Park Estate into the racecourse which he proposed to sell to the body-snatchers, once it was established. Minnie wouldn't sell the place because she did not need to. William's gift had saved her from the mess she had got into by accepting Tonker's offering, and if only William lived until November there wouldn't be any serious catch in *his* present. Miss Pinkerton knew all about this. She did all the work on both sides. She was an over-efficient person who must have suffered acutely from the exasperating set-up down there with Minnie changing her mind about selling every two minutes." He paused and touched Luke's arm. "That afternoon Miss Pinkerton pottered about William's room and must have seen him lying there looking useless, incurable, and an abominable old nuisance who was holding everything up. At the same time she saw a very simple method of getting rid of him. She took it. My bet is that she deceived herself into thinking that she was being merciful."

"Also," said Amanda frankly. "She could almost blame Uncle William for making the dormital poisonous. I mean, if he hadn't taken alcohol with it—and Pinkie didn't approve of wicked old men taking alcohol, anyway—it wouldn't have hurt him any more than it hurt her, and she took it regularly."

"Right!" Luke laughed briefly and without amusement. "I know that mentality, and I recognize the type who believes that a rich man's business is sacred. The richer the man the holier his affairs. I suppose Miss Pinkerton merely thought of Smith as someone working for Genappe and therefore all-important. You're quite right, Campion, she would have got away with it if Little Doom hadn't looked through the window. How much did he see, I wonder?"

"Not very much," murmured Mr. Campion. "I don't think Miss Pinkerton thought he had, either. But when he dashed round by the drive in an attempt to cut her off and came up with her at the stile, she was feeling guilty and so she panicked. When he touched her she hit him with the first weapon which came to hand. Unfortunately it was a ploughshare and he hadn't the right sort of skull to withstand it. I don't think she thought he'd seen her with the dormital."

"Don't you?" Luke turned to him. They had come to the place where the path divided. One arm led down to the garden of The Beckoning Lady and the other meandered towards the single plank footbridge which gave to the uplands and the Indian camp. "Why not?"

"Clear and limpid thought," said Mr. Campion modestly. "If Little Doom had mentioned medicines when he caught up with her she would have rushed back to restore the position before harm was done. She did nothing of the sort. Why? Because when he suddenly appeared beside her on the bridge I think he started talking about something else, something she thought was an impertinence."

"Oh. What was that?"

"Frankly, I do not know." Campion sounded regretful. "But having made an intensive study of the lad and his methods, I should guess that he asked her why he had caught her dusting the sick room when she was employed at ten bob an hour, or whatever it was, for purely secretarial duties. She snubbed him and he caught hold of her and it happened.''

"Horrid," said Amanda with a shiver. "I'm going back to the garden; I'll meet you there, Albert."

She vanished into the shadows and Luke and Campion continued on to the plank bridge where they paused for a moment looking down into the moonlit water. Lugg and George Meredith were at the camp with the body, and they had little doubt that by this time Old Harry would have joined them.

From the boat house came the sound of music.

"The woman couldn't have seen Little Doom fall," Luke said presently. "She must have simply hit out and fled. Then, when she heard no more about it, she put the whole incident out of her mind as people do. No wonder the sight of the body a week later sent her over the edge. A rum business. So simple and ordinary. It might have happened to anybody."

"Not *anybody*," Mr. Campion protested gently. "Only an extraordinarily beastly woman would have tidied Uncle William out of existence." He paused. "If you're not going to need me at the Indian camp I think I'll go back to the party."

Luke glanced towards the boat house. "You go along," he said. "I'll follow you. As far as I can see I'm only going to be an embarrassment to the local boys from now on. Keep an eye on Prune, will you?"

It was the first time that Mr. Campion had ever heard him use her name and he tried not to resent it. He was irritated by his own reaction and when he collected himself he found Luke was talking about the girl.

"Prune has been designed to be a smashing wife for a man with a Manor," he was saying unexpectedly. "Mine may not be quite the kind that was originally envisaged but it's much the same as the others in essentials. Don't let us worry you, my dear chap. It's all right. You'll see. We'll go places, Prune and I."

Mr. Campion blinked. A vista of years had opened before him in which Luke's genius backed by Prune's influence carried the remarkable couple to heights as yet unguessed.

"I . . . Good gracious me, yes! I believe you will!" he ejaculated.

Luke's smile flashed in the half light.

"We're both quietly confident," he said magnificently. "What a wonderful girl, Campion! Seriously, have you ever seen anyone like her? Anyone in all your life?"

Mr. Campion went back to The Beckoning Lady.

When he arrived on the lawn the crowds had thinned but an inner core of revellers remained and the proceedings had developed a new intimacy.

Tonker and Minnie, with a sleepy Westy and Annabelle, were sitting on a couch which had been brought out of the drawing-room, listening to Lili Ricki, the new Swedish Nightingale, singing Sydney Carter's lovely song against a lightening sky.

Tonker had relented and put on the beaded waistcoat to please Emma, but he still wore his beautiful blazer and Minnie's posy was pinned to his lapel, where it looked like a loofah in the cold light.

As Mr. Campion came up he was just in time to see him put out a foot absently to trip up an August who was flitting past, but his voice was sad to the point of unsteadiness.

"The youth of the heart and the dew in the morning,
You wake and they've left you without any warning."

He quoted the lyric softly. "Oh Minnie, how tragic. How awful, Minnie!"

Her snorting laugh echoed quietly in the shadows.

"Cheer up," she said, putting out a hand apologetically to the man who had stumbled. "It hasn't happened yet. Come on, Tonker, we've got to cook these people breakfast."

At long last Mr. Campion left the car for Lugg, and he

and Amanda walked home through the dawn. For a long time she was silent, but when they were completely alone she paused to look at him.

"I suppose it's going to be all right?" she said.

"All right?" His glance was sharp. She was far too clever; he had observed it before. "What did you notice?"

"Only," said Amanda calmly, "that Miss Pinkerton spelled 'judgement' *just like you do*."

Mr. Campion was silent for a long time. Finally he hunched his shoulders. "What a horridly odd coincidence, little Over Intelligent," he said softly. "You will kindly shut up about that one—unless, of course, you want to come and grin at me behind bars. What else could be done? The suicide note had to be found. In what other way could the truth be made so apparent to South? Like all good officials he had to have a bit of paper to convince him."

"Oh quite," Amanda was affable. "Do you think the carbon was much like the fair copy?"

"Good heavens, I hope so!" Mr. Campion sounded both dignified and hurt. "My sincere bet is that it is almost exact. I may be unethical but I am not criminal. The only person who could tell us would be the S.S.S. man and then only if he read the letter to the Coroner before he destroyed it. Perhaps he didn't. Anyhow, I don't think he'll offer much comment."

"No." Amanda spoke thoughtfully. "Sidney Simon Smith has his own troubles just now, since Fanny has found him out."

By the time they reached the Mill they were talking of other things.

"I went in to look at Rupert before I left," Amanda remarked, "and I tell you, Albert, I think we ought to have some twins."

"Now that is a thought," said Mr. Campion.